"The four main characters in *Pickle's Progress* seem more alive than most of the people we know in real life because their fears and desires are so nakedly exposed. That's because their creator, Marcia Butler, possesses truly scary X-ray vision and intelligence to match."

—Richard Russo

"Butler's debut is character-driven…starts with a crash then slows as the characters' personalities develop. In this study of how childhood experiences shape perception, and how deception keeps people caged, Butler shows that nothing need be set in stone."

—*Kirkus Reviews*

"Oh, what a pickle *Pickle's Progress* puts us in--a duke's mixture of villainy, deceit, betrayal, and, Lord help us, romantic love--all of it rendered in prose as trenchant as it is supple. Clearly, Ms. Butler is in thrall to these fascinatingly flawed characters, and by, oh, page 15 you will be, too. Let's hope this is just the first of many more necessary novels to come."

—Lee K. Abbott, author of *All Things, All at Once*

"How does healing happen? Sometimes in quirkier ways than you might expect. Butler's blazingly original debut novel is a quintessential moving, witty, New York City story about the love we think we want, the love we get, and the love we deserve. I loved it."

—Caroline Leavitt, NYT bestselling author of *Pictures of You* and *Cruel Beautiful World*

"Written in brave and startling prose, Butler has crafted a fast-paced tale of tragedy, passion and love. Throughout this surprising work, we see NY in all its beauty and raunchiness, so that the city itself becomes an integral part of the complex and compelling plot. Rare is the brilliant memoirist who also writes fiction with the same sure hand, but Marcia Butler is such an author."

—Patty Dann, author of the bestselling novel, *Mermaids*

"*Pickle's Progress* is a wild trip into the heart of New York City with wonderful, complicated, highly functioning alcoholics as tour guides. Marcia Butler's characters are reflections of the city they live in: beautiful but flawed, rich but messed up, dark and hostile - but there's love there, if you know where to find it. Butler's sharp, artistic sensibilities shine through here, and the result is a brutal, funny story of family, regret, and belonging."

—Amy Poeppel, author of *Limelight*

"Like the first icy slug of a top-shelf martini, Marcia Butler's debut novel is a refreshing jolt to the senses. Invigorating, sly and mordantly funny, *Pickle's Progress* offers a comic look at the foibles of human nature and all the ways love can seduce, betray and, ultimately, sustain us."

—Jillian Medoff, bestselling author of *This Could Hurt*

"Marcia Butler's debut novel, *Pickle's Progress,* is funny, sharp, totally original, and completely engrossing. It joins the pantheon of great New York novels. I loved every page."

—Julie Klam, NYT bestselling author of *The Stars in Our Eyes*

"You'll laugh, you'll cry, you'll shake your head, but you'll keep turning those pages to find out what happens to Karen, Stan, Junie, and Pickle in this riveting, dramatic version of musical chairs."

—Charles Salzberg, author of *Second Story Man* and
the *Henry Swann* series

PICKLE'S PROGRESS

A NOVEL

MARCIA BUTLER

central
avenue
publishing

2019

Published by Central Avenue Publishing, an imprint of Central Avenue Marketing Ltd.
www.centralavenuepublishing.com

Published in Canada
Printed in United States of America

1. FICTION/Literary   2. FICTION/Family Life

PICKLE'S PROGRESS

Cloth: 978-1-77168-154-4
Trade Paperback: 978-1-77168-155-1
Epub: 978-1-77168-156-8
Mobi: 978-1-77168-157-5

1 3 5 7 9 10 8 6 4 2

For Ralph Olsen

And the Lord said to her, "Two nations are in your womb, and two peoples from within you shall be divided; the one shall be stronger than the other, the older shall serve the younger."

Genesis 25:23

1

TWENTY BRIDGES CONNECT THE ISLAND OF Manhattan to the rest of the world. Only one spans westward, over the Hudson River, and spills onto the lip of America's heartland. Each year, more than one hundred million vehicles make their way onto eight lanes on the upper level and six lanes on the lower level of the George Washington Bridge, travelling back and forth in the name of a dollar, perhaps for some manner of love, maybe just for the view. And if cars and trucks aren't enough, walkers, runners, cyclists, skateboarders, bird-watchers, and jumpers alike can also enjoy the scenery from the walkway known as the South Sidewalk.

The eastbound on-ramp from Leonia, New Jersey offers a surprisingly short approach. Suddenly, as if from thin air, steel cables loom above, swinging like silver-spun jump ropes playing Double Dutch over the vehicles. Massive and audacious, the bent cords ascend and seem to evaporate into a vaulted sky. On a misty night, the terra-cotta buildings to the east, in Manhattan, appear as boxy smears of potter's clay, notched out with squares of glass, reflecting an occasional head-light hitting the mark. Be it a reveler returning from a late-night party, or a sleepy trucker clocking a twelve-hour overtime shift, the George

Washington Bridge suspends many disparate lives during the early hours of a Sunday morning.

Karen and Stan McArdle pulled onto the George Washington Bridge, headed toward the Upper West Side of Manhattan. It was just after three a.m. and they were cranky, probably because they were drunk. They'd stayed at the dinner party far too long and Karen had a few more cocktails than she'd needed, placing herself in that vulnerable corner where Stan could prick her with his épée of marital righteousness. That's just how their relationship felt—sharp and sometimes dangerous. Yet strangely alive as they explored those moments, when one or the other might lunge forward and twist that bright, cold metal a tad, then deftly retract the sword. The trick was to know how far to penetrate the dagger, and how long it could linger without bleeding out the heart.

The urban élan of Manhattan still appealed to Karen and Stan while most of their friends had left years before, joining the ranks of Leonia-Teaneck-Hackensack-Weehawken-Hoboken converts. For a long time, Saturday night yuppie dinners had been the way they'd managed to stay in touch. Recently though, the gatherings had felt more like a gloomy obligation. Their friends, now annoyingly sober, continued to pop out one indulged and irritating child after another. This was not a lifestyle trend Karen and Stan subscribed to.

Some might have considered them to be "working" alcoholics. Karen preferred the term "highly functional"—certainly a few notches up from the category known as "pre-twelve stepper." At least, that's what she liked to tell herself. Labels didn't matter at this moment though, because Karen and Stan itched and scratched as they approached the bridge and that inevitable descent down a mountain of alcohol into a gully called "hangover."

Karen glanced at Stan, noticing a determined grimace on his face. "What's wrong *now*?"

"Don't ask me to go to these dreadful parties ever again. I'm done. Cooked. We've absolutely nothing in common with any of those dullards. Zilch. The conversation? From diapers to college SATs and back again. Numbing. I'm brain-dead just thinking about it. Okay?"

"Whatever. But yeah, you're right. It's gotten boring."

"Hallelujah. *Finally* we agree on something."

"Shut up. I just said I agree with you—that's a *positive*." Karen slid down in her seat with her fingers massaging her temples, attempting to head a migraine off at the pass.

The traffic proved as smooth as crushed velvet, the weather a depressing drizzle, and Stan's classic thirty-year-old Volvo hummed, with over two hundred thousand miles under the hood. He usually kept well under the speed limit—an attempt to avoid cops who might pull them over and sniff the yet-to-be-metabolized vodka pooling in their gullets. But as they drove through the 5 mph E-Z Pass lane, Karen heard Stan gun the engine. She glanced at the speedometer: 30 mph. Gripping the steering wheel at ten and two, he began to count the cars passing on the left, ticking them off by lifting his fingers one at a time. At the count of ten, with all his digits sticking in the air and using only his palms to steer, he curled them back down and started over. Counting was just one of Stan's "things."

Karen's eyelids drooped as she mused about the remainder of the night ahead of them. At this pace, they'd be home in about ten minutes, the Volvo tucked snug in a neighborhood garage. A fight was then sure to erupt over who'd walk their dog. The Doodles could hold it like a flyweight champ, and a typical Saturday night found him holding a topped-off bladder and pawing at the front door while Mommy and Daddy sparred. A typical spat began with Stan slamming his keys on the foyer console, declaring, "I did it last night."

"But I did it last weekend—both days. Stan? Just take The Fucking Doodles *out.*"

Stan would relent with, "Oh God." Or, "Why me?"

Tonight, Karen dreaded a rerun of their tired sitcom. She wanted to bank at least six hours of sleep, because they'd made plans for a Sunday breakfast with Pickle to discuss the brownstone the three of them owned together. Details of the joint ownership had become a prickly point, and Stan's twin had demanded a sit-down. So, Karen made a tactical decision that when they returned home tonight she'd just take The Fucking Doodles out. One of them had to be somewhat coherent for the breakfast meeting.

Karen relaxed, satisfied with her preemptive concession. Her head lolled back and forth on the car headrest, the motion nicely paced, reminding her of the pulse of some music she couldn't quite name. Then there were the *chunk-ker-chunks* of the tires as they rolled over the regulated patches of asphalt repair, creating a jagged counterpoint. The two rhythmic worlds almost never synced up. But if she waited long enough, eventually, they did. Then she'd start over. It was a surefire way to get her head together, and for a few moments she even forgot she was drunk.

Suddenly her heart quickened; she opened her eyes—wary.

"Stan?"

His fingers continued to work the steering wheel and he didn't answer, still wrapped inside his universe of one through ten.

"*Stan!*"

"Huh? Wha's wrong?"

"The oil."

"What oil?"

"The *car* oil—the slick theory. We just started levitating. I can feel it."

"Please. Silence—I'm begging you. I'm *counting*."

"No, listen. This is serious. Remember the oil slick theory? It's worse in the first two minutes of a rainfall and we've just entered minute number three."

"Now *you're* counting?"

"I have to. The cops. Plus, we might die."

Stan blew out a thin stream of air. "Jesus, Karen. I've never crashed the car, as you well know. Just close your eyes if you need to. Anyway, I noticed you went way over your martini limit tonight, so your perceptions are not, shall we say, to be trusted?"

"Ugh. You're disgusting. I hate you." Karen crunched further down in her seat, disheartened that she'd even engaged in the futile exchange. Stan always managed to trump her with some kind of straight flush.

He patted her hand. "The hate keeps us close, dearest. Just like the love. Right?"

"No comment," she hissed. But she took Stan's point because she did trust him. With a brain born for calculation (even when they'd been drinking), he'd determined the travel distance when they'd first started attending the dinners in New Jersey. At just over six miles, door to door, Stan figured they could make it without being stopped for speeding, or getting into a crash due to the weather. Or the oil. Or the alcohol. That's what drunks did: they planned. And counted. Sometimes, they even prayed.

Karen saw Stan's fingers resume whatever it was they needed to do on the steering wheel. She drifted back to her tire-pulse samba (or was it a waltz?), waiting for that reassuring sync-up, and hoped that the Volvo was gripping the road.

"Are you asleep yet?" He couldn't leave her alone.

Karen, irritated, grunted. She turned her body, sidled closer to Stan and considered an answer worthy of his idiotic question. "I thought you preferred me dead to the world. But since you ask, I was dreaming of someone."

"Who?"

"You sure you want to know?" She whispered into his ear.

"Shit. This is stupid." Without looking at her, Stan palmed Karen's forehead and pushed her back.

"No, *you're* stupid." Karen's voice began to rise with irritation. "And now I'm wide awake, thanks so much, and a tad this side of sober. That doesn't exactly feel good. Now slow the fuck *down*."

"There's no one on the road. Calm down."

"That's not true; you've been counting the cars nonstop."

"My fingers have been working at a very. Slow. Pace. Pay attention."

"First you want me to sleep—now it's pay attention. Make up your mind. You're insane—" Karen broke off mid-rant. "Stan. What's that?"

"What?" He looked in the wrong direction.

"Straight ahead!"

A woman was standing directly in front of them, perhaps five hundred yards ahead, with her hands at the sides of her face, mouth open, like the Edvard Munch painting.

"*Jesus!*" Stan jammed the brakes and the Volvo immediately spun out. Karen's oil theory held water after all because she felt the car skim the road, then pick up speed. Though no longer in control, Stan pumped the brake, and after performing a 360-degree pirouette, they bashed into the side guardrail. Neither had worn their seat belt and Karen's upper body flew squarely into Stan's. Their faces mashed together with a force that punched a simultaneous grunt out of them.

The impact jarred Karen's senses—first, a throb at her gum line, and then a pain digging straight into her front teeth. She rimmed her lips with her tongue, tasting tin mingled with vodka breath. And then she heard herself begin to whimper—not only for her bloody mouth— but also because she *was* drunk and her heart couldn't quite bear the shame. Just as quickly, things felt oddly serene—church-like—with only a rapping of gentle rain on the hood, puncturing the quiet of the car interior. Her world felt freshly precarious, as if the planet were indeed flat and teetered on a spiked axis. Karen was afraid of tipping over, terrified to even move, unsure of the damage to herself, Stan, and the woman outside. Yet, cars passed them at a good clip. The accident was apparently a fender bender and not worthy of real concern.

She let her head drop and pressed her face into the crook of Stan's elbow, into the fabric creases of his dress shirt—that crisp, white, 100% cotton, usually ironed by Stan to within an inch of its life—now soaked with his dank sweat.

He whispered into her hair, "Karen? Tell me you're okay."

She felt tears springing but didn't want to be vulnerable. "My mouth feels weird," she mumbled into his elbow.

Stan pushed her up and scrutinized her face.

"My God. Your front teeth are bloody."

Karen's eyes opened wide with astonishment. "Shit. Stan—I stabbed you with my teeth. I can see the dents."

Blood oozed from Stan's forehead, dribbling down along the creases of his nose, coagulating at his lips. Enamel to flesh. The irony was not lost on her; this accident had provided more physical contact than they'd managed in a long time. Stan tentatively prodded Karen's wobbly teeth and stroked the blonde fuzz on her upper lip, then kissed her bloodied mouth. She didn't wince, but leaned forward, accepting the pain.

Just then the rain abated, and she heard a primitive sound outside the car.

"NOOOOOOO!"

It was an inhuman wail—one that would have been hard to identify in nature, if not for the fact that Karen could see the source. The Munch mouth produced the howl again.

"NOOOOOOO!"

Karen pushed away from Stan and climbed out of the car. She stumbled to her knees, momentarily forgetting how drunk she was, and from this vantage point was surprised to discover the extent to which the car was damaged. The front grill of the Volvo was bashed in and steam pissed out from the bottom of the car at several locations. One of the tires was flat, and another, was also headed for that fate. After scrambling to her feet, Karen ran over to the woman, grabbed her arms, and shook her. "Are you all right? What happened?"

The woman wrenched herself from Karen's grasp and bent over, hugging her own waist. She aimed the next words straight into the asphalt. "Jacob—Jacob—Jacob."

Karen backed up, giving the woman some distance. "Okay, okay. But please. What's wrong? Just tell me what happened."

"He's gone. He jumped. He ran and went over the side." The woman spoke with almost no inflection, like she was reciting a grocery list.

"You mean somebody jumped off the fucking bridge? You're kidding me, right? Tell me this is a joke."

"No joke." The woman dropped to her knees and folded up.

Karen ran back to the car and thrust her torso into the passenger-side window. Stan appeared to be asleep, or perhaps he'd lost consciousness from the hit to his head. His toothy wound frightened Karen and she wished, for what seemed like the ten-millionth time, that they were sober. Reaching over, she poked at his arm. "Stan."

He started awake, trying to reorient himself. "Wha?"

"Call your brother, right now."

"Why?" He winced as he touched the gash on his forehead, then stared at the blood on his fingers.

"That woman says a guy jumped off the South Sidewalk. Call him."

Stan shook his head back and forth, bewildered. "God's sake, Karen. I'll just call 9-1-1."

"No. I want Pickle. He's close by. Plus, we've been drinking and I don't want this to get complicated. He'll know what to do."

"But he's in the *city*. We're in Jersey. He won't have jurisdiction."

"No, we just passed the state line—look."

Stan turned around. There it was behind them on the opposite side of the bridge roadway: "Welcome to New Jersey."

His head bobbed with recognition. "Yeah, I see your point. Okay. Pickle."

Karen dragged her head and shoulders back out of the window, then turned to find the woman now propped against the guardrail, utterly still, with her legs stretched in front, her feet canted out in balletic first position. She was drenched, even with the light rain, so Karen surmised she must have been on the bridge for hours. The woman's in-scrutable expression unnerved her. Crouching down, she tried to rouse her by seeking eye contact and gently shaking her shoulder. When she got no response, Karen put her arm around the woman, who then be-gan to moan, "Jacob." A goner, for sure.

"What happened? Miss, can you just tell me what happened?"

The woman looked up, stared at Karen for several seconds, then jerked her head to the side and dropped her eyes to the pavement in what Karen took for embarrassment. And with that gesture, Karen was instantly grateful, because she realized she didn't want to know the answer. Any explanation would have been a falsehood, the true reason surely unknowable. The kind of agony that might propel a man into the Hudson River stirred Karen in a place she could not acknowl-edge, and an awful gush of newly sobered reality pinched her heart. It was always strange, this spiked alertness, occurring on so many early mornings when nothing was certain and everything felt at risk. As she looked into this woman's face, she recognized some aspect of herself, and Karen wondered how the hell she'd gotten to this place in her life.

She glanced over her shoulder to make sure Stan hadn't drifted off again, and noticed his fingers punching at the phone. Pickle almost never answered on the first, second or third try, and she saw Stan's frustration as he redialed. Finally, his lips began to move. He wiped his mouth and grimaced at the blood on his palm. Karen sprinted to the car and grabbed the phone away from Stan, putting Pickle on speaker.

Pickle's voice boomed into the car. "*Fuck*. It's three in the god-damned morning, Stan. Why are you calling me?"

Stan rested his forehead on the steering wheel, then jerked up with pain. "Pickle. Thank God you answered."

"What . . . Stan, this'd better be good 'cause I got a lot going on—"

"Wait. Karen's here too. I . . . we've been in an accident. On the GW Bridge. We're on the New York side, heading into Manhattan."

The pause was long enough for Karen to wonder if they'd been cut off. Pickle finally broke the dead air. "Okay. *And?*"

Stan sighed. "Yeah, we're loaded."

"For Christ's *sake*, Stan. Get some help. Get some therapy. Get to the AA rooms. Do *something*. I'm begging you—"

"Wait, Pickle," Karen interrupted. "It's not what you think. Some guy jumped off the bridge."

"Hold on—lemme turn on the two-way."

Karen heard crackling and mumbled voices from Pickle's police scanner.

"Right. I hear it now," Pickle said, his voice softening. "Somebody must have called in your accident, but there's nothing about a jumper yet. Okay, you guys hang tight. I'll be right there. And for the love of God, don't talk to anybody till I get there. Got it?"

The phone went dead and Stan gave Karen a wounded puppy expression. She crossed her eyes and smiled sarcastically as she threw the phone into Stan's lap. "See? I told you he'd fix it."

"God, Karen. Yes, yes, yes. You were right. Let it go. For once." Stan tried to breathe through his nose. He hawked up a big snuff, aimed his head out the window and spit. With that effort, he let his body slide down to the right, landing across the gearshift between the seats. "*Ow.*" He waved his hands at her to back off. "Lemme sleep."

Karen felt a body come up behind her and then a hand on her shoulder. Turning around, she was surprised to see how tiny the woman was—a few inches shorter than Karen, who was petite herself.

"Help me. Please? Can you help me?" The woman's face, expressionless, and her voice, a low monotone, caused a curious hyperawareness in Karen. It was a contrary sensation of being badly needed while at the same time having no agency over what was happening. She ushered the woman into the backseat of the Volvo, then clambered in next to her. The woman slumped forward, her head down at her knees, lips touching her sodden wool coat. Red hair billowed around her head, illuminated now by a beacon of light from the very top of the bridge. The glow made the woman's tangled hair look like a spiderweb, with no order to madly spun strands. Karen placed her hand on the woman's arm and gently squeezed. The woman took in a shuddering breath and turned her head to the side. It was then that Karen realized the woman was just a girl, really. Not one crow's crease at the edge of her eye. Her forehead was unlined like an ingénue, and a sparse set of ochre freckles smattered a thin, upturned nose.

Karen tried once again for information. "What's your name?"

"Junie."

Stan jolted upright, quickly turned around, and seeing the two women in the backseat, shook his head. "Karen. Sit up here."

"No. It's better if I'm in the back. For the cops."

"But I need you *here*. I don't feel good."

"Not now, Stan."

They sat—almost at military attention—like waiting for the firing squad, while Karen willed herself into sobriety. She listened intently for Pickle's distinctive siren, always sounding a half pitch above the others. He'd refused to get it repaired. Pickle McArdle was like that.

2

WHEN APPROACHING THE GEORGE WASHINGTON
Bridge from the Manhattan side, the Bridge Apartments rise improbably out of asphalt, cement, and oil slick. The building serves as
a New York City landmark for radio heads announcing congestion at
rush hour. "Traffic is backed up for two miles approaching the Apartments," is a frequent warning to any driver heading out of the city on
a typical Friday afternoon. The high-rise is deeply ingrained in the
psychic architectural lexicon of New Yorkers who own a car and have
a need to travel to New Jersey on a daily, weekly, or monthly basis.

Living in the Apartments requires a certain amount of shoulder-
shrugging resignation. Air quality is dodgy most days. The floors shake
continually from eighteen-wheelers rumbling underneath the building on the Cross Bronx Expressway. Yet, despite these atmospheric
and automotive tectonic shifts, residents—solidly middle- to lower-
class—remain stoic, or better, sanguine. Perhaps a reflection of the
flexibility of New Yorkers, the building is mercurial—simultaneously
in-your-face yet off-your-radar.

Pickle gazed out the large window in his apartment, tossed his cell
phone into the pillow at the head of his bed and flicked off his police

scanner. If he looked down, his current view of the bridge and the Hudson River might reveal a one-car demolition derby or a swan dive into the water. But he felt disconnected from what he knew had just transpired: both. That was the curious paradox about living thirty-two floors above river level—the panorama that excited him also made him a witness to an occasional tragedy. But most days, he considered his view as just a wide country road dangling from metal marionette ropes, all manipulated by some version of God.

He assumed his twin brother and sister-in-law were holding up traffic. But then he noticed that cars were, in fact, moving steadily in both directions. Through the fog, the glow of headlights engorged as they moved toward him, while red taillights fizzled to nothing. This meant, of course, that their accident was negligible. No one crossing the bridge would know that a man had leaped to his death, unless they stopped to ask. And no one in his or her right mind would stop, or even care, at this hour of the morning. He fumed; let them wait.

Pickle burped. The Indian food he'd eaten a few hours earlier sat leaden in his stomach. Yellow-orange curry had dribbled down the front of his sky-blue Mets T-shirt—not a nice blend of colors. And he stank. Of saffron, of body odor, of someone else's cigarette smoke, of his own fetid breath. Yet the woman asleep under his bedcovers, not having moved an inch during the call with Stan and Karen, hadn't seemed to mind the offensive scents escaping from various parts of his body. Hasty sex and the late hour had thrown her into a hard sleep. But not Pickle. Sex always woke him up and made his brain go a bit mad—pinging on all pistons.

He walked to the other side of the bed, kicking a shoe with a stiletto heel out of his way, and poked at her through the covers, guessing at the location of her ass. She didn't move but snorted in disgust.

"Come on. Get up," Pickle barked.

"No." The pillow muffled her voice.

"You have to go."

"Why?" Now she canted her head, eyes like slits, toward Pickle.

"Because I have to go to work."

"You said you had the day off." She propped her torso up on both elbows, her heavy breasts swinging like Newton's Cradle.

"Something's come up. You gotta leave."

The woman finally turned over, tossed the comforter back, stood up buck naked, and began gathering her clothes. After a quick stop in the bathroom for a pee, she threw a parting shot over her shoulder. "Pickle, think a hundred times before you call me again."

Pickle locked the door with a snap of his wrist and turned to consider his jumbled studio apartment. The bed was front and center, because that's where he spent most of his time during the few hours he wasn't working his typical sixty-hour week. A Parsons table doubled as a surface for a laptop and meals, one armless chair tucked underneath. He'd jammed an old dresser inside the only closet, shoving his hanging clothes, mashed and wrinkled, to one side. But what did he care? He wore jeans and T-shirts most of the time, anyway. With the kitchen taking up one wall and the west-facing window soaking up another, the remaining wall space was dedicated to a flat-screen TV mounted directly opposite the bed. This 400-square-foot room was the sum total of Pickle's personal life since he'd joined the police force, straight out of cadet training. At the time, one room and low rent was all he could manage and even needed. But through the years he'd come to prefer it, love it, in fact. Because his eyes owned the near and distant horizon, like a bird in an aviary where, in at least one direction, there were no limits. Dumpy as the place was, Pickle had a surprising million-dollar view.

Before he left to rescue Stan and Karen, he returned to the window and stood dead center of the bridge's crossed steel trusses, like enormous see-through Legos anchored deep into the ground. Pickle cast his eyes to the westernmost point and pondered what it might feel like to *not* be Stan McArdle's twin.

They were truly identical—the rarest—indistinguishable even at third glance. As infants and then as toddlers, their mother had been reduced to dressing them in *different* colored outfits just to tell them apart—they were that interchangeable. On fourth glance, the one distinguishing mark was a red mole on Stan's leg. That dermatological miracle was the only indication that they were different—and to Pickle's young mind, like midnight and noon.

Growing up, Stan gave Pickle searching rights whenever he felt the urge. Lying on the bed, pliable as a damp rag, Stan allowed Pickle to inspect his body to locate that dot, again and again, which Pickle saw as important as an Eagle Scout merit badge. But it was impossible to share with the world, as the thing lived on Stan's uppermost thigh. So, when the public at large pointed out for the ten-millionth time— *Look! They're completely identical!*—Stan refused to drop his drawers on command, much as Pickle pleaded.

They were adults now—still the same weight, wrinkles appearing at the same pace, temples greying not at all—still utterly identical. And ridiculously handsome. The swivel-headed stares continued— now not so much for being twins—but for their Clark Gable looks. With emerald eyes, coal-black hair and clear, wan complexions, the brothers could pull a noisy room down to a whisper.

Pickle turned to the mirror glued to the back of the front door of his apartment and scrutinized his face. Sure, he was good-looking— that part was easy and didn't even count, because he wasn't responsible for that luck of the genetic draw. The problem was he didn't feel smart enough, and not nearly clever enough. He wasn't terribly ambitious and though he'd risen in the ranks on the police force, he couldn't even acknowledge that small amount of success. The truth was, he'd just never live up to the *way* of his brother.

The corner of a framed photograph poked out from under the bed and caught his eye. Pickle had kicked it there months ago, for what reason, he couldn't exactly remember. Bending down, he pulled it out, dragging along with it an unused condom covered with dust balls. It was an eight by ten, black-and-white image from Karen and Stan's wedding. They stood in a line—Stan at the left, Karen in the middle and Pickle on the right. The shot was not posed; they were all in mid-motion, but the lens's focus landed squarely on Karen. The photographer knew his craft and had zeroed in on her beauty. That left Stan and Pickle a bit fuzzy. Still, the composite impression was decidedly a trio shot.

Pickle strained to recall the exact moment, and what might have caused Karen to glance away from the camera. Her gaze, aimed skyward, left her mouth in a crooked, slightly ironic smirk. Her eyebrows slanted in a concerned parenthesis, as if a hawk were about to swoop down, grab her by the hair and drag her off. She looked just this side of afraid, dressed in virginal white.

This was the only image Karen had given Pickle from the dozens taken that day. There were so many that perfectly captured the wedding, now in evidence stacked across the mantel above the living-room fireplace in the brownstone. But this one was not exceptional, with expressions that didn't particularly flatter any of them. It was such an odd selection, and he had pressed her about it.

"This is a *shitty* photo. Why'd you even bother framing it?" he'd asked.

Karen had flatly dismissed him. "I don't know, Pickle. It just looks like who we are. Okay? Let it go."

He did let it go, for a long time. Now, before coming to their aid once again, Pickle suddenly understood what she meant. Karen was the only one in focus.

3

FOUR EVENLY PLACED ORANGE TRAFFIC CONES
blocked one lane of the Manhattan-bound off-ramp from the George
Washington Bridge, allowing for police to travel west toward the accident, and for eastbound traffic to filter through. With all windows
opened wide and a soggy breeze passing through, Pickle idled his car
for a few minutes on the Manhattan side of the bridge. He took a
deep, wet breath. He was headed toward a tragedy, yes. Someone was
dead and that was, of course, a pity. Yet Pickle couldn't help but feel in-
vigorated, almost hopeful, because the night itself was glorious. Bulky
rain clouds floated above him and the moisture at street level shimmered. Chilled droplets from the invisible mist clung to the hair on
his arms and he rubbed the sky's sweat into his palms, hoping to create
energy from the friction. Pickle gunned the gas in neutral; the engine
roared, yet nothing moved—an inert power he admired. He shifted
the gear into drive and deftly swerved around the cones.

"Assholes," he muttered to himself while jabbing at his siren. With
each successive punch to the horn, Pickle hoped to dissipate the feelings of frustration that arose when he thought of Karen and Stan and
the brownstone. A century-old piece of Upper West Side real estate,

it was truly a gorgeous hunk of Queen Anne architecture, albeit a wreck. In spite of the need for a gut renovation, Karen had explained to him, the brownstone was ideal for two units. She and Stan would occupy the parlor floor and sublevel with access to the garden, and Pickle would live on the two upper floors where skylights flooded the top story with sunlight.

How nice. Sounded perfect. But it hadn't happened. Karen and Stan's space had been renovated first and they now lived there. The second phase—Pickle's—continued to languish into an endless stall. Which was all the more irritating because initially he hadn't particularly wanted to buy in. After all, Pickle had argued, he'd be giving up his view. But as Karen kept at him in her usual nudgy fashion, he gradually came around and eventually found himself excited by the prospect. So, he'd forked over a considerable chunk of his savings.

Now their meeting, scheduled for the next morning when Pickle had hoped to lay his frustrations out on their lovely mid-century modern dining table (in the very house he was supposed to be living in, but wasn't), was in jeopardy. All because some dumb jumper and his brother's subsequent drunken fender bender had collided on *his* bridge. He glanced down and was reminded again of his last meal, staring up at him from the front of his T-shirt. Pickle absently scraped the crud off with his fingernail. A crusty remnant flew onto the dashboard and slid into the defrost air vents. "Fuck them!" he yelled to no one in particular, and thumbed the siren once more—this time with feeling.

As he slowed to a stop, Pickle took it all in—the experienced cop—guessing who might feign innocence and who was surely not guilty. On the face of it, the scene presented as deceptively serene: people sitting in a car, each banged up, but both easily repaired. Several cruisers fanned out with their noses abutting the Volvo, splayed like half of an all-black color wheel. While Pickle waited for someone to notice his arrival, he watched his crew from a distance. They stood lined up like matchsticks at the barrier to the Hudson, looking south toward the Battery. Some joked as a coping mechanism, while others were obviously sobered by the assumed fate of the jumper.

Finally, a few heads turned his way, sides were poked with elbows, and they busied themselves. A uniformed officer strode up to Pickle's car, shaking his head with a grim expression on his face. "We just got here. It's a mess, Pickle."

Pickle stared over the rim of the steering wheel and then glanced up into the officer's expectant eyes. He wanted to hear about the jumper from his crew because the scanner hadn't leaked that information. With a jab of his chin, he prodded the cop to continue. "And? What's so messy? I heard the scanner—it's a simple accident."

"Well, sure, that's what we thought, too. But the woman in the car told us that somebody went off the bridge. We just called the Coast Guard. Fat chance of living through *that*—the Hudson is high and rough as hell tonight . . ." The cop lingered on the potency of the river's tide status, then looked both ways and leaned in closer. He brought his voice down to a whisper. "But, Pickle. It's your *brother*. In the car, I mean. That's why we waited for you."

Pickle widened his eyes for maximum effect and snorted. "My *brother*? Okay. Let me get in there and talk to him."

The officer shuffled away and Pickle began to toy with how to approach this. For a nanosecond, he considered the glee he'd feel by a future filled with schadenfreude, as he considered throwing Stan and Karen, metaphorically, under the Volvo. He'd expose them as the drunkards they were and it would serve them right, but good. He'd already fixed a bunch of their DUIs and was damned weary of bailing them out of serial drunken fracases. Then again, he thought . . . they *were* family. Resigned, Pickle sucked air in through his teeth and picked a strand of *saag* from between two back molars. He wiped it against the windshield, crawled out of the car, and sauntered over to the Volvo.

Bending down at the driver's-side window, Pickle's eyes silently commanded Stan and Karen to not utter one word. Not yet. They looked back at him, dumb and smug, like a couple of cows getting a last-minute reprieve from the slaughter. He then gave himself three full seconds to sniff the booze and determine the damage. Not too bad, actually—he'd smelled worse from them. This was a rare moment when he could claim dominance, and he relished the feeling, lingering just long enough to notice someone else in the backseat: a small woman, slumped to Karen's right. The detail lodged in his brain but he had to get on with business. Pickle made a quick about-face to his crew and stated only what was necessary.

"Back off, guys. It's family."

Now the cone of silence descended—for cops and victims and perps—before the timeline began and circumstances were recorded. When stories got straight and tight. Where people took the room to breathe and assess and consider. And get sober. It might take three minutes or thirty minutes, but that invisible buffer was always there to aid and abet. And it was needed. Pickle understood too well that most people, even cops and their families, were just bottom-of-the-barrel human.

Karen watched Pickle deal with the logistics of the jumper, pointing here and there, getting his crew in order. While they'd waited for him to arrive, she and Stan had tried to pose as the sober people they wished they were. They barely took a breath. But now that Pickle was here, she felt untethered from the knots of tension inside the car. She slowly exhaled and relaxed a bit.

Junie finally lifted her head and scooted her body closer to the open window. She looked out toward the Hudson and pushed her hair back from her face. With this new perspective, even in the pitch of night, Karen saw Junie's red hair crackle with dappled refraction as strobes from the cop cars bounced off the curls. Stunning. Junie must have been embarrassed by Karen's scrutiny because her body dropped back down and she draped her arms up and over her head with fingers twitching, hiding herself—if I can't see you, you can't see me. She rocked her body and moaned the jumper's name, "Jacob."

Stan turned around. "Karen. Jesus. Keep her quiet. I can't have this woman going surreal and nutty on me," he implored.

"She's not nutty. She's practically a child. Where's your compassion? Don't be such a self-centered monster." Karen rubbed Junie's back with one hand and poked the back of Stan's head with the other.

"Ow! Dear God, what I wouldn't give for a belt right now."

"Right. Your solution for *everything*."

"And yours as well—"

Their voices had picked up volume, and Pickle's head popped back into the open window. "Shut up. No arguments. *Nothing*. Think Helen Keller. We're almost done."

The young woman stopped rocking and slowly lifted her head to meet the new voice. She narrowed her eyes to examine Pickle—then turned to see Stan's profile. Back and forth. The oddness of seeing identical twins seemed to draw her out.

"I don't want to go home," Junie whispered.

"What do you mean?" Karen asked.

"I can't. I'm all alone. I don't think I can handle it."

"Don't worry, Junie," Karen reassured her. "You'll come to our house."

Stan stiffened. "Jesus, what are you *saying*?"

Karen rubbed Junie's hands as she reasoned with Stan. "How can we expect her to go home, Stan? Look at what's just happened." She turned to Pickle, who was unusually silent, staring at Junie with an odd expression on his face. "Pickle, tell him. Tell him it's okay for her to come to our place. You'll fix it, right?"

Pickle thought about what to do and he lingered on the fact that the girl's fate was in his hands. He began to inspect her more closely—this Junie someone, who was now staring him down, clearly afraid that he might decide to ruin her life. Her eyes were not the predictable green to complement her hair, which he imagined would turn a brilliant orange in daylight. No, they were the swimmiest blue possible, firing off shards of sapphire as light shot past her face. And those eyes were the shape of overgrown almonds, presenting a soft and somewhat surprised expression. And then *June*—his favorite month, of all things.

Now, on the bridge, in the rain, with the musty odor of Junie's wet wool coat enshrouding them inside the car, Pickle sensed that something utterly beautiful and possibly life-altering was close at hand. His breath quickened. He would pull this woman out of the abyss of a dreadful night and a jumper's death, and deliver her into the breaking light of day.

Pickle nodded at Junie, then turned to Karen. "Yeah, sure. She should stay at the brownstone. I'll fix it."

Junie squeezed her eyes shut. Stan groaned. Karen smiled imperceptibly. Pickle felt a rustle of motion behind him as the cops crowded in, having given him all the time he and the cone were due. One cop stepped forward and tapped him on the back. "Pickle? What's it gonna be?"

Pickle pulled out of the car window and faced his men. "Okay, the woman says the guy ran from her and went over on his own. I need to get her to the station for a statement. You guys stay here and take it up with the Coast Guard police. I'm gonna drive her in. My brother and sister-in-law will come with me. Get the Volvo towed. Let's move it."

The orders were given, yet no one moved and a few yawned.

"Let's *go*, for fuck's sake! There are no mysteries here. This is not a happy story."

The cops dispersed to a million corners. Karen helped Junie into the backseat of Pickle's car and Pickle directed Stan to the front seat. Pickle revved the engine and took off toward Manhattan as the rising sun, cresting over the top of the Bridge Apartments, blinded him.

4

DURING THE DRIVE TO THE PRECINCT, PICKLE
had called in his partner, Lance Burke, to assist with Junie's interview.
Now, as he ushered her into the room, Lance was prepared with coffee and had already set up a recording device in the middle of a table.
He and Lance had been an effective duo for a decade now, with an
easy give-and-take. While Pickle was known to bend rules, Lance, for
the most part, played straight, which somehow leveled everything out.
They were known as Frick and Frack at the precinct, because Lance
was as memorable as Pickle. His ruddy face, tracked with premature
wrinkles, was topped off with an unruly mop of greying red hair which
seemed in perpetual need of a barber. He wasn't exactly a bad-looking
guy, Pickle conceded, but Lance's glow was not the brighter of the
duo. Additionally, their differing statures gave them a comedic Lau-
rel-and-Hardy appearance. Pickle stood over six feet and Lance barely
reached five foot five. Because they presented as opposites, people often expected them to think and behave differently, as well; tall-hand-
some cop vs. short-average cop somehow translated to good cop/bad
cop. Or maybe it was the other way around. Pickle wasn't sure how it
all worked—he didn't particularly care. All that mattered was that he

trusted Lance in the most sensitive of arenas: criminals and women.

They seated themselves so that Junie could see them both, and Pickle and Lance could make eye contact without moving their heads. Lance shoved inkless pens and stubby pencils to one side. He pressed "record" and, after the preliminaries of date, time, and place, he prompted Junie to begin. "Ms. Malifatano, please tell us in your own words what led to this incident on the George Washington Bridge— and the subsequent death of Jacob Kalisaart."

Junie shifted uncomfortably in her chair, rubbed her eyes, then gathered up her hair. She plucked a longish pencil off the table and dug the tip through her hair and against her scalp to position a messy bun at the top of her head. Pickle, poised to just listen, watched her preparation. He'd be the witness to her recounting of the facts, or what she believed to be the truth, which he knew could be mutually exclusive. He sipped lukewarm coffee and tipped his chair onto its rear legs, with the back splat resting into a corner of the small room. And he thought about the blunt tip of that pencil making a dull grey mark on the skin of Junie's skull.

She began with a sigh, sad and resigned. "We were both going to do it. Kill ourselves, I mean." She closed her eyes, as if to remember, or forget. Or maybe to lie. Pickle pushed these usual notions away because in his fantasy, Junie was on the earthly side of angelic.

After several seconds, Lance nudged her. "You wanted to kill yourself."

Her eyes remained shut, perhaps in embarrassment, Pickle assumed.

"Yes, I have the note and we signed it. I have it—here."

Lance leaned in. "You have the suicide note with you?"

"Yes. And the blue tape."

"*Blue tape*? For what?"

27

Disclosure of a note and the tape seemed to open a floodgate. Junie's eyes popped open, wild and frantic. She straightened up in her chair and wrapped her arms around her midsection in self-protection. "I really can't talk about it. It's private. You wouldn't understand. When can I go?"

Lance reached over and slid a beat-up box of tissues toward her. Junie grabbed a few in quick succession, blew her nose, and then wadded them in her fist.

"I know we won't understand . . . of course," Lance reassured her. "But we have to get a statement from you. Someone has died, so this is now a police matter. We want to get you out of here as quickly as possible. So, the sooner you tell us what happened, the sooner you'll be able to leave. Okay? You were saying something about a note and blue tape?"

"Okay. Right. I'll just tell you, I guess." She blotted the corners of her eyes with the tissue ball. "I was going to tape the note to the bridge to let everyone know what had happened. That we'd done it. But it was raining and the tape didn't stick, and we got into an argument about it. Jacob said I hadn't planned well enough. And of course, he was right . . ."

Lance cocked his head as a subtle signal to Pickle: listen up—be vigilant. Junie's recounting seemed to cause her to forget herself and where she was, so her recitation tripped along like a wife relaying the mundane details of her day to a disinterested husband. But Pickle knew that under duress, people often said things that sounded odd, mixed up or facile. Too pat. He rubbed his nose as an indication to Lance that he'd understood the cue.

Junie pulled a damp, folded piece of lined notebook paper out of her pocket, along with a small roll of blue construction tape, and placed them on the table.

Lance leaned toward the microphone. "Let the record reflect that Ms. Malifatano has produced a piece of paper with writing on it and a roll of blue tape. Go on."

"Well, we hadn't planned on the rain. Or *I* hadn't, anyway. And that's when we started to fight. About the blue tape."

Now she became animated—very different from the collapsed girl Pickle had met on the bridge. She paused to put her finger to her lips. Her eyes widened with a fresh memory and then her finger wagged in midair. A correction. "No. Wait. It was more like he was mad at me for not checking the weather report. But it never occurred to me that rain would be a problem for the blue tape. I mean, it's an obscure thing to prepare for, you know? I'd checked for everything else. I knew when to walk onto the bridge—which day was best and what time. Drivers aren't as alert in the middle of the night, and particularly a late Saturday night. So, I hoped they wouldn't notice us." As she talked, Junie's voice continued to notch up in pitch.

"How do you know all *that*?" Lance grunted.

She smiled, as if happy to finally have an interested listener. "I researched it—on Google. And Wiki. Plus, I knew that the barrier on the South Sidewalk is only waist high, so it'd be easier to jump. The Brooklyn Bridge has much higher barriers. Did you know that? The George Washington is the best, even though everyone thinks most suicides happen on the Brooklyn Bridge. Like in the movies. But that's not true. Anyway, there's lots of terrific information on Google, and ... *ohhhh*."

Pickle leaned forward. The front legs of his chair smacked down on the linoleum floor, causing both Lance and Junie to jump. She let her head drop, with her chin to her chest, and then slowly rolled down and set her forehead at her knees. The pencil in her hair slipped out, fell to the floor, and inched toward Pickle's chair. Her bun gradually uncoiled itself from a tight twist and spilled forward over her head. Clusters of orange snakes fighting each other. He leaned down, tweezed the pencil with his fingers like an undetonated grenade, and gently deposited it into his jacket pocket.

Lance rolled his eyes at Pickle and then broke in. "Okay, Ms. Malifatano. Take a break for a moment. Is it all right with you if we read the note?"

She rocked her body forward as a sign of consent.

Lance nodded to Pickle. The room was only about ten by ten, so any movement would feel intrusive and Pickle didn't want to slice into the potent mood. He silently lifted the paper off the table, nudged the note open and read the words he knew she had written:

Dearest World,

We are not sorry. No, we mean what we've done. We're not sure who we loved or who will love us after we jump. But you all did matter, if only for a bright second or two when we were able to know our minds.

Goodbye.

Junie and Jacob

Handing the note to Lance, Pickle spoke for the first time during the interview. "You wrote that." He stated it as a fact.

She grunted a confirmation.

"It's beautiful."

"Thank you," Junie mumbled into her knees.

Lance's head snapped toward Pickle's as he motioned a silent "*what-the-fuck*?" gesture with his hands.

Pickle ignored Lance. "But I'm—we're—very glad you're alive. I understand that this must be difficult. But without going into the reason why you both wanted to kill yourselves, can you tell us how Jacob happened to jump *without* you?"

He'd just floated the money question. Simultaneously, the feeling in the room shifted as rays of the early morning sun broke through the windows—high on the walls, skirting the ceiling. Pickle knew this particular light as a perceived indication of progress by the unfortunate individuals who found themselves here. He had witnessed this phenomenon over the years. The emergence of sunlight, for some reason, prompted the assumed guilty to fold and throw their chips on the table. They were weary and ground down, not to mention hungry and possibly amped up from multiple cups of coffee. So, after a very long night, it made sense that sunlight equaled hope, and suspects could then reasonably deduce that a bunch of sunlit words might get them *out* of this room and into another, perhaps bigger and better room. Or maybe even out of the fucking building. Fat chance. Sunshine, Pickle thought, was one clever son of a bitch.

"Please go on, Ms. Malifatano," Lance encouraged.

Junie straightened up, shoved her sweater sleeves to her elbows and rubbed her hands up and down her face—smudging mascara, or what was left of it. Taking in a slow breath, she raised her eyes to the ceiling and squinted from the sunlight.

"We fought. About the tape and some other things. Jacob was out of sorts and kind of nasty. And that hurt, because on the subway ride

31

up to the bridge we'd held hands and were close. The subway car was empty, so it felt private. Then, on the bridge, things started to change, mostly with Jacob's mood. I remember thinking it was all so irritating but also strangely typical—like we were standing in the kitchen, bickering like any old couple. But Jacob was unpredictable, generally. He began to run around in small circles and shake his hands, and I realized then that he might have taken a speed pill. He did that on occasion—the speed—to cut into his depression. Anyway, I tried to get him to stop. I pulled on his arm and then both my hands slipped down to *his* hand. I held on really tight—like playing that game where you have teams pulling on a rope. What's that called?"

"Tug of war," Pickle said as he leaned forward, his elbows on his knees, his hands cupping his chin—really fascinated now—like watching the endless last ten seconds of the Super Bowl. Lance's foot poked him in the shin under the table and Pickle shot back up, regaining a pretense of appropriate decorum.

"Right. That game. Then I noticed that my feet were on an area of the pavement that for some reason wasn't too wet. The rain had been coming, off and on, but mostly a drizzle. I noticed this because I had very good traction. And then I remembered that I'd worn my new sneakers. I bought them just the other day and the soles were still rough—you know—good for gripping? Anyway, I set my legs apart and pulled, and managed to stabilize Jacob so that he stopped twirling."

Pickle winced. Why would she buy a pair of sneakers if she were planning to kill herself a few days later? It was the obvious question and Pickle sensed Lance's eyes trained on him. But people did all sorts of things that were perceived as *normal*, before they offed themselves. Such as, "Oh, I had dinner with Uncle Joe last night. He seemed to be doing better and I noticed he had a healthy appetite." Only to discover Uncle Joe a few days later, lying in bed with a self-inflicted gunshot wound entering through his mouth and exiting out the back of his head onto the upholstered headboard. And then, finding his wife stuffed in the closet with her throat slashed. Something like that, anyway.

Pickle avoided Lance's stare and tried to rid himself of his tendency to overthink things. He didn't want to be a cop right now. Because mostly, people were just too weird. They'd give ice-cold or emotionally overwrought versions of both horrific murders and simple fender benders. And then talk about the shoes they wore. Okay, he reasoned silently, the sneaker purchase was simply not an issue.

Junie paused to pull her hair around to her left shoulder. "When I finally got him to stop, I let go of his hand and turned around because I heard a car coming closer—from New Jersey. We were on the South Sidewalk. I told you that already, right?"

"We know. Go on," Lance encouraged.

"Well, it's just that I hadn't seen a car for a few minutes. Or at least I *think* it was a few minutes. Maybe it was just a few seconds. But I remember being surprised about the sound of the engine—kind of like an older car, or diesel fuel. Anyway, when I saw the car approaching I was suddenly embarrassed about even being there. Because just at that moment I felt exposed—out on a limb. Maybe even crazy. Here I was on a bridge, ready to kill myself, and the most mundane things kept popping into my head. It's hard to explain. You know?" She dispensed a defeated sigh.

Pickle was back to tilting on two chair legs with his fingers interlocked behind his head. He was listening with half an ear now, more preoccupied with her face—wondering what gene pool was responsible for birthing that head of hair and those wondrous eyes, and her clotted beige freckles. With a neck so lithe, so swan-like, it was hard to imagine she had the strength to hold up her skull, let alone that thick mane of hair. Her body—as much as he could see—looked very thin. Pickle concluded she didn't have muscles worth a damn. Her only obvious strength seemed be her ability to sit there and tell two strangers what clearly embarrassed her.

The humid atmosphere had made all three of them clammy. Junie's wet coat, hanging on the back of her chair, must have increased the dew point in the small room. Lance's forehead shone with sweat. Pickle's armpits were drenched and he surely stunk, but was too self-conscious to take a quick whiff. But floating on top of everything rode *her* peculiar body odor—a feminine stress smell—feral, really. It comforted him that her smell dominated his. "We're almost finished. You're doing fine. Just push through and you'll be out of here," Pickle assured her.

Junie shot Pickle a weak smile, then her face retracted back to a blank façade. "Okay. When I turned to see how far away the car was, I let go of Jacob's hand. And that's when it happened. He ran and climbed over and jumped, all in what seemed like one motion." Junie put her hand to her mouth and swallowed with difficulty. "I need water, please. I feel sick."

Lance quickly reached to the floor, scooped up a bottle of water and poured a few inches into a paper cup, then set the bottle beside it. Pickle scooted a metal wastebasket closer to her chair with his foot. She drank, slowly first, then refilled, gulped, and wiped her mouth with the back of her hand.

"Thanks. I'm okay now. When he jumped, at first I was surprised, because I was alone. See, we were always together—we had that kind of relationship. I guess you'd call it codependent, overly so. Anyway, that was my first reaction—surprise. Like, this couldn't be happening and we needed to have a huge do-over. Because we'd planned it together and now he hadn't held up his end of the bargain. I'd been deprived—tricked out of something that was *my* right, too. And just then, I wanted to be where he was. In the river. Dead. And now I'm alive, and I don't know what I'm going to do. And that is *SO. NOT. FAIR.*"

She hurled the last three words at Pickle. He flinched. And for the first time, she bawled, from the very bottom of her lungs. It was a wretched sound, like some kind of cog mechanism with interlocking parts made in different centuries. The crunch and grind of her howl was unlike anything he'd ever heard before. And wrong, like an early death. Pickle clasped his hands together, fingers laced, placing them over his crotch in the prayer position.

It was nearing late morning by now and the next shift would soon gather in the precinct room down the hall for their daily directives. Pickle had no idea what internal clock he was running on, but he'd never felt more awake—*alive*—in his life. His palms itched badly and it was all he could do to not pull a comb out of his back pocket and scrape them raw. His mind buzzed as he imagined drinking her hot tears, salty as they surely were. He'd rock her quiet, like the baby/girl/woman he knew she was. He wouldn't press her. No, he'd coax her back to the living. And when she was ready, she'd meet his gaze, with her almond eyes and her blue irises and her orangutan-colored hair and her past life of hurts. Then she'd see him, and know him.

Pickle looked at his watch, then reached over to the recorder. "Terminating at 10:14 a.m." He pressed the button. *Click.*

5

KAREN'S HEART ALWAYS CAVED A BIT WHEN STAN was at his most vulnerable. Having returned to the brownstone, she surveyed the state of Stan's special universe through his eyes. Not only were his shoes strewn from here to there, but clothing lay scattered, willy-nilly, across the floor. The kitchen sink brimmed with crusty dishes and the bedclothes were sullied by an unbearable clump of soiled towels. Karen truly felt for him, but only to a point. Because that was what Stan perceived as the hurricane he imagined swirling around him. In reality, one shoe was proud by two inches in a perfectly lined up row of Tom Ford loafers, a pair of trousers had ever so gently slipped to the floor from the back of a chair, a partially eaten piece of toast sat on a single plate in the otherwise empty sink, and a dry hand towel lay perfectly folded on their pristinely dressed bed. While Karen sympathized, she could not exactly empathize. Stan lived in his head, while Karen was, above all else, a brutal realist.

They'd gone straight to the emergency room from the police precinct, once Pickle had been able to release them as innocent bystanders who'd unwittingly witnessed a bizarre incident, through no fault of their own. And coming off a stinking drunk notwithstanding, that *was* technically true. The diagnosis? Stan's forearm had a deep bone bruise, the tooth gash in his forehead would heal, and he was anemic—a chance discovery from routine blood tests taken at the hospital. Karen would need to see a dentist; her front teeth wobbled. Their alcohol levels had passed muster at .05%. All told, Karen was relieved that they'd dodged yet another in an endless fuselage of drunken bullets.

Once back at the brownstone (after Karen had taken The Fucking Doodles out), they'd collapsed on the bed for a five-hour-post-drunk sleep. Hungover and dehydrated, late morning now throttled them.

Karen stabbed a finger toward the sofa. "Sit *down*."

"I can't. I need to do this." Stan scampered around the living room in his pajamas and robe, wincing mightily with each jostle to his bum arm, as he attempted to restore his imaginary disheveled world to lockstep order. Prodding the odd shoe into place with his toe, he inadvertently jumbled the others.

Karen pressed, "I understand you feel you need to, but this is going to fly differently for a while."

Stan halted in mid-mania and gave a mighty kick to his shoes in frustration. He chugged deeply from a bottle of Icelandic glacier water. While his right fist clamped the neck of the bottle, his left arm was wrapped in an ace bandage supported by a sling, rendering it useless. Stan was a southpaw. He heaved a tortured sigh and looked at Karen as tears began to slip down his cheeks.

Not wanting to witness a flood worthy of Noah, she turned her back to him and continued with a barrage of reasoning. "Stan, please. I don't want to have the same conversation every hour on the hour, so let's review one last time. You're taking pain pills, so you're going to have to cut out the drinking. And you can't use your left arm, not to mention the computer or even a pencil. Come to think of it—"

"Oh Jesus, Karen. Kindly shut up and stop being my mother or whoever the hell you think you need to impersonate. You know very well what the real problem is. I'm seriously *compromised*. And I couldn't give two shits that I can't write or use the computer, or do much of anything . . . although I'm sure that reality will descend upon me soon enough when I go back to the office. Because on top of all *this* . . ." Stan made a broad gesture with his bum arm and the torque of the sweep caused him to commit an unintended twirl. Karen spit out a laugh.

"Yeah, go ahead and laugh your ass off," Stan said, attempting to recover some dignity. "Reduce me to a blithering mess, why don't you? But you're right about one thing: I can't drink. Unless I stop the pills, as you've advised ad nauseam. So instead of infantilizing me, try to be my wifey-wife for a change—you know, the supportive soul mate I married? The one who's supposed to know me better than anyone?"

Stan paused, and Karen knew this was her big cue to step in with some words of comfort. Instead, she remained silent with her back to him, arms crossed and foot tapping.

"Okay—*be* like that," he soldiered on. "But you're on notice: I'm officially in withdrawal from alcohol. You know what that feels like. You're lucky I'm not going into the DTs. Remember Sue Ellen in *Dallas*? Her 'tremor scene' in the drunk tank when she was screaming hysterically? When Miss Ellie and Clayton came to see if it was really her? Because she'd gone missing for a few days? Her makeup was so perfect . . . mauve . . . I think it was season eight. No, maybe the ninth . . . Remember?"

Karen rolled her eyes to herself. "How could I forget? We've only seen that episode about four hundred times—"

"You love it too, so don't go all high and mighty on me. But that's where I could be right now—in the drunk tank. And you seem to have no conception, no compassion for everything I'm juggling. I mean really. *Look* at this place!"

Karen turned around and sliced her throat with her forefinger. "Stop all this shit right now. We had the accident less than twelve hours ago and you're acting like the place has devolved to . . . to that place that starts with an A."

"Arma*ged*don. I can see it right in front of me—the official end of my world." Stan picked up the sash of his silk bathrobe with his good hand, wiped his eyes, blew his nose into the fabric, examined the mess, and then let it drop. A stunned look crossed his face as he realized what he'd just done. "This is what I'm reduced to. Where are the fucking *tissues*, for Christ's sake?"

She didn't feel like even acknowledging his redundant question; a box of Kleenex was sitting right in front of him on the coffee table. Instead, Karen deflected and softened her tone. "Since you brought up the bible, it's Sunday—let us rest and be grateful in it. Dear God in fucking Heaven. Anyway, The Doodles has been seen to and, at the moment, that's all we need to worry about."

The Doodles, who'd been sitting in a corner of the room, heard his name mentioned. He sauntered over and plopped down onto Stan's trousers—only after first clawing at the fabric to make his nest. His lower jaw protruded—a classic characteristic of the Brussels Griffon breed—and he heaved a wheeze of contentment. Then, as if to press the point of his pleasure, he spent a few moments licking his chops, which caused a few viscous dribbles to land on Stan's pants.

Stan promptly grabbed his trousers out from under The Doodles and skulked to the back bedroom. "Is nothing sacred in this house?" The Doodles followed the trousers.

Now the living room became a welcomed vacuum of quiet. Shafts of light shimmered through the front windows and trees from the sidewalk blew dappled shadows across Karen's arms. She stepped into the path of the sun's rays to warm her face. Normally she loved early light, but this morning it was all she could do to keep her pounding head upright. Her hands clenched as she tried to regulate her breathing. Then she caught a disturbing glimpse of herself in the mirror over the fireplace. What a fright; like a morning facial mask dabbed with hot oil, every line seemed exaggerated.

Karen's beauty was not orthodox. Her oval face resembled fourth-century BC Etruscan bone structure; indeed, her features seemed carved from different eras of antiquity. Admittedly, her nose was a bit Roman, her lips a tad thin and her eyes a nondescript brown. Still, while one could pick apart the details, the composite was a heart-stopper.

The brownstone, too, was a flawed masterwork, yet it also worked. Whenever Karen felt the burn of imperfection in herself, she simply looked up to the archways, which consistently measured a few inches off symmetrical. The hardwood floor borders didn't quite match up in the odd corner. Then the ceiling, where century-old tin tiles had been patched in through the years with modern replicas, failed to blend under close inspection. Karen felt reassured that, *yes*, beauty just might come in complex packages.

The amalgam of beauty and design were common ground for Karen and Stan. Their architectural firm, called simply *McArdle*, had grown into a sassy and well-respected powerhouse. At the masthead, Stan was considered to be a straight-up genius—his personality quirks mere trifling annoyances to be noticed and then tolerated. The tricky line in the sand was that Stan would not—*could* not—tolerate any deviation from his design concepts. Just one of Karen's roles, as head designer, was to assuage the clients and patiently explain that accommodation was not a word Stan ever used or was even willing to admit was listed in Webster's. And she'd remind them, at regular intervals, why they had walked through their office doors to begin with: to live in a one-of-a-kind *McArdle* environment.

Within this rarified world of creating space, Karen and Stan connected deeply with one another—ironically, as twins might. They seldom needed to verbalize a design concept; their intuition was perfectly in tune, like a Steinway concert grand sitting on stage at 7:59 p.m. in Carnegie Hall. Often a simple sketch (on a bar napkin, like Stonehenge in the movie *Spinal Tap*, they joked) was all that was needed to communicate an idea. And Karen understood what a relief it was for Stan to be *known* immediately, and so thoroughly. He'd spent a lifetime explaining the "way he was" to, it seemed, everyone on Earth. Stan wore the cloak of the brain trust and Karen ironed it all out.

Karen held her breath, waiting for the theme song of *Dallas* to emerge from behind the bedroom door. Then, as a twang of the country bass guitar thwacked, she released her air. Stan would be occupied for at least the next episode, or, forty-seven minutes.

She stretched out on the sofa and smoothed her white terry-cloth robe, cinching the sash a bit tighter. Her mother had also worn just such a robe. As a young girl, Sunday morning was the best day of the week with her mother. Karen let out a weak giggle, realizing that here it was—Sunday morning—*right now*. And how odd that a piece of clothing had brought her childhood to mind.

When it was early enough that the weather was still unsure of what it wanted to do, she'd creep downstairs. Then she'd turn the corner to see her mother's hourglass silhouette in front of the window at the kitchen sink, wearing that white poly-fleece robe, blocking the seven a.m. light. Her mother sought a horizon young Karen could not yet imagine.

One morning in particular, when her parents had been up all night with the card games and her father had just gotten to sleep on the sofa in the living room, Karen walked up behind her mother and wrapped her arms around her impossibly tiny waist. She squeezed her mother's hands, which were clasped together at the heart level, as if praying. After a few moments, a gesture came back to her—a slight pressing. It was her mother's way of saying, "Yes. I can have you with me now. I can even tolerate your touch." They stood together like nested spoons while Karen waited for her mother to offer the words in a small voice, meant only for her, the rules Karen needed to remember for when she'd grow older.

"Power over a man is simple: Be pretty. On second thought, be beautiful if you can manage it."

Karen nodded, and her chin rubbed into the plush robe on her mother's back. It was not yet certain that she would be a beauty of any sort, and this worry kept Karen awake at night. Her younger sister, Betsy, resembled her mother's Garbo looks. Karen favored her father, or so she was often told. But it was difficult for a girl to translate the handsome and angular face of her father onto her own, and call it beautiful.

"If you can be lovable, that will help things along, of course."

Karen wanted to be lovable—tried her best. But she wasn't quite sure what that looked or felt like. Or, whether she could even learn it, because wasn't lovability something someone else decided?

"You must be sneaky. This will, without question, be necessary."

Sneaky confused Karen terribly. What was it? She'd just crept down the stairs and took some comfort in accomplishing that. So, she could only hope that sneaky was already a part of her.

"And always, always go for the money."

Money was still a mystery, an alien notion. She'd seen a lot of it on the dining table during the card games. The piles created feathery green mountains whose tufts occasionally floated to the floor. This looked beautiful to Karen. But when the men reached across and grabbed the bills and then crumpled them, hard, in their fists, Karen felt disturbed by their apparent urge to destroy something of beauty.

Afraid to move a muscle, Karen took in her mother's words, thinking and wondering, but mostly worrying. She blew a warm breath into the back of the robe and felt her mother's shoulders settle down. She wanted so much to ask questions. But for now, she would have to be satisfied with understanding just small portions of each rule. She imagined if she rolled all the parts she *did* understand into a tiny ball, they would make sense, and explanations might not be needed after all. Maybe she could even figure out the rules on her own.

The last Sunday morning, before the house caved in on itself due to the vanishing of her mother, Karen came down to the kitchen expecting to see her at the window. The sun blazed fully into the room; her mother's body was not there to shape the morning light. She saw the fleece robe lying over her father's slack form as he slept on the sofa. The robe collar was tucked snugly under his whiskered chin. *Her* chin. She saw, just then, that she actually did resemble her father and it felt like a hot poker to her eye. Karen blinked. A piece of green paper poked out of the robe pocket and she became brave. She reached down and plucked it out: a one-hundred-dollar bill. The paper found its way into Karen's fist—crumpled hard—just like the men. And then all the rules finally tumbled together: clear, concise, and now understood. She might, after all, live as her mother had instructed.

Lying on the sofa in the brownstone, Karen watched the sky morph into a grey color she'd never seen before. What part of her mother did she remember most vividly? Was it her godless praying hands, her bewildering advice parsed out in a monotone voice, or the swing of her body? None of that. No, it was the warp and weft of the robe fabric. Karen rubbed her hands up and down the cloth as the end of morning, now devoid of any sun, seemed to ease her headache. She stood on wobbly legs and made her way toward the stairway to the lower level. Stan must have heard her footsteps on the creaking floorboards. He cracked the bedroom door open.

"Karen, don't go down there. Not today. Look at my clothes—all over the floor." He opened the door wider and gestured around the bedroom for emphasis. "And The Doodles. He's on top of my stuff. I need your help. My *arm*."

Karen dismissed him with a swat to the air. "You'll be okay. Go back to bed. I want the space downstairs to be comfortable for Junie. It's almost noon and they'll be here soon."

Stan walked out of the bedroom and positioned himself between her and the stairway. "Why in God's name are we bringing this clearly damaged woman into our home? You seriously need to think about this. We know nothing about her. She could be untrustworthy, maybe even a thief. You saw her in the car . . . like a ghost. She's strange and odd."

"Strange and odd? Listen to yourself. Sounds like someone I know."

The Doodles skulked over to Stan and sat on top of his right foot. Stan rubbed The Doodles with his left toes. "Well, you don't have to get personal. It's just that I honestly don't understand your reasoning."

Karen had to think about this, because she understood that her current decisions were being controlled by something other than common sense. "Okay. I admit this is impulsive and it probably *is* ill-advised," she conceded. "God only knows why I'm taking her on. I don't know . . . I just feel I must . . . that somehow it's necessary."

"This is very unlike you. You clearly haven't thought it through. For example, she must have family that'll take her. Have you even thought of that? They'll be wondering what's happened to her. C'mon, Karen, call this shit off before we get in too deep."

Stan reached over and stroked her cheek. Karen, jerking back from him, shook her head. She couldn't tolerate physical contact and noticed a tremor in her fingers. They quivered from not enough sleep or, more likely, a hangover. A strong Bloody Mary would solve all of this. Instead, she made fists and roughly stuffed her hands into her robe pockets. Laughter from the street outside caught her attention and she walked back to the front window to watch a street scene below the partially lowered blinds. She saw fingers holding cigarettes from swinging hands, baby strollers being pushed along followed by sneakered feet. Even a basketball bounced by. Everyone in the world was propelling the day forward, except her. Karen looked down at her bare feet—the polish on her toes had chipped. She'd gotten a pedicure just the day before, and couldn't remember how or when this had happened.

With her back still to Stan, Karen grabbed at some final reasoning, mostly for his benefit, but also for her own. "Look, we can't let her go back to her apartment when her boyfriend just killed himself. That would be insanely cruel. And besides, she told me she has no family. She's an orphan."

Stan laughed, raucous and cutting. "An orphan? You *believe* that crock?"

Karen reached over and picked up a plastic tumbler from the dining table. Feeling the weightless goblet in her hand, she swiveled and heaved it toward Stan's head. He managed to duck in time and the plastic ping-ponged off the wall behind him, bouncing several times before it rolled back to Karen's big toe.

"See?" Stan said with disgust. "You're a mess. You can't even hit me. But I promise you this girl will be a disaster. Mark my words."

"Whatever. But it'll be my disaster. So today you're gonna do something for somebody else for a change. And if you can't do it for Junie, you'll fucking well do it for me. Today, you are going to be *nice*."

She picked up the glass and placed it, just so, on the table. Stan stepped back and bumped into the wall as Karen walked past him to head down the staircase.

"That's good, Stan. Do your rope a dope, just like Ali."

Karen flicked on the light to the lower level. As she reached the bottom of the stairs, she saw shadows through the frosted glass at the outside door. Curious, she unbolted the latch and found Junie in Pickle's arms.

"Dear God, Pickle. What the hell are you doing at this entrance?"

"We just got here. I rang the doorbell upstairs—I don't think it's working. We came down here to try this bell."

"Why didn't you knock upstairs?"

"I'm not an idiot, Karen. I *did.* You and Stan were screaming at each other and couldn't hear me. But forget that. Just let us in. Junie's a mess."

Karen pulled Junie into the vestibule and then shoved Pickle back outside. She slammed the door shut and locked it.

Pickle began to pound on the door. "What the hell, Karen? Don't do this!"

She ignored him and shepherded Junie into the bedroom at the back of the brownstone. Karen plunked her down on the bed, one of the few pieces of furniture in the room. She knelt down and positioned herself at the young woman's knees, then pushed Junie's hair back. She wanted a good look at her face because up until that point, she'd viewed Junie only through dim light at the bridge.

Suddenly Junie draped her arms around Karen's neck and they hugged. Each time Karen made a motion to disengage, Junie would claw her closer. As they remained in their entwined position, Karen thought back to Stan's words of warning. Perhaps this wasn't the best idea. Junie was not a stray pet that would adapt after just a few nights. Enveloped in Karen's arms was a thoroughly distraught human being. For the first time in a long time, Karen had no idea what tomorrow would bring. A chill crept up her back.

"Do you have to pee?" Karen whispered into Junie's ear.

Junie shook her head.

"Do you need to eat?"

"No." Junie finally pulled away and stared into Karen's eyes, waiting for directives.

Karen looked down at the front of her robe and noticed Junie's mascara smudges on the lapels. On impulse, she pulled off the robe, exposing herself in only a bra and panties. She then undressed the girl, who limply complied, and tucked Junie into the robe, knotting it loosely around her waist. She dragged the covers back and positioned Junie onto the bed. She pushed the girl onto her side and smoothed the covers over her body. Then she lifted Junie's head and placed a plump pillow underneath. Karen climbed over Junie, lay on top of the covers and brought the girl close into her body, like melted granite slices. Her exposed back hairs prickled from the chilled air. Gradually, the warmth of Junie's body bled through the covers and reached Karen's chest and belly. Somehow the contrariness didn't bother her. She stroked Junie's hair and the girl began an intermittent whimper, which gradually turned into a sustained wail. Karen held on hard, as she witnessed an explosion of grief she wished she herself could feel.

6

SQUARED-OFF GRIDS DEFINE NEW YORK CITY, making navigation around town fairly easy for locals and tourists alike. But there are occasional streets that disturb the geometry. Roosevelt Avenue in Queens slices the patchwork asphalt at an angle. Broadway rips up the very center of Manhattan, beginning at the Merchant Marine Building in the financial district, then ascending into the Bronx and beyond.

The Flatiron Building, situated at the triangle of Fifth Avenue and Broadway, whose chignon-like acute angle measures just six feet wide, was Pickle's favorite New York City slice of pie. He stood close to the curve of the building and placed his hands on the limestone façade, cool to his touch, stubbly in texture. Then he looked to the structure's top. Wherever his eyes landed, carved decorations reinforced his admiration. Eagles spread their feathered wings, ready for flight. Military shields stood at attention, prepared to do battle. Acanthus leaves twined around classic ball-and-dart edging. And it then occurred to him that this building, which capped off at just twenty-one stories high, was a reasonable height for a skyscraper. Though little else was reasonable at this moment, because he was about to do Karen's bidding.

When Pickle had delivered Junie to the brownstone the previous day, Karen managed the handoff in her usual pushy fashion, spiriting the girl into the lower level, then slamming the door in his face. After sitting on the stoop for a few minutes to assuage his bruised ego, Pickle decided to try the parlor-floor entrance again. This time he pounded like a firefighter. Stan let him in without a word and they sat around with coffees, eavesdropping on some painful sounds emanating from below. Stan appeared numbed to his apparent future living arrangement, while Pickle could barely contain the excitement he felt about the possibility that he might actually have some sort of chance with Junie.

But soon it was obvious there was to be no inclusion or even discussion about Junie, according to battle plans laid out by Karen. After an hour, she'd come up and shoved a list of furniture items and her credit card into Pickle's hand. Then, she shepherded him to the front door and pushed him out with the parting shot, "Pickle, I really need your help. Go buy all this stuff tomorrow. The salesman, Darren, knows Stan and me. He's older and bald—you can't miss him. It'll be easy."

Pickle left the comfort of the Flatiron, walked a block south, and entered Design Within Reach. He looked around, walked up to his mark—the only bald salesman on the floor—handed him the list, and tossed Karen's credit card on the desk. "Ring this up, and make a note that this is for *McArdle*, so I want the fastest delivery possible."

The man, startled, stared at Pickle. "Stan?"

Pickle remained stone-faced and silent; he was in no mood for niceties, let alone explanations.

"It's Darren—remember me?" The man, confused, blinked for

a few seconds and then continued. "We've worked together several times—all the Knoll furniture you and Karen installed in that triplex in SoHo a few months ago?"

Pickle sacrificed a perfunctory smile, then crossed his arms. Waiting for . . . what? He didn't really know—just that he wanted the guy to suffer. Why this guy? Well, he was standing in front of him. Poor sap.

Darren, clearly floundering, tried again. "I think the address was the Printing House, just above Houston Street. Does that ring a bell, Stan?"

Pickle felt himself cave. After all, it wasn't this guy's fault. "I'm not Stan. I'm his brother, okay? But I don't have time for chit-chat. I want this stuff delivered by the end of the week. Per Karen and Stan."

Darren cocked his head to the side, and then squinted his eyes. "Oh. Sorry. Ah . . . you're twins. You're *identical*!"

Pickle bristled, returned with a cold stare and pointed to the paper in Darren's hand. "The *list*, please?"

Darren examined the paper for a few seconds, logged onto his computer and scrolled around for inventory. He looked up, uncertain. "Well, there is a lead-time on several of these pieces. At least four to six weeks from day of order."

Pickle looked up toward the ceiling and shook his head. "I just told you this is for *McArdle*. You gotta move this to the top of the line for Karen. Is there going to be a problem?"

"I'll see what I can do," Darren stammered.

"Don't see—just *do*. Obviously, this is an emergency, or she wouldn't ask."

"Right. Let me talk to my manager and we'll try to work something out. I'm sure it won't be a problem."

"I hope not, because Karen already told me that they can get this Knoll shit, whatever *that* is, over the Internet—and probably for less money." Pickle paused for effect. "Do you want the sale or not?"

"Of course, Stan. I mean . . . Mr. McArdle. I'll call Karen this afternoon with the confirmation and try to have it delivered by Friday."

Darren wrote up the order and ran the credit card through. "Can I just trouble you for your signature?" He pointed to the paperwork and Pickle reluctantly grabbed a pen off the desk and signed.

Darren handed Pickle the credit card and stared at the signature. "*Pickle?*"

Pickle slipped the plastic into his jacket pocket. "Yeah. Tiny Vlasic Pickles. Just like your dick. Have a nice day."

He walked out of the store and wandered north into Madison Square Park, past a bronze statue of the casually seated former New York State governor, William Seward. The day was fair, with a breeze somewhere between cool and warm, and infant buds on branches brushed the governor's head. Pickle eased himself down on a bench next to the beat-up sneakers of a homeless guy who'd covered himself with cardboard. He looked right and left, noticing several vagrant men prone on the benches, grabbing much-needed rest that, Pickle knew, was difficult to achieve when homeless in the city. Cookie-cutter scenes fanned out in front of him: mothers with infants in strollers, swings filled with kids—their nannies pushing them from behind with varying levels of disinterest plastered on their faces. And with each belch from municipal buses behind him, starting-stopping-starting-stopping, Pickle imagined bombs primed to explode in his head.

The twins had lived in apartments in Nassau County, where they spent their early childhood. Their mother raised them, the father having disappeared shortly after the twins' birth. Pickle had only seen one photograph of him, displayed on a table by the sofa, holding both scrawny, premature infants—with either arm folded up in between their legs. His father's eyes bore into the lens, assured—almost smug. And eventually Pickle saw that he had his father's eyes, so it was as if he was looking at himself. Those eyes, like the Mona Lisa's, seemed to follow his body as he walked through the living room on his way to the kitchen. This troubled Pickle and sometimes, when no one was looking, he'd crawl through the room just to avoid his father's stare, or his *own* stare—self-similar—like a menacing fractal.

Pickle had only a vague awareness of his mother's precarious financial state. Just that things were never quite right, as she struggled to feed and clothe the family. They were not allowed second helpings at meals, but since Pickle knew nothing different, this was normal enough to him. Though he was often hungry again at bedtime, he knew not to ask for food. But as Pickle got older, something shameful seeped into his growing awareness of himself and his family. One day in the future he would name it: they were third-world white—very poor, fatherless, and secretly hungry.

They'd never had a yard like other kids, not a swing set or sandbox in close proximity. So, his mother made a point of getting the twins to the local town park at least twice a week. That park became the equivalent of their absent backyard. She picked them up after school, drove to the playground and unleashed them to the grass and dirt. There were two small fields—one for soccer and one for baseball. It was understood that the twins would always participate in separate sports, mostly because no one could tell them apart. They were known as the "baseball twin" (Pickle), and the "soccer twin" (Stan). For that unbridled hour or so, they exhausted themselves while their mother went to an automat cafeteria across the street. Pickle imagined that she kept track of their games by watching through the thick plate-glass window, covered with chunky black lettering.

Pickle tipped over on the bench and stretched out. The anonymity of Madison Square Park felt sweetly familiar; governor Seward, now his friend. Then a faint odor of decaying feet from his bench neighbor, like a rancid batch of smelling salts, startled him, and his head jerked in a disgusted reflex. The comfort from a few moments ago shifted and suddenly he felt like a released fish that was desperate for a gulp of watery oxygen to sift through its gills. The distant scream of a fire engine circled Pickle's mind like barbed wire—a rescue attempt, but for someone else. Pickle turned his body toward the back of the bench.

One spring evening, the other parents had gathered at the park to take their kids home after the scores were discussed and the losers placated. Pickle strained to see his mother exit the cafeteria. He waited on one end of the field—Stan at the other. Pickle saw the glass doors open, splitting the black letters in half. His mother said goodbye to a man with a prim peck to his cheek. They held onto each other's hands as they separated, with their fingertips the last point of contact, and then walked in opposite directions. His heart pounded in anticipation, wanting desperately to tell her that he'd scored the winning run that day—something he'd never accomplished before.

Her car was parked directly in front of the cafeteria, closest to Pickle. As his mother pulled out onto the street that flanked the park, Pickle gathered up his gear, readying himself to get into the car. But she made a U-turn and drove by, wiggling her fingers at him. He watched her speed to the other side of the field to pick up Stan, who jumped into the front seat beside her. She then made another U-turn. Pickle crossed the street and climbed into the back seat. Discussion of Stan's game was already in progress. He never told his mother about his game-winning run.

Of course, Pickle came to understand that his mother favored Stan. But he learned to ease the burn of it, to make it reasonable, and over time almost normal. And very, very small. He planted all the bones of his pain in a shallow grave, a skeleton that might one day spring back to life.

Cars swished behind Pickle as he lay, cradling his head, on the park bench. Worn wooden slats chafed his hip bone through his jeans, so he turned onto his back. A nap was near and he imagined he could sleep. Then he thought better of the whole thing. Pickle stood up and leaned over the homeless guy he'd almost shared a cardboard blanket with.

"C'mon. Nap time's over buddy. Let's go," he ordered, pulling his badge out of his breast pocket and waving it under the man's nose.

Pickle took the cardboard off the man and saw that he wasn't wearing a shirt. Just jean cutoffs and sneakers, no socks. His entire torso was filthy, his arms blistered from infected injections.

"Never mind. Sweet dreams." Pickle re-nestled the cardboard over the man, who'd not moved a muscle during the exchange.

7

KAREN STEPPED IN FROM THE RAIN, SHOOK OUT her umbrella, and stashed it in the Art Nouveau bronze urn by the front door. She fluffed out her blonde hair, which had frizzed a bit from the humidity. She sloughed off her raincoat and hung it on a hook next to Stan's various outer garments, neatly lined up according to the color wheel and length. Karen scrutinized her appearance in the floor-to-ceiling Art Deco mirror opposite the entrance console table.

She'd soon turn forty-two, but was often taken for early thirties. Her signature clothing style helped: restrained bohemian with a hint of eccentricity verging on Galliano for Dior. But she couldn't reasonably take any credit; nature alone had given her this odd beauty she'd grown into. And just as her mother had advised in her rules, much of Karen's influence in business, and by extension with men, rode square-ly on the back of her looks. Beauty trumped talent and even hard work. So, she worked at it—in fact, was ferociously dedicated to it. Karen stepped closer to the mirror to assess her bust: side view, front view, then back to side view. She nodded to herself and opened one more button at her bra line. Then she smiled.

It was just over a week since the accident, and Stan still hadn't made it into the office. Karen knew he was milking his maladies, plus, he'd maintained a regular diet of pain pills to keep him on the other side of coherent. But Karen, who'd learned the true meaning of the word "sanguine" since marrying Stan, wasn't particularly worried. They had no new projects beginning—just four in current production. The *McArdle* staff, well-oiled in the challenges of New York City construction management, was more than capable of propelling things along. Indeed, Stan's absence had allowed for a festive atmosphere in the office. The staff particularly appreciated this—as if they were able to let down their collective hair.

The brownstone was unusually still and Karen wondered if anyone was home. Her bedroom door was closed; no sign of *Dallas* or The Doodles. This bode well. Karen welcomed the lull before the hurricane: all things Stan McArdle, when he'd certainly grill her in detail about her day at the office. Tucking into her slippers, she padded into the kitchen to consider what to prepare for dinner.

She heard dense chords filter up through the radiator vents from the lower floor—Mahler, Symphony No. 5—music she knew well. Karen had been introduced to it in college via the questionably classic 1971 film *Death in Venice*, starring Dirk Bogarde. Visconti, the director, had used Mahler's music as emotional background texture for the grim plot. The day after she moved in, Junie had asked Karen to bring down a dozen or so CDs so she could listen to music. This particular disc seemed to be at the top of Junie's playlist.

Karen opened the freezer and stared at four unopened bottles of Stoli, stacked on the upper shelf, like dead trout with lifeless eyeballs glaring at her. Stan hadn't had a drink yet—she'd monitored all their liquor every day. And she'd managed to abstain, as well, now eight full days without. Karen fingered the iced surface of the bottles, her body heat instantly thawing the beautiful crystals. Quickly retracting her hand as if a burn had singed her flesh, Karen thought again of the movie—the final beach scene. Bogarde, whose brown hair dye drips down his whitened face, is ill from cholera. But this doesn't stop him from lusting after the young boy. And that unrequited longing always squeezed Karen's heart. Maybe that's why she saw the movie whenever it played in art houses. The music reminded her of a quality of sadness that she simultaneously sought and avoided. Sought, because this sadness was how she knew herself to be. Avoided, ironically, for the very same reason. When the movie was over, she'd usually go to a bar and get hammered.

Karen slammed the freezer door shut and pressed the front of her body against the cool surface of the Sub Zero. She rubbed her forehead into the metal and felt her breasts flatten; her pelvis connected and she became vaguely stimulated as the music downstairs ended with a whispered nothing. Confusion muddied her thoughts—booze, sex, music; she couldn't seem to disentangle the things that both moved her and hurt her. Her mother had not given her a rule for this particular quandary.

Now Mahler segued into the last movement. Junie must be awake—who could sleep to such bombastic music, she wondered. But all Junie *had* managed throughout the last week was to sleep—most of the day, according to Stan—and through the night, as well. Meanwhile, Karen had attempted to wrap up Junie's loose ends by paying the final money owed on her rental apartment and arranging for her humble possessions to be moved into the brownstone. The young woman braided herself into what fate had planned for them all, and limply agreed to everything Karen proposed without question. It seemed that Junie was, indeed, alone in the world. Though Stan continued to voice suspicion.

The hundred-year-old stair planks creaked as Karen descended to the lower level. She stopped halfway to listen for movement, then continued, stepping past shoes lining the hallway. What a difference a week had made to the lower level of the brownstone. Not only had all the furniture been delivered, but stacks of books towered high in corners of the front room. Clothing hung on hooks by the door to the backyard garden. The bath smelled of a recent soak with lavender soap. All this trace evidence of a life buoyed Karen, and she silently committed herself to one more day of sobriety.

Karen knocked, waited a few seconds, and then pushed the bedroom door open to see Junie, awake and reading. The Doodles, also stretched out on the bed, popped his head up. Junie jolted forward, dropped the book to the floor, and quickly dialed the Mahler down.

"I'm sorry, I didn't hear you come in upstairs. Was the music bothering you?"

"No, no—not at all. I just wanted to see how you're doing," Karen assured her.

Junie remained quiet, grabbed a brush from the bedside table, and began untangling the snarls in her hair. Karen turned the music back up a bit, then perched at the end of the bed next to The Doodles, who presented his belly for a rub. She plucked an orange ribbon off the floor and handed the silk strand to Junie, who used it to gather her hair up into a bushy ponytail. They sat quietly for a while, as music saturated the space between them.

"I'm going to make dinner," Karen announced presently. "We have a whole chicken I can roast, or I can make pasta. Anything appeal?"

"Either is fine," Junie said without enthusiasm. "Don't go to any trouble. You've done so much . . . I feel like such a freeloader."

"Please, Junie. Stop. We've been through all of this before and you just have to accept that we're going to take care of you for the foreseeable future."

The future. Karen let the idea sit heavy in her head. She and Junie talked at the end of each day and Karen had gradually learned general details about her sad new housemate: life with Jacob, and how she'd grown up. Though Karen had assumed a terrible upbringing, Junie's story was not particularly tragic or even unusual. It seemed that Junie was a person who, for the most part, allowed others to influence her, and that she wasn't particularly goal oriented. She'd drifted into the relationship with Jacob and was taken with his persuasive personality, until the night she found herself on the bridge. They didn't talk much about the incident. Surely Junie was changed by it, though she appeared to be embarrassed more than anything. But Karen liked Junie, who displayed a quirky sense of humor once in a while. By the end of the week, Karen felt that she was making inroads to what she hoped would be a friendship.

Junie gave a weak shrug and Karen softened her voice. "Junie, don't you believe in fate? Kismet? That things might happen for reasons that we can't immediately understand?"

Junie tossed the brush to the end of the bed. "I don't know. Maybe."

"Well, I honestly believe that meeting you on the bridge was just that. Kismet. It could have been the car behind us, or the one in front. But it wasn't. We stopped, or crashed anyway, and there you were. And as much as the event has been horrible for you, with Jacob's suicide and all, I'm here, *now*, to help you in any way I can and for however long it takes. I want you to try and accept this. Do you think you can?"

Junie hesitated and then gave Karen a doubtful smile. "Okay. As much to thank you as anything."

"You don't have to thank me. Actually, you being here is doing something for me too."

"Oh? I just thought you were a saint and a really nice person."

Karen laughed and relaxed. She stretched across the bottom of the bed, propping her head up with her hand. The Doodles belly-scooted over and rooted his nose into her neck.

"Yeah, well that's nice of you to say, but I certainly don't see myself as a saint or even a 'really nice person' most of the time. I've got a lot going on with Stan, as you might imagine. And the business, too. It's stressful and on many days, not a lot of fun. But there's something I want to tell you. Then, maybe you'll understand a bit more."

The next disc had just begun with more Mahler: *Kindertotenlieder—Songs on the Death of Children*. Karen hesitated for a moment; maybe the music was a warning. A sweat came up and she wiped her forehead with the palm of her hand, but was cold at the same time. Turning to lie on her back, Karen pulled her cardigan tight around her waist. Now she felt modest and followed the S-curve of the cove molding where the wall met the ceiling, looking anywhere but into Junie's eyes.

"I didn't help someone when I was young. A man—he was sort of a friend of my father's—was abusing my younger sister. And one day, by chance, I discovered that it was going on. I was about thirteen at the time and couldn't completely comprehend what I saw; I was only vaguely aware of sex. The man's back was to me, but I knew who he was."

Karen coughed and fixed her eyes on the ceiling light fixture, a stationary orb. "She seemed to let it happen. There was no resistance and no indication of discomfort, so it was somewhat unclear to me that this was wrong or bad or even harmful. But I never said anything—kept it to myself."

Karen knew that this version, as difficult as it was to admit to, was deeply watered down, nowhere close to the truth. In spite of the fact that Karen *was* naïve to any manner of sex, or that, yes, her view of Betsy was blocked almost completely by the man's body—this bedroom scene was, still, horrific. But what she could barely think, let alone say out loud, was that Betsy never recovered from her trauma and died of a heroin overdose several years later.

Karen let the piece finish. Then, she reached over and shut off the CD player. She didn't want to know what might be cued up next—certainly more wrong music—and she was grateful for the thinness of the silence. As she lay on the bed, Karen's breathing slowed to its lowest point, as if the autonomic nerve system had failed her and she had to consciously pump air down to her diaphragm in order to stay alive. The effort felt like a punishment. She turned and met Junie's eyes. "That has largely defined how I see myself, Junie. A coward."

Junie shook her head. "How awful."

Karen slammed her eyes shut, tight.

"No, no," Junie jumped in. "Not that you didn't tell, but that you've tortured yourself all this time. You were young. You weren't in charge."

"Well, I suppose that's true, but I was the older sister. Our mother was gone by then and Betsy didn't have anyone else but me. Anyway, I haven't forgiven myself."

"I can understand that. Guilt is a pretty bad house to live in."

Karen took those words as Junie's way of acknowledging what her days might be like thinking about Jacob; he was gone, and Junie was still here. She sat up and grabbed Junie's hand for emphasis. "You see now? Why I want to help you?"

Junie offered Karen a quick, encouraging smile.

Footsteps clomped above them and The Doodles poked his head up, then jumped off the bed and scampered up the stairs. They both waited a few minutes until Stan left the brownstone to take The Doodles out for his pee before they continued.

Junie's eyes suddenly brimmed with tears and Karen moved closer. "What's the matter?"

"Nothing."

"What nothing? Is it what I just told you?"

"Yeah, that's part of it. But hearing Stan upstairs . . . he hates me."

"Stan?"

"Yeah."

"Stan doesn't like anybody. Even me, at times."

"You're at work, so you don't know. But when I go upstairs and he's in the kitchen or the living room, he just turns around and goes into the bedroom. He hardly talks. It's uncomfortable."

"But think about it, Junie. You don't talk much either."

Junie paused to take this in. "I know . . . Okay, I get what you're saying."

"Look. I'm not saying you need to engage in some kind of phony conversation at every turn. But you must have gleaned by now that Stan is not like other people."

"He does seem odd." Junie lowered her eyes with this admission.

"To say the least. And he can't help it. He's not in control most of the time. So, this transition—with his bad arm and you being here—it hasn't been easy for him. It's not in his nature to consider others, but it doesn't mean that he doesn't like you. Just give it some time. That's exactly what I'm telling him—to give it time. He'll come around and so will you."

"How can you be sure?"

"I'm not. But part of what Stan relies on me for is to act as if I *am* sure. And I suppose I'm asking you to do the same. Trust me just a little, maybe?"

Junie sat up with resolution. "Sure. Let me get dressed and I'll come upstairs and help you with dinner."

"That would be lovely."

Karen's cell phone rang from the upper level. She disengaged herself and trotted upstairs. Seeing the familiar number on the screen, Karen picked up. "Pickle?"

"I'm around the corner and I'm coming over."

"Wait, not tonight."

"Why the fuck not?"

"The timing's off. Please, not tonight."

"You've been putting me off, Karen. All goddamned week. I'm comin' over. Now."

Pickle hung up on her just as Stan returned. The Doodles was dripping wet. Karen threw a dishtowel at Stan. "Wipe The Fucking Doodles off. And get out of that robe. Get dressed, for God's sake! You look dreadful—that robe could stand up by itself and take a bow."

Stan knelt down to rub The Doodles dry. "What are you talking about? This is only its second appearance. Plus, it works perfectly with my pajamas."

"Whatever. Get moving. Pickle's coming over in five minutes."
Karen looked at the freezer door and imagined the Stoli bottles inside.
One more day, she thought. Better yet, one more hour.

8

PICKLE PACED IN FRONT OF THE BROWNSTONE
as cars whizzed by, spraying the sidewalk with oily rainwater. He
danced back toward the building, dodging a few spritzes. He combed
his hair, sprayed his breath, and popped in a mint for good measure.
Then he cinched up his pants by the belt and tucked in his shirt. He
looked down at his belly and smoothed his hand along his flat abs; at
least he didn't have a paunch like most men he knew. Finally, he re-
flexively brushed non-existent dandruff off his shoulders and began to
muse about the injustices that surrounded his life.

Pickle found it difficult to swallow the claim that Junie had been
asleep in bed for the entire previous week. But that's what Karen had tried
to force-feed him every time he'd called. She'd painted a touching portrait
of the young woman buried under the covers, in the pitch dark, much too
disturbed to entertain a visit from the likes of him. Karen talked a tidy
story. So, the past several nights he'd come down at midnight to conduct
his own private drive-by. He was not above spying on them. And good
thing, too, because unless Junie slept with every single light bulb turned
up to eleven, and there was a ghost living on the bottom floor pacing back
and forth behind the front curtains, Karen was a big fat liar.

He shook out his hands to ease his frustration and focused on the evening ahead. Making a good impression was important—Pickle knew this. Female and male alike had advised him that it wouldn't do any harm if he made more of an effort with his appearance. Because handsome as he was, Pickle was a slob. But for the most part, Pickle didn't care a whit about his looks. As a matter of fact, he secretly relished taking inventory of his past meals via the slop that had dried up south of his chin. He'd reminisce: Oh yes, Chinese—soy sauce from a few days ago. Italian—pasta grease from yesterday. And always, black coffee with his breakfast. He considered this quirk his birthright—and at least he wasn't in Stan's peculiar hell of perfectionism. But tonight, Pickle had cleaned up, because he thought he'd found the woman to push him over his own personal cliff of filth, and he was ready to do a swan dive worthy of a ten from the Russian judge.

The rain had mostly abated, leaving a fishy scent from the Hudson River mingling around him. A new moon fizzed through the almost-bald branches, which clawed at the dewy air. The evening could almost be a noir movie set, if not for the suspicious pedestrians who looked Pickle up and down as he stood staring at the brownstone, muttering to himself.

Pickle stuck his tongue out at the next ogler who gave him a sidelong glance. "What're *you* looking at? I'm talking to myself here!" he yelled into the guy's back.

Suddenly Pickle felt foolish and began a well-worn litany of second-guessing. Was he *too* well dressed? Who did he think he *was*? And what was the *point*, anyway? Because, if he was honest with himself, how could someone like Junie take to someone like him? Since that morning at the precinct, he'd built her up in his mind as the Queen of Sheba. Now, as he stood at the steps of the brownstone, his sense of deficiency roared through like Amtrak, on schedule for a change.

It was all Karen's fault—the whole lot of it. He didn't even have keys to the damned house he partially owned. The meeting that was supposed to iron out all this delayed renovation bullshit had simply evaporated, as if the elephant ambled out of the room and sailed the Queen Mary back to Africa. He was at Karen's mercy and felt no agency in his life. Then he reminded himself that Junie was not some far-flung fantasy—she was about fifty feet away. This helped to calm him, and Pickle again scrolled through the only things within his control: his hair, his breath, a mint, a clean shirt, a belt, ironed trousers and finally, no dandruff. For good measure, he pulled out a pocket mirror to check his nose hairs. Clipped. Good.

Just as he was about to race up the steps to make his entrance, the front door opened and Stan, dressed in matching celadon green sweats, T-shirt, and sneakers, breached the upper landing. His bruised arm, in the bandage but out of the sling, swung heavily at his side. Stan hesitated, sniffed the air, then clomped down the steps to meet Pickle.

Usually the kempt twin, Stan appeared haggard—like out of last week's police lineup. A yellowing bruise from Karen's teeth stretched across his forehead. His unshaven beard, possibly due to shaky hands from withdrawal, clouded his cheeks. All of this pleased Pickle to no end. He straightened up and smiled broadly at his brother.

Stan brusquely pierced Pickle's optimism. "Don't smile at me like that. I'm doing worse than I look. And what're you doing standing here talking to yourself—out loud, no less? I've been watching you for ten minutes. Karen's got the dinner almost on and that girl is *finally* awake and about to come up for air."

Pickle cocked his head in disbelief. "You mean she *has* been asleep downstairs this whole time?"

"Well, not the *whole* time, but yeah, she sleeps a lot. But I think she stays down there because I get the feeling she doesn't like me—at least that's what Karen has intimated. Wait. Correction: the girl thinks I don't like *her*. But what's the difference? Bottom line? We don't communicate well. Anyway, in case you care at all, I'm miserable. I can't work. I can't drink. I'm on pain meds. Ergo my intestines are at a standstill. I haven't showered—only baths are allowed and I can't tolerate sitting in dirty water. Bathtubs are all wrong."

"Bathtubs are *wrong*?" Pickle prepared himself for a Ted Talk on ablutions according to Stan.

"Yes, as a matter of fact they are dead-to-rights wrong. My client, the one in 15 Central Park West? He's Indian—from the country—and they have four full bathrooms in their apartment. He's having us gut out every tub in the place. He'll only use showers. I told him it was bad for resale—they should leave at least *one* tub. But he was adamant, and didn't give a shit about the resale. He's filthy rich, so what does he care? But ideologically, he agrees with me. He won't take a bath. It's unhealthy—the germs breeding like bunnies in tepid water—"

"Bad metaphor—rabbits don't spend quality time in water," Pickle interrupted.

"Quiet. I'm on a roll. Anyway, now I'm sitting in a filthy bathtub every stinking night. I can't even shave, and God knows when this dreadful bandage will come off—"

Pickle'd had enough. "Stop, for fuck's sake! Listen to yourself. *Bathtubs*? Do you actually believe this nonsense?"

Stan paused to consider. "Yes. Yes I do."

"But wait. Wait a damned minute. I thought your clients in that building were Brazilian." Whether he liked it or not, Pickle heard all about their projects, so it was relatively easy to store this drivel in his subconscious and cough it up when it suited his cause—like an opportunity to throw an inconsistency in Stan's face.

"I fired them," Stan scoffed. "They were whiners. I'd never heard such moaning—day in and day out. But that wasn't the kicker."

"No? Oh, goody, tell me how evil you were." Pickle also had to admit that he vicariously fed off the fact that Stan was in a position to tell people to go to hell without passing Go. Which he did frequently and with blithe satisfaction.

"With pleasure. What pushed these South American goats off the Andes was that they had the gall to object to what I wanted for the space—"

"Stop. These people are from Brazil. The Andes are in Peru."

"Don't bother me with topographical details. Anyway, it seems they had 'ideas.' And most of them stemmed from predictable mother projections they were exploring with their current four-hundred-dollar-an-hour shrink. How dare they work out their inadequate breast-feeding issues on me! My God, how I could make money analyzing these people. I could retire tomorrow with the shit I've had to sift through. So, they had to go. Even Karen agreed, and she's loath to fire *anyone*. Anyway, the Indian guy was in the building already and had just bought an apartment on a higher floor with better views. I told them the place would need to be completely gutted and that they'd have to do what I wanted. They agreed immediately. Of course."

"Oh, of *course*," Pickle said with sarcasm.

"Look, I have my standards. But what do you want from me? I'm a mess." Stan bandied his bad arm up and down in a demonstration of disability.

Pickle grimaced with disgust. Why did people think Stan was such hot shit? It must be his fashion plate: celadon—a trendsetter. "Forget about the stupid bathtubs. Let's get back to Junie. Seriously, Stan. What the hell's going on in there? I've called Karen every day and she's been putting me off like crazy."

"Nothing's going on—*seriously* nothing. Not that I'd know much anyway. I haven't descended to that level of the brownstone since we moved in. I don't like environments that are underground, even halfway."

Pickle grunted in acknowledgement. He knew Stan had an aversion to basements, maintaining that only people in coffins should spend any time at all below grass level. Another one of his "it's wrong" convictions—like the bathtubs—prime fodder for another "Talk." And who was this "Ted" bastard anyway, Pickle wondered.

Stan laid his bad arm on the wrought-iron railing. "God, this thing's heavy. But since you ask, all I know is the girl, who by the way isn't such a girl—I think she's in her late twenties—is recovering from her 'trauma.' This is all according to Karen, of course. I've barely uttered a word to the nymph."

Stan paused to scrutinize his fingers at the end of his bandaged arm. "Jesus, even my cuticles are a disaster. Look, Pickle. A word of advice from your older brother by sixty-eight seconds: Don't get ahead of yourself. Don't overblow things. It's only been a week. To be honest, I think Karen's right to hold you off."

"You and Karen: the undivided force of nature."

"I understand you've taken a liking to her, but you can't expect to charge in and swoop her up."

Stan reached over and patted Pickle's cheek. "By the way, you look good."

Pickle jerked his head back. "Thanks."

"No, *really*, you look good."

"I *said* fucking *thanks*. Stop acting like it's a miracle from the baby Jesus."

"Well, you have to admit I don't see you shaved, showered, reeking of Mentos, and in trousers and a sport coat very often. With a belt."

"What the hell do you expect? I'm a cop who's usually in civvies. We don't dress up. We try to fit in, blend with the crowds?"

"I cannot relate to the crowds to which you refer," Stan stated with indignation.

"Stop the uppity shit, Stan. Try to remember your humble beginnings—the good old fucked-up years." Pickle tapped his forefinger to his lips. "You know what? You should be a cop for about ninety seconds. Your entire view of humanity would change instantly. Rich or poor—people are people. Period."

"God. This drivel. Were we even raised by the same she-wolf? Please, remind me."

Karen popped her head out the door and screamed in a whisper, "Dinner is served!"

Stan started up the steps, but Pickle held him back. "Wait up, Stan. Karen, we'll be there in a minute."

She eyed them both, sniffed the air, threw them a phony smile and closed the front door.

Stan sighed. "See? Even Karen smelled your breath from fifteen feet. You're going to have to sleep that mint off. Now, what?"

"You know what. I'm begging you to take advantage of this latest episode of demolition derby to dry up."

"We'll see."

"I looked up your record of DUIs and you're at the limit. One more and bye-bye car for a year. Not to mention other considerable inconveniences. Trust me, you do not want to tip into that world."

Stan remained silent, nodding his head incrementally, and Pickle couldn't tell if the gesture meant agreement or if he was just placating him.

Pickle pressed. "And it's not because I judge you . . . really—"

"Oh no you don't! Don't you dare throw me that deadbeat line about *no judgment*. We both know there's not a person on the planet that doesn't judge a drunk. You work with them and I *am* one. So, there's that. Second—"

Pickle raised both hands to halt Stan's freight train of deflections and justifications. "Just shut up and let me finish? Okay, I won't stand here and torture you with all the reasons you already know."

"Well thank God for that!" Stan smirked and murdered a mosquito on Pickle's hand with his bandaged arm.

"I'm just saying this could be the time that you stop. For real."

Pickle paused and stared at his twin's face, which was actually *his* face, and an odd realization occurred to him. At that moment, Stan looked like the disheveled Pickle, and Pickle could easily pass for the natty Stan. They were ghost twins and always had been. A clever immersion into one another's psyche began early on when Stan began to trick his mother. He'd impersonate Pickle, dress like him, take on his persona completely—all in order to absorb the fierce blows she'd meant for Pickle. This was a debt Pickle knew he could never repay.

Stan shook his head with his hands over his ears. "Goddamn it, Pickle. I know you're about to wax poetic about our childhood and ... it's manipulative ... and frankly, beneath you."

"I don't give a shit. I'm here because of you."

"What*ever*!" Stan heaved a sigh and lowered his voice. "Well, it's been over a week now. Let's not jinx it."

"No drinking? Really? That's great," Pickle whispered back.

"I said, don't mess me up. I don't wanna talk about it. Let's just go in."

They found Junie sitting at the dining table with The Doodles perched on top of her feet. Cloth napkins peaked like triangles at each place setting, the salad had been tossed, and glasses brimmed with sparkling water.

Pickle eyed the water and then Karen.

She waited a beat. "Do you want a drink, Pickle? Wine perhaps? Stan and I are drying out a bit." Another three beats. "Junie knows all about our current sobriety. Good things can come out of tragedy sometimes."

"Cut the platitudes, Karen," Stan groaned. "I'm barely holding it together over here."

"Nothing to drink for me. Water's fine." Pickle thought it best to stay sharp.

He took the seat opposite Junie, nodded to her as a greeting, and looked around the open-plan space. Karen always came up with interesting stuff to display on the live-edge walnut shelves above the kitchen counters. In fact, everywhere he looked, Pickle couldn't help but admire Karen's sense of color, style, and her overall sophistication.

The place was ridiculously lovely. How nice for them.

Karen stood at the end of the dining table and began carving into a roasted chicken. The Doodles took his cue, gave up his short-lived devotion to Junie's feet and strolled over to Karen—the dispenser of the tidbits—for a chance at a scrap of poultry. As the knife slid back and forth across the meat, Karen stabbed at small talk. "I heard the weather is supposed to be nice tomorrow. Thank goodness."

"What the hell difference does that make in *my* life, Karen? I can barely go outside with this thing suffocating me," Stan snapped, waving his arm up and down like C-3PO.

Karen plopped down into her chair and put her head in her hands.

"Sorry." Stan pushed his hair out of his eyes with his left paw. "I'm just really having a hard time. I can barely feed myself with my right hand. I'm hungry all the time."

Karen looked up and her eyes drilled into Stan. "Then stop complaining and keep shoveling in the food."

As Stan and Karen devolved into their most familiar characters—Albee's Martha and George—Pickle began a game of cat and mouse with Junie. He'd catch her looking at him and he'd smile. Not too much. Just enough to impersonate a guy she might take to—on alternate Saturdays, every three months—if he was lucky. But as soon as the corners of his lips went north, she'd look away. Then he'd admonish himself for the attempt. This eye banter continued while the odd couple excavated some disturbing aspects of married life. Their voices rose and they soon began screaming at each other. Pickle barely took notice; he considered their arguing like background noise. But he saw Junie cave into her seat, little by little.

"Jesus, you guys. You're giving Junie the wrong impression. Can't we have a nice family meal?" Pickle gave Junie a sarcastic wink. "See how the McArdle clan shows its love, Junie? All the dreadful fodder is fair game. And speaking of manure, Karen, Stan reminded me while we chatted outside that he has an aversion to basements. And bathtubs, but we'll leave that topic for another meal. Anyway, this made me wonder why you guys took the two *lower* floors of the brownstone. See Junie, I'm supposed to have the two *upper* floors."

Junie piped up for the first time. "You mean you own this place, too?"

"Yup."

Karen stared at Pickle, blinking several times. "Pickle, now is not the time for this discussion. But if you must know, Stan is fine with the arrangement—parlor floor and basement."

"I am?" Stan said with bewilderment.

"Yes, you are. We discussed this."

"We *did?*"

"Yes, we did. That's the end of that."

Stan shot up, causing his chair to fall backwards. "*No.* No, no, no. Waiiiiit a goddamned minute, Karen. Pickle's got a good point. I don't remember this so-called discussion and anyway, why would I agree to something that doesn't make sense? I won't go into basements—and you of all people know this very well—so why *are* we living on the two bottom floors? You're taking advantage of me, Karen. I miss things and then you railroad me!"

Pickle began to laugh. Karen slammed both hands on the table.

"Pickle, shut up. And Stan? Sit. Both of you calm the hell down. You're acting like idiots. This is embarrassing. We have a *guest* in the house."

Stan righted his chair and, chastened, slumped into his seat. Pickle leaned in, wondering exactly how she was going to finesse all of this. But of course, Karen proceeded with Socratic reasoning.

"Stan. Listen to me. We did talk about this and decided that it would be easier if we kept you and all of your needs to one floor. You know—the organizing, the counting, the color-coding, the lining up, yadda yadda. If all of that bled to another floor, then there'd literally be no place for me. So, the basement is perfect. And further, we both decided that it would be nice for Pickle to enjoy the better light upstairs."

Karen fixed her face into a pout as if she'd had to beat her children after they'd been bad boys. "*Jesus.* You're both so suspicious of me, and neither of you has a memory worth a dime."

"Pickle, she's right. I remember now. I think," Stan acquiesced.

While all this bickering went on, Junie had slowly risen from her chair and backed up toward the stairway. Her hands found the railing behind her and she gripped for stability. Pickle recognized the look on her face—one he'd not been able to forget all week, since the precinct. Her inability to bear the sway of her world, when her lungs were about to explode from grief. And he was now helpless to rewind this dinner mayhem, which he'd helped to create.

Junie called for The Doodles and they disappeared down into the basement.

Stan, clearly exasperated by the sudden departure of two-fifths of the dinner crew, muttered, "Jesus, that dog never goes down there. One week with that girl and he's turned rogue on me. I can't count on anyone anymore."

For a few moments, no one moved. Then Stan began to press Karen for his nightly recap about what had happened at the office that day and she obliged with excruciating detail. Pickle pushed it all to the background—it sounded like the worst elevator music ever plagiarized.

9

THE DINNER ENDED WITH A LIMP FIZZLE. JUNIE slunk back into her Mahler, and Stan receded to the bedroom for a soak in a tub of filthy water followed by some *Dallas*. Pickle remained in the kitchen to help Karen clean up. They worked quietly, as a team—clearing the dining table, washing and drying the dishes, then stacking them onto the shelves. Karen didn't like dishwashers— too noisy, the cycle too lengthy, she maintained. In fact, she eschewed many trappings of domestic convenience. A purist, or just a micromanager, Pickle wasn't sure which.

He stood at the sink and rubbed the goblets clean of potential water spots, the way he knew Karen liked, while she went into the living area to call for her car service to take him home. And he stewed. He'd not made any headway: to make an impression on Junie, to speak with her privately, to make plans. But perhaps more importantly, to get back on track with the brownstone renovation. Pickle was the twin who was always on the wrong side of some threshold. He threw the damp dish towel across the room. It hit the wall and slithered to the floor. Exhausted from an evening of defeats, he closed his eyes and shook his head.

Stan had been their mother's helper in the kitchen; she appreciated the way he applied his obsessive fastidiousness to mundane house-work. While the clatter of dish washing rang though their apartment, Pickle labored over homework at the dining room table. He was expecting a call from a boy down the street who'd asked for his notes on a test to be given the next day. Pickle was a good student—not brilliant like Stan—more workhorse, more dogged. But he was always prepared and classmates frequently called upon him to help out with assignments, a spirit of generosity his mother maintained had no intrinsic value. Stan, on the other hand, had a phenomenal memory, never wrote anything down, and was therefore useless to help anyone. This was part of his emerging savant brilliance and it delighted their mother endlessly.

The dish noise momentarily ceased when the phone rang. Expecting to be called to the phone, Pickle scooted his chair back, gathered up his notes, and made his way down the hall to the kitchen. He stopped just short of the doorway, still hidden from view.

His mother answered. "Hi, Paula. Sure, I've got time ... Oh, I'm *so* sorry. What a shame. How does Bob feel about it? Well, at least you're in agreement. Do you need me to go with you? Sometimes it's easier if you're with a woman, and I know Bob's a bit squeamish. Okay, just let me know when and I'll take a sick day. And Paula? You won't regret this. I can honestly say, two are a burden."

As he listened, Pickle's knees turned to oatmeal. His legs buckled and he slid to the floor with his back against the wall. He felt slightly sick to his stomach. On any other day, he'd call for his mother to help him. But now, holding back the urge to vomit, he remembered that he should place his head between his knees. Pickle stared at the floor, as he listened to his mother continue to encourage her friend to have an abortion.

"The day of their birth? What a mess. I was hysterical. Out of my mind. Stan was already in my arms. He was enough. When Pickle came, I just screamed, 'Put it back in—put it back in!' Well, what are you going to do? Okay—talk tomorrow. Bye."

Stan's feet appeared. He gripped Pickle by the elbows, his hands still wet from the dishwater, pulled him to a standing position, and brought him back to the dining room.

Birth order, Pickle thought. It's a bitch. He heard Karen come back into the kitchen and sensed her body near him. Pickle snapped his eyes open and stepped in front of her.

"Karen, we need to talk."

She crossed her arms with defiance. "What, Pickle? It's been a long day and I'm exceedingly tired. You have no idea what I've been juggling. Stan's not coping well—"

"Fuck Stan," Pickle said, his voice a steely whisper.

Karen rubbed her hands on her skirt fabric with impatience. "What? Hurry up. The car will be here in a few minutes."

"Don't you dare rush me, you little bitch."

She backed away, knocking into a stool, and landed with her back against the opposite kitchen counter. Pickle stepped forward and pressed into her, forcing her to bend backward. He reached his arm around to the back of her head, and, holding on tightly to a clump of her hair, jerked her head further down to the counter. From a distance, they might have been attempting a tango dip.

Karen let a soft grunt escape as Pickle continued to pull at her hair. "Pickle, *please*. Junie's downstairs—Stan's in the next room."

"Then be quiet. I'm just gonna talk to you."

She tried to look at the floor.

"*Look* at me," Pickle hissed.

She met his eyes. "Okay. Just let go of my hair. You're hurting me."

Pickle released Karen's head and allowed her to straighten up. He arranged her hair—bringing the blonde wisps to the front of her shoulders, and then fluffed out her bangs. Karen's shoulders relaxed and she added a few feet of distance.

"Feel better? You look good, Karen. Beautiful, actually. But you already know that. Now, here's what we need to get straight. Who do you see? Do you see me? Or do you see Stan? *Who am I?*"

"Pickle," she whispered.

"That's right. And I've had just about enough of this shit."

"What shit?"

"C'mon. Don't play it that way. You're too smart for that."

She sighed, exasperated. "What do you *want?*"

"The brownstone. I want in. I'm way overdue."

She began to object, but Pickle grabbed her arm and clamped his hand over her mouth.

"Don't say anything. All that crap at dinner about Stan being held captive on the parlor floor? You may be able to spoon-feed that twaddle to him, but not me. The *real* question of the day is why the fuck I'm not living in the building I half own. This shit is going to stop today."

Karen clawed his hand away from her mouth and pushed away from him. "It's not that easy. These renovations have to be carefully planned—"

"Fuck the planning—you've been doing squat about it, and I've let this go on for too long."

"I don't know. I think the timing's wrong, with Junie—"

"Jesus, Karen, listen up. The next time you speak any words to me, I wanna hear THE plan. I wanna hear that you've told Stan, and that you have your contractor lined up with a start date. All that good stuff you know how to do so well. I'll give you four days. Not five. Not three. Four. So, today is Monday. Call me on Thursday at three. You got that?"

She jerked her head in a nod.

"I'm gonna say goodnight to Junie. Remember: Thursday. Are we clear?"

Karen stifled a cough and he took this as an affirmative response.

Pickle reached to an upper shelf, pulled down a half-empty bottle of vodka, unscrewed the cap and set the bottle in front of Karen with a bang. Then he placed a freshly washed and dried goblet next to the bottle.

"Drink up, Karen. Knock yourself out."

Karen watched as Pickle went downstairs. Murmuring voices rose up through the radiator vents. The inflections sounded like plans, agreements, maybe the future. And then she heard a sound she realized she'd not heard all week—Junie laughing. Shortly, the downstairs front door opened and clicked shut.

Karen coughed and wiped moisture from her eyes with her hand. Then she dragged the warm tears across her lips. She tasted salt and noticed the dregs of red lipstick, leftover from hours before, now embedded into the heart line of her palm. She looked at the bottle and the glass and found herself pouring two fingers of vodka. Karen preferred her booze almost straight. She opened the freezer, removed one ice cube, and dropped it into the glass. The sound startled her, like an intruder. Her hands shook as she raised the glass up and smelled the liquor that supposedly had no odor. Then, with willpower she had rarely known herself to possess, Karen extended her arm and dumped the vodka down the drain.

10

KAREN WAVED TO HER CREW AS THEY TOOK their lunch in the noon sun. Multinational armies of men languished on the sidewalk along the perimeter of the building, speaking to each other in hushed native tongues. They laughed in bursts at private jokes she didn't understand. Across the street, Karen looked up and saw a crane cantilevered off the roof as if it had no physical connection to the building. They always seemed to swivel just when she looked away—like a missed double play—like everything important in life.

She rode to the tenth floor and plopped her purse on top of some newly delivered Sheetrock stacked against a wall. Before she spoke to her site manager, Karen would need to pull up her beauty britches. She dug through her purse and grabbed a small cosmetics bag, then touched up her lipstick, blotted excess nose oil, and spritzed on some perfume. Patrick wasn't going to like what she had to say.

"I'm going to pull some guys off this job." She spoke the words as a declaration, while he was still in motion—walking toward her. Karen had found that, when lowering the boom on a man, this approach was a fairly decent predictor of success.

Patrick stopped short and craned his neck in disbelief, and she felt satisfied that he was temporarily befuddled. "You're kidding. What for? We're behind schedule as it is. Nope. I don't think we can do that, Karen." He shook his head, as if he were the boss.

This was also a good sign: when the man said several sentences, all strung together, and then ended with a head movement. Karen made a point of remaining still and not countering his movement, which would be seen as weakness.

"It's not negotiable," she said.

"*Why?* This'll completely screw up my schedule!"

Let the man become frustrated. "I'm sorry about that, but I wouldn't do it unless it was urgent," she apologized, without explaining.

"Well, I don't know . . . is this a new job?" he asked.

"It's gutting out my brownstone—the top two floors."

"Oh, please. How can that be urgent? You've been living there for, what, a year? Why now?"

"That's none of your business," she said. Never let the man assume knowledge of your life.

Patrick dropped his empty coffee cup to the floor and stepped on it, twisting his construction boot. "Okay—go ahead. Lay it on me."

The trick was, in a very short exchange of words, to make the man question the very nature of the business relationship he thought he understood. Karen was a master; she had him, and she dug in.

"It needs everything—kitchen, bathroom—basically soup to nuts. The plans are all set at the office. Stan and I designed both units when we did the first phase. I'd say you could get the demolition done in less than a week—then you'll need about two weeks for the rough plumbing and electrical. I don't want a day to go by without substantial work happening, and I need it to be in move-in condition in two months.

Max," she deadpanned.

He chewed on her words, then gave a wry smile. "That's a lot of 'needs,' Karen." He paused. "Does Stan know about this?"

She was at the point of play where she'd get personal, which was, she knew, what Patrick actually needed from the beginning. Some kind of confessional—better yet, a collusion, and at Stan's expense.

"Patrick. You know very well that Stan's never privy to the scheduling of our projects. But no, he doesn't know. Not yet. He's been a mess since the accident. So, before I do tell him, I need assurances that you'll be all over this. I've just *got* to finish the brownstone." She pushed out her lower lip and raised one eyebrow simultaneously. "I'm *counting* on you." When placing the power back in the man's palm, he'll close his hand like a fist.

Patrick turned and walked to the other side of the room. He sat on a windowsill and looked up to the view, which she knew was the Deco spire of the Chrysler Building. Typically, men like to think about something phallic before they agree with a woman.

He shrugged in defeat. "Understood, Karen. But I'm reluctant to take any of my guys off this job. The clients are adding extras right and left."

"*Tell* me about it. Give me options." Now they were equals, and in cahoots. And the crazy thing was that she had to repeat this nonsense nearly every other day.

"Well, we have that crew finishing the small job in the Village. I was going to put those guys into 15 Central Park West just to speed that along. Gutting those four bathrooms—it's become massive. But at least that client still has his apartment on the lower floor. I'm thinking I could send the Village guys over to you."

"The Village job will be done in, what, three or four days. Right? That'll work." She'd given him his bone and allowed him to gnaw on it. Then it was easy: just wait until he came up with the solution, which Karen already knew was the correct option.

"Yeah, maybe sooner. We're just about finished with the punch list." Patrick scratched his beard with stubby blackened fingernails, thinking. "Send me a PDF of the plans. It'll take me the week to organize and order stuff. We'll load into the brownstone next Monday. I'll get the dumpsters set for that entire week. We're lucky because you own the whole building. We didn't have to go through the DOB when we did the first phase, so let's just act 'as if.' But Karen, you've got to give me ten to twelve weeks."

This was to be her only concession. But she didn't really have a choice because construction was like a weather system; it couldn't be predicted from one day to the next. Pickle would just have to swallow it.

They walked to the elevator and Patrick thumbed the service button. Dust pushed through the bottom of the metal doors as the lift began to rise. When he walked into the blanketed shaft, Karen held the doors open for a moment longer. "We understand each other—right, Patrick?"

He dropped his head with deliberate weight, and she was gratified at speaking the last words.

As the doors closed, Karen pivoted on her kitten heel and walked to the back of the apartment, into a small room designated as a cozy study. She looked out the window and saw the crane pluck a piano from the sidewalk and lift it with pincers. It then prepared to maneuver the piano into an enormous window across the street, at the same level as her floor. Obviously, there was no way to get the thing up through the building. She found herself mesmerized by the sheer audacity of such a solution to someone's personal need. That's what life seemed to be reduced to, Karen thought. If there was a hole, a gap, *any* opening whatsoever—the effort would be made. *Men.*

The piano began to spin, and a man at street level screamed instructions into a walkie-talkie to the crane operator. Karen turned away. The scene made her woozy and she lost her balance. Suddenly she was on her hands and knees, heaving up her breakfast into an empty plastic paint bucket, conveniently within range. Her heart felt as if it might punch out of her chest and she had a familiar feeling of overwhelming and futile dread—that she was losing something she'd never owned. Karen hung her head and sobbed.

A plumber, working in a nearby bathroom, came running with a wrench in his hand. He stopped when he saw Karen, and waited about ten seconds as she continued to cry.

"Jaysus. Karen. What in Christ's name's wrong?"

Waving him away, Karen shoved the bucket across the floor. He leaned over to look into it, grimaced, then picked it up and headed back to the bathroom. "You take care, now."

Karen kicked the door shut after him, slumped down to the dusty floor and splayed her legs out in front of her. She kicked off her shoes and they flew in opposite directions, the heels landing with sharp thuds. It was after the noon hour and Karen's joints ached, as if in need of a lube job; she felt mentally barren and almost imbecilic. She crawled about ten feet across the floor to an enormous fireplace. It was new—never been fired—so she curled up inside it and could almost imagine the warmth of a benign blue flame. Her head found a nearby sack of dry cement for a pillow. Thoughts of Junie in the Volvo on the night of the crash came to mind, with her arms curled up around her head so no one would see her pain. Karen reached into her purse, turned off her phone, cradled her arms up and over, and rocked herself to nowhere.

The late-day sunlight warmed Karen's face, waking her with a start. She looked around, slightly bewildered, and saw that the window across the street was now shut with curtains drawn, and she imagined someone playing Chopin mazurkas on a freshly tuned piano. Grit from the cement bag had adhered to her cheek; the granules had mixed with her sweat. She troweled off the slurry with her forefinger, dragged it into her mouth, bit down on the rough sand and swallowed. Vodka was on her mind.

Digging into her purse, Karen found her phone—4:30 p.m. She'd slept over three hours. Ten texts and one voicemail stared at her. Scrolling down, she saw that most of the texts were from Stan. No one left voice messages anymore—so she looked to see who it was from. Pickle.

Karen rolled onto her back as Pickle's soft voice bounced against her eardrum. "I knew you wouldn't pick up and don't bother calling back. Just this: Thursday."

She punched Stan's cell number.

"Where the hell have you been? The office has been calling me all day. I didn't know what to tell them. Karen, where have you *been*?"

"Dear God. Shut up already. Everything's fine. I was stuck in the subway for hours and then I got something to eat. It's been a rough day, Stan. I don't want to discuss it, okay?"

"Whatever. I just don't like getting calls from people in the office. I don't know them. It's uncomfortable for me."

"Well, if you made an effort to actually introduce yourself to your employees, then that little problem would be cleared up. How's Junie?"

"How the hell should I know? She's down there, I guess."

"Is she playing Mahler still?"

"Yes."

"Really?" Karen mewled.

"*Yes*. She came up and asked for more CDs. I showed her what was left in the living-room cabinet. She cleaned the shelf out. Greedy little thing. Though I have to admit, her taste in music is impressive. When're you coming home?"

"Calm down. Right now."

11

PICKLE STROLLED NORTH OF THE APARTMENTS.
He headed up Cabrini Boulevard until he got to 190th Street, turned
onto Margaret Corbin Drive and approached the entrance to the
Cloisters. The reassembled French abbeys rose in front of him, massive and earthy, with chiseled façades. Pickle visited the Cloisters often, but not so much for the twelfth-century museum—rather, for
the unobstructed view to the Palisades cliffs across the Hudson River.
Rounding the perimeter of the grounds, he headed toward the far-
thest bench and sat.

The day was azure clear—an end to a spring afternoon like none he
remembered in a long time. The Hudson, cresting high with whitecaps
from the recent rain, roared, swift and urgent, below him. And as he
turned his gaze left, toward the GW Bridge, a sliver of setting sun re-
flected off one of the suspension cables, blinding him. Pickle shivered.

Lance Burke rounded the bench and sat to Pickle's left, blocking
the light shard that had just pierced Pickle's face.

"No. No. Sit on my right, Lance."

Lance sighed, did as he was told, and moved to Pickle's right. But
the sun had dipped a fraction, causing the ray to move on to infinity,

or another target. The moment evaporated, and Pickle grimaced as if disappointed. "Oh well. It's gone now."

"What's gone?" Lance turned to consider his partner's profile. "Pickle, are you going batty on me? First you go AWOL from work for a day. Then you call in and take a week of sick leave. Now you want a meeting in some godforsaken park on a bench, like you're in an outdated film noir. Give me a crumb here. I'm dying from the suspense." Lance yawned.

"First, film noir cannot be outdated. That's an oxymoron. And second, this is not a godforsaken park. It's part of the Metropolitan Museum of fucking Art."

"Or the location of a mugging at gunpoint two weeks ago. *Or* the set for the next Bond movie, if that makes you feel any better. Take your pick."

Pickle waited for his partner to release all the sarcasm he must have been collecting throughout the last week. He couldn't blame him.

Lance poked Pickle in the shoulder. "I'm waaaaiting."

Pickle twined his hands behind his head with elbows flapping to either side and stretched his legs in front of him.

"I was supposed to do some shit with the family today," Lance said with irritation. "My wife is pissed. Not that you could relate. But go ahead—get comfortable. By. All. Means." With each word, Lance flicked imaginary lint off his trousers.

Pickle sat forward and turned toward Lance. "Don't rub it in. The family stuff. I'm sensitive."

"Then why all the cloak-and-dagger? We're cops, remember? We don't do shit like that. What's going on?"

"I met someone."

"Ah."

"And I think she might be *the* one."

"*Ah.*"

"I'm *serious.*"

"Ahhhhh." Lance's voice swooned with disbelief.

"Okay—make fun of me. Then go fuck off." Pickle got up and started down the path, but not before kicking Lance in the shin.

"Pickle, wait! C'mon back. I wanna hear."

Pickle returned and kicked Lance again, harder this time.

Lance canted his leg across his knee and rubbed the skin. "Don't abuse the father confessor. Bless you, my child, for you have sinned. I'm all ears. Who is she?"

Pickle pulled out his comb and slicked back his hair.

"Candice? From Property?" Lance prodded.

"Nope, not Candice. That fell apart, at least in a way. I prefer phone sex with her."

"*That's* a comfort. Then who?"

Pickle dug out a handkerchief from his hip pocket, blew his nose, and then stared in the direction of the bridge.

Lance eyed Pickle with suspicion. "Wait. Hold on. Not that crazy red-headed chick from the bridge. Malifawhozzitsname?"

"Correct."

"Dear God. Say about three billion Hail Marys and you might survive this one."

"Praying won't change anything. She's glorious."

"She's a dead-to-rights, fuckin' crazy, whackadoodle lunatic."

"She's an angel."

"Pickle. You were there. Googling the bridges? The sneakers? That joker who took a dive? The *blue tape?*"

Pickle took in a swift breath. "Did you find him?"

"Yeah, we fished him out down by Battery Park the next day."

"But you didn't call Junie to identify him?"

"We didn't have to. His ID was still in his pocket. And he was in decent shape so the picture matched."

"Good." Pickle smiled, nodding in approval.

Lance twiddled his thumbs. "So. Tell me about the happy couple."

"What'd you find out about them?" Pickle deflected.

"Nothing. You specifically told me to, quote, 'Leave this one alone.' So, that's what I did."

"Right. I remember. But now I need to know."

"I just told you. I followed your orders. 'No need to investigate,' you said. 'Simple case,' you said. 'Let me handle this,' you said."

"Good. I know. But just tell me what you found out."

Lance pulled out a black notebook from his hip pocket and flipped through some pages. He zeroed in on a few cryptic notes. "They lived in Brooklyn—Greenpoint. He had some money—not a lot—but they'd blown through most of it."

"Where'd he get the money? Was he rich? Trust fund?"

"Nope. His grandparents died about two years ago and left him a chunk. About a hundred grand, which is easy enough to munch through these days. It seems that's just what they did."

"What about her?"

Lance licked his thumb and pushed past a few more pages. "Okay. She's most recently from Maine. Parents are dead—no sibs. She's educated. Almost completed a BFA in art history from Bowdoin College. On a full scholarship, too. But she left in the last semester and never finished. Then she came to New York a little over a year ago. She's twenty-nine years old, which surprised me because she looks more like nineteen. Here in the city she worked at the Met Opera Shop, and then as an usher for a short time, so she's a bit of an artsy-fartsy type."

Pickle's eyes brightened. "She's an artist, you say?"

"No, I said she was artsy-*fartsy*. But maybe it's the same thing. You'd know better than me."

"Hmmm." Pickle grunted. "What else? What about him?"

"Nothing."

"Dirt?"

"No, none. And I dug. He had an estranged family from New Jersey. They seemed like average folks, who were, by the way, devastated by the news of the guy's death. But I don't think there's anything fishy there. My guess is it was the standard thing of the guy hating his parents for all the mundane reasons. None of which made any sense to his parents. Per usual."

"No dirt. Are you *sure*?"

Lance slammed his black book closed. "Fuck, Pickle! *Nothing*. No prior acts, no arrests, no lockup in the loony bin. No weirdness at all. We even looked at his phone and computer. The guy was basically a boring sad sack—a depressive who couldn't seem to get a grip. And he brought your girlfriend along for the ride."

Pickle grabbed the notebook from Lance and began to flip through the pages. "There's got to be more. Gambling. Porn. Something—"

Lance snatched it back and whacked Pickle on the head. "It's very simple. He was living off this inheritance, met her, and they shacked up. He went through his dough. End of story. Until he offed himself."

Pickle took out a breath spray, gave himself a shot and handed it to Lance.

"No thanks."

Pickle pushed it into Lance's palm.

"Okay. Whatever." Lance took a shot and attempted to hand it back to Pickle.

"Keep it—it's a present."

Lance glared at him.

"Hey. I'm just looking out for you, Lance. Your breath is bad, and you should know these social skills."

"I'm married with kids. I don't need skills anymore."

They sat in silence for several minutes. Kids played a ball game directly behind them and Lance's foot jiggled with irritation each time their footsteps came near. Pickle propped his elbows on his knees with his fists under his chin and stared at a tug pushing a barge up the Hudson, against the current.

Finally, Lance broke the tension. "What the hell does all this have to do with me?"

"I'm seriously considering early retirement."

"Fuuuuck!" Lance groaned. "You can't do that. You just met her. Even if the sex is phenomenal, what's the rush? Pickle, this is crazy—" Lance stopped mid-rant and softened his voice. "Okay. Tell me something so I can understand. What's she like?"

Pickle turned his body away.

Lance twisted him back. "I'm your partner, Pickle. I'm on your side. But you have to give me something. Have you seen her every day? Is this some kind of ramped-up speed dating?"

"To be honest, I've actually not seen her yet. Technically. She's staying with Karen and Stan. I had dinner with them last night at the brownstone."

Lance whistled. "Wow. So, let me get this straight. You want to retire early, all for a woman you've spent a couple of hours with. And to boot, she's living in your brother's house, which, by the way, you own half of, but don't even live in. *This* is worthy of early retirement? No, this is beyond fucked up."

"I just have a very intense feeling about her—Junie. It's hard to explain."

"Try."

Pickle rubbed his eyes and thought about the question, which was, he had to admit, reasonable. He trotted out the list he'd been compiling in his mind for a week. "Well, she's small. And lovely. And I like the sound of her voice. And she's not pretentious. In fact, she seems unspoiled. Like from another century. A Victorian. Kind of like—"

"Wait," Lance stopped him and squinted. "Downton Abbey?'

"That's not *Victorian*. Look, I'm just attracted to her in a way that's different. Like, I find her pristine. Like, she's at arm's length, unattainable. Like, it wouldn't matter if I never had sex with her. You know?"

"Like, no I don't know. Like, thank God for that. Like, I'm lost."

"Well, that's all I've got for now, because as I said, we haven't had any time together. But I'm seeing her tomorrow. We have a date. Sort of."

"So, go on the sort-of date and see if you get off home plate. But you're just a couple years from making your twenty. Why would you throw that away?"

"I'm not sure. It's our work, I think. I want to be clean for her."

"If you want to be clean, take a shower. But retiring is out of the question."

Pickle hated what Lance was saying. He was logical and reasonable, and even correct. But those were middle-of-the-road concepts that didn't reflect his current temperament: Pickle wanted to race around a track in reverse at a hundred miles an hour.

After several minutes, Lance proffered a new roadmap. "Consider this. Take three weeks. Or double it—take six if absolutely necessary. Get this woman out of your system—or into it—whichever comes first. Then we'll talk."

A worm in Pickle's brain told him this was an apple he should bite on. Everyone was entitled to a breakdown or breakthrough, and if he was honest with himself, Pickle wasn't sure which was the truth.

"Okay. I'll wait. Fix it for me at work. Six weeks, though."

"You got it." Lance cuffed him on the shoulder and walked away.

Pickle looked back to the Hudson and noticed the tug hadn't pushed the barge more than a quarter mile. The river held a camouflaged power, and he recognized the disguise.

12

KAREN HAD STOPPED OFF AT A STARBUCKS TO chug down a triple espresso and use the ladies' room, clean up, reapply makeup, and regroup from her lost day. It was after seven by the time she reached the brownstone, where she found Stan in his robe, standing at the kitchen counter rearranging the spice bottles. He tilted his head toward Karen, grunted, and then continued with the task of assessing and selecting. She knew his challenge too well: he needed to decide if the spices should be arranged in alphabetical order, or alternatively, in the order most frequently used. But there were complications. If he chose the latter, he'd then have to anticipate which spices were used the most and the least. Stan didn't cook, so that would be an abstract choice, which never pleased him. In either case, the flakes needed to graduate up and down, and be pleasing to his eye at any given moment. Karen girded herself for a discussion on the verisimilitude of minced stalks of shrubbery. She tossed her purse on the sofa, and waited.

Stan squinted at the bottles. "Which way, Karen?"

She positioned herself under the centered lighting fixture, took a few steps back for perspective, and pondered the art of the flake.

"Make them alphabetical."

"But that's boring. There's no *whimsy*."

"Then do the 'as used' option if that makes you feel any better," she said dismissively.

"You're placating me, and this is crucial. It's the first thing I see when I enter the kitchen. It has to be right, and I need you to care."

"I really don't care about your urge for whimsy tonight, Stan. Anyway, why are you focusing on the spices? Do something with martini glasses—an object that has some tangible meaning in our lives."

Stan swatted the bottles back toward the tiled backsplash with his bad arm. They chimed a xylophone melody and a few ricocheted forward and fell to the floor, spinning like pinwheels. Stan loped around the kitchen trying to corral them with his good arm, and ended up tipping over, landing on his back with his head next to the trash can. He peered up at Karen, expecting assistance. She shook her head.

Stan stuck out his tongue. "I can see I'm not going to get anything useful from you, which is typical." He heaved himself up and brushed phantom dirt off his robe lapel. "By the way, which subway was stalled? I didn't hear anything on the radio."

Stan missed very little and Karen, anticipating a grilling, was prepared. She took a deep breath and summoned up the phony script she'd memorized on the way home. With Stan, the more complex the lie, the better.

"It was the L train."

"What in God's name were you doing on that train? I forgot there even *was* an L. It's so far down the alphabet."

"It's weird, I know. But I got a call early this morning from a potential client in Brooklyn. They said the L was close to their house.

I guess the MTA doesn't care enough about that particular train to bother with an announcement. But eventually I got there."

"Anything interesting?"

"It's not up our alley. They seemed to have plenty of money but it's not what we like to do—too traditional. I should have vetted it out more fully before I took the time, but you never know. Brooklyn's so hot right now. It was a bad impulse on my part."

She added that detail, admitting to sloppy judgment, at the last second. This would further placate Stan by adding a fresh notch to his belt of brinksmanship.

"Speaking of martini glasses, can I have a status update about our mutual passion for a minute?" she asked.

"What passion would that be? I wasn't aware we had one."

"Don't be hateful and sarcastic. I'm referring to our drinking."

"Hateful, certainly, but not sarcastic," Stan bristled. "Neither of us has had a drink since the accident. But since you bring it up, I'll add these crucial details. I've been off the pain pills since yesterday. Today I reached for the Stoli exactly twice and resisted. My fingers are still shaky, but with Herculean effort, I've managed to shave. If I take one more walk around the block to 'clear my head' as you've advised every half hour, I'll start popping pills with a beer chaser. I've been inside all day, avoiding that female inhabiting the lower level. And I managed to organize the cleaning supplies by size and color. Which was practically impossible. Can I get some credit around here?"

"Fine. I get it. You're sober. Happy?"

"It's all in the details. Now, let's get back to you. Why *were* you so late tonight? Should I be suspicious? You could have met someone and had a drink. Come here. Let me smell your breath."

Starbucks espresso sizzled down in her gut like a spatula pressing meat to a fire, and Karen's stomach ached. She walked over, stuck her face into his, and gave him a powerful puff directly up his nose.

"No booze—but a *lot* of coffee. You're exonerated," he relented.

"Small mercies." She looked around. "Where's The Doodles?"

"Downstairs. With *her*. That dog is one more breathing entity that's abandoned me for that creature. You've adopted her as a surrogate daughter, and Pickle seems to want to get his paws around her, too."

"*Shhhhh*. She'll hear you. The radiator vents," Karen whispered and pointed to the back wall of the kitchen where the heat came up.

"Oh, don't worry about that—listen."

She hadn't noticed until Stan pointed it out, but faint music, which Karen couldn't identify, filled the air. "What's she playing?"

"Just every single dreary post-Brahms composition in existence. Mahler. Wagner. And Schoenberg. Before the tone row, of course. All day long. No wonder she wanted to off herself."

"You're cruel. Be on notice that I find you very unattractive at this moment. I'll see how she is." She started toward the stairway.

Stan hopped over to Karen to intercept her and pulled her into the living room, where he directed her to sit on the sofa. He sat next to her and arranged his robe with modesty. "Now, my darling. Don't crush a vulnerable man's heart. It's not nice. Especially when my entire world has crashed down on me. August, or whatever her name is, can wait. Anyway, I've been waiting for you. Are you game?"

Karen shivered. "Maybe."

"What would tip you over into the 'land of yes'?"

"I'm not sure. Right now, I hate you too much."

"Hatred is the fleetest of emotions. Just brush it away. But be quick about it." Stan reached over and tickled his forefinger across Karen's waist. The sensation felt like a knife and the coffee in her belly turned viscous. Her insides began to swell.

"I might consider a tryst," she said.

Stan eyed her with interest. "It's been far too long. Sixty-six days, actually. But who's counting?" He smiled at his own joke, unknotted the sash of his bathrobe and let it fall open. He was fully erect, with no boxers on.

Karen sidled closer. "You sure this doesn't have to do with the fact that there's another female in the house? The added estrogen in the air?"

"Nope."

"Then why are you particularly hard?" she asked.

Stan touched the back of her neck, and Karen's shoulders and arms went board stiff.

"Don't you know?" he asked.

"Tell me." As Karen said the words, her tongue felt thick in her mouth.

"Because you're the best fuck in the city," Stan explained.

She detested sex talk. And though her body and face continued with animation, in her mind Karen shook her head—no, no, no. The thing in her belly would produce the necessary words.

"You can do better than that," the voice scolded. "That's too much of a cliché for any kind of realism I'd ever believe."

"Well then, let's narrow that statement down and say you're the best fuck I've ever had." Stan sat back on the sofa, satisfied with his correction. "Better?" he asked, needing encouragement.

Karen managed to blink once, and her feet made an involuntary shuffle on the floor. Some sensation returned to her shoulders, arms, and fingers. Just enough for her to do what was necessary. She grabbed Stan by the penis and began to pull him toward the bedroom, like a stallion on a lead. Stan shrugged off his robe and, naked, followed her, slamming the bedroom door behind him with a kick of his foot. He lay on his back diagonally across the bed, while Karen began to undress.

"C'mon, you little bitch. Bring it here," Stan demanded.

"Why'd you call me that?" the voice asked.

"Well, you're certainly little. And I guess in the hip-hop vernacular, you're my bitch," he explained.

"Let's get some things straight. I'm going to fuck you silly. And I might even give you a bruise or two," the voice warned.

"Sounds wonderful," he swooned.

"But don't ever call me that again," the voice cautioned.

Karen ripped off her blouse and bra, her breasts buoyant, nipples hard. She crawled on top of Stan and straddled him. Her insides now spun like a whirling dervish. Karen flew up from the bed. She spent the next hour pressed against the ceiling, watching her body below.

13

THE CITY, NOW ALMOST EBONY, HUMMED AT A flaccid pitch. Their bedroom at the back of the house overlooked the garden, and Junie's lights from the level below provided a burnished glow to the room. Karen's hovercraft body had made a soft landing from twelve feet above. She'd then showered and oiled her body. She'd massaged her fingers and her toes and rubbed a chamois cloth all over her skin. Her belly had receded to nothing and she felt her limbs reattach to her torso. Finally, she tested her voice, and it sounded reasonably familiar—like a sibling.

Karen detected strains of orchestral music seeping up from beneath the bed—maybe a Brahms symphony. The heartbeat of tympani rumbled across the support beams, up the bedposts, and fluttered into the mattress. Fresh from her ablutions and lying on the bed, she gathered the bedcovers close to her breasts and observed Stan as he dozed on his back. He always softened after sex; a defensive veneer would abandon his face. Karen examined Stan's features from the side and noticed that his mouth was almost smiling. This rare time, when his obsessions loosened their grip, allowed for a benign neutrality between them, and this presented her with the possibility of accomplishing her real mission tonight. She lightly traced her finger along Stan's eyebrows. "Darling?"

Stan's eyes popped open. "Whoa, Nellie. What'd I do now?"

"Why do you always go to that place when I use an endearment? Please don't screw this moment up."

Stan tried to look the other way, but Karen pulled his face back toward hers. "What's wrong?" she asked.

"I'm afraid."

"Why? Of what?"

Stan seemed to weigh his answer. "Of everything. We're not drinking, for one thing. And that girl downstairs—"

"Her name is Junie."

"Okay—this Junie whoever. I'm still not sure this was a good idea. We're stuck with her now."

"Did it ever occur to you that her presence is one of the reasons that we've been able to stay sober for a few consecutive days? Maybe even longer, if we're lucky."

"That sounds like far-fetched psychobabble. Which disgusts me on every level. I don't believe in luck. You know that. But I'm uncomfortable in my own home. And I have no idea what to say to her."

"Didn't you tell me she'd been upstairs for more CDs? You must have talked to her."

"Yeah, I did. She seems to know a lot about art."

"See? She's not so bad, and it looks like you have something in common."

"Well, let's not get carried away. But I'll grant you, she does appear to be intelligent."

"Good. Now what else? You've not told me everything."

"Well, it's your sweetness tonight. I have to be honest; I don't trust it."

This unnerved Karen, because she was unaware of how she'd actually behaved. While she'd floated above the bed, the woman below did the usual things expected during sex. And Stan had appeared to be satisfied, at least from a distance. So, she had to wing it. "You never trust. That's your nature. I'm used to it."

"That weak reasoning may help you—"

"Stan, the way we are with each other—the jabs, the barbs—that's not a compulsion. It's a habit. You need to be able to make the distinction. Think of it as concrete that has to be chipped away in order to dissolve and then be reconstituted—"

"Please, Karen, you're making us sound like a new construction project. Spare me the analogies. I detest them. They're for those who can't express ideas accurately." Stan sat up and scooted back against the headboard. "Sorry for the lecture. Anyway, what were you going to ask me? Right after the 'darling' part?"

Karen turned over on her stomach to face Stan. "Okay. I have to tell you something and it's already a done deal, so don't get crazy."

"I'm listening."

Karen squeezed her eyes shut. "I've arranged for Patrick to start the renovation on Pickle's half of the brownstone." She opened one eye.

"Huh. Really? *Why?*" Stan asked, incredulous.

"We're starting Monday."

"That's not 'why.'"

"It's been a long time, Stan."

"Nope. I can't allow it. I barely lived through our phase. And Pickle's never seemed to care."

"But he *does* care. And I have a sense that he might feel competitive. You know—Junie's here and he's not. He'd never admit to it, of course; he's much too proud. So, I talked to Patrick about it this morning."

Stan was still for a few minutes, and she held her breath as she watched him work it out.

"Does Patrick have the manpower? I don't want this interfering with any of our jobs."

"Patrick's just fine. He agreed to it immediately," she said.

"Okay. But only if you have his complete assurance."

Karen silently let out her breath. "We've gone through the scheduling and have it worked out. And Stan? I want it to be a surprise, so don't say anything to Pickle. I'll tell him later in the week after I get all the details settled."

"Lips sealed." Stan made a "lock the key" motion to his mouth.

He tried to yank her back on top of him, but Karen pushed him away, rolled onto her back, and reached for the video remote. "Let's watch the end of season two. Sue Ellen's in the sanitarium when Bobby comes to visit, and she tells him that Cliff Barnes is the father of her unborn baby."

Stan smiled. "*Won*derful. Sue Ellen's makeup. Lashes. Bronzer."

They relaxed into the Ewing family saga. Karen strained to hear Junie's music under the sound of Sue Ellen's tears. Nothing came from below, so she focused on the tremble in Sue Ellen's voice as she gradually revealed to Bobby her fatal secret, which would ultimately undo her and Cliff Barnes.

14

PICKLE STOOD ACROSS THE STREET FROM THE Solomon R. Guggenheim Museum on Fifth Avenue at Eighty-Ninth Street. The swirl of the nautilus stood out as unique to any other building in New York City. Pickle stared at the top for several minutes and realized he was slightly jealous of the architect, Frank Lloyd Wright. Audacious: the man and his structure. Pickle and Junie had made vague plans the previous evening at the brownstone, and then, learning that she was an "artsy-fartsy" type from Lance, Pickle chose this museum for their first date. Now he wondered whether he could live up to the man, the building and the art. But he had to start somewhere.

Pickle leaned against the thick stone barrier to Central Park while he waited for Junie and, exhausted, yawned three times. He'd not slept more than an hour or two the night before. At three in the morning—fitful and anxious—he'd pulled out his penis and his cell phone and called Candice from Property. Over the next couple of hours, and only after Candice had given him two happy endings, Pickle was finally able to quiet his essential body part and sleep. Now, he imagined bags under his eyes and willed himself not to pull out his pocket mirror. Instead, he glanced down at the front of his shirt to make sure he was presentable. No stains. Well, there was always the comfort of knowing that he looked just like Stan, who, admittedly, was a handsome bastard.

Pickle appreciated the architecture and art of New York City, a fact he'd managed to keep hidden from Karen and Stan. When they discussed their business, or the latest art exhibitions they'd attended, Pickle understood the subjects, the aesthetics, even the history. This was a language they assumed he had no fluency in, and the fact that he'd hidden his knowledge over the course of their marriage, thrilled Pickle. Kind of like the secret satisfaction of sitting on the subway where two people suddenly break into Spanish to be private, but you know enough Spanglish to understand that the woman is fucking her husband's best friend. Pickle smiled to himself at the thought: fooling Karen and Stan over and over. Still, to reveal nothing had been a hard-learned lesson—an inheritance bequeathed by his mother.

Their mother had noticed Stan's emerging brilliance from very early on, as did most everyone. So, Pickle had been seen as the normal twin, and by extension, the lesser twin. When they were about ten years old, the school had selected twelve of the brightest students for a spelling bee. In these situations, Pickle was always included, deserving or not, because teachers didn't want him to feel inferior or left out, time and again. Stan excelled beyond Pickle in all subjects, and this was their way of being kind.

Pickle and Stan sat next to each other in a circle with the rest of the students, while the parents were placed directly behind their child to be supportive, but unseen, partners. As the quiz began, the words were simple enough and most of the kids shouted the spellings in unison. This exercise was meant as a warm-up.

The room smelled of sour milk breath emanating from the children, and nervous sweat from the adults, who were understandably invested in their children's accomplishments. Their faces belied a competitive streak—alternating glee and disappointment. Gradually, as the words became more challenging, the rules of the game changed. The children were now required to raise their hands in order to be called upon for the answer. And soon the bee was down to three students: Stan, Pickle, and a girl.

Pickle felt a sharp pinch to the back of his upper arm just as he was about to raise his hand to answer. He flinched, startled by that first pinch. Stan zoomed in with his arm and then the correct answer. Pickle's eyes burned with tears, as he looked halfway back toward his mother, whom he noticed had moved her chair directly behind his.

The next word proffered produced the same result, and with it an understanding that a pinch from his mother equaled a victory for Stan. He might not have been able to ultimately beat his brother in the quiz, but he understood that he was not to even try. Not only would he receive a pinch, but surely even more confounding punishments from his mother when back at home.

Learning to hide smarts at a young age took an intellect of a different sort—from the secondary brain center in the gut. For young Pickle, perfecting this body-level intuition proved to be a coping mechanism that helped him survive his mother. He'd always held onto that backup intelligence, which he later honed into an ability to wrap himself in a blanket of his own secrets.

Pickle turned to see Junie walking toward him. Her hair was carved into a braid that slid down the side of her neck, the tufted end landing just above the crook of her elbow. With her face washed clean and not a hint of makeup, she radiated a simplicity that Pickle wanted to devour. He placed his hands on her upper arms, squeezing them in affection.

She gave him a wry smile. "I'm here."

"I see that you are."

"I almost didn't come. I've been inside all week. But then just to-day I felt a small opening, or possibility, and I walked out the door."

"I'm really glad you made it. But you're not obligated to Karen and Stan, *or* me, for that matter. You're free to do whatever you want. You know that—right?"

"Yeah, I know. But I'm grateful, because standing here right now feels almost okay."

Pickle knew what that felt like. "Almost okay" was better than shitty and worse than not bad. He was just about to roll that deflating thought around in his mind, when nature came to his rescue. The sun broke out from behind clouds and fell on Junie's face—like a Rembrandt painting with the pearliest of shimmers usually dedicated to his rendering of slick oysters. Grateful, Pickle laughed at this mental image, and scrutinized all her freckles, like the Milky Way.

"What's so funny, Pickle?"

"Oh nothing, I was just thinking about something fishy."

Junie perked up. "Fishy! Not me, I hope. I'm not a fishy type."

"No, you're not fishy. Wanna see some art?"

Pickle pointed to the museum and her eye followed his gesture.

"Yes. Art would be fantastic."

They jaywalked across the street and Pickle gained them entrance with his membership card. Beginning at the top of the spiral, Pickle and Junie then drifted down for about an hour, silently pointing when the urge crept up. They were quiet with each other and Pickle was encouraged that she wasn't a talker. No words were needed in a building like this, not about the art, or anything else.

Cezanne, Gauguin, Braque, Klee, Degas. Each artist caught their interest through differing brushstrokes that seemed perfectly suited to the colors and forms within the frames. They stopped at the Kandinsky titled *Seven Circles*. Elemental and spare, the black background drove into a visual infinity. Junie traced the outline of the frame with her finger. Turning to Pickle, she wondered aloud, "Why is everything in life divided into squares?"

Pickle looked back up to the top of the spiral, where they'd begun, and then faced Junie. Her eyes, worn out, told him that she expected him to tell her the truth—which meant there was already a burgeoning trust between them. He somehow found the courage to risk an answer that might cause her to regret even asking this question.

"Squares are my friends," he said.

Junie smiled at his unexpected and surprising declaration.

"They interest me because they're a geometric volume with an implicit memory," he further explained.

She gave him a puzzled look and Pickle couldn't believe he was about to share his private understanding of the world with a virtual stranger.

"Most people stop at corners and simply turn right or left. But I see those corners as my chance to pause and reflect, or question—maybe even regret."

Pickle pointed to the top of the spiral and twirled his finger. She laughed, possibly expecting a joke.

"Circles are different. They propel us forward and we can choose to move quickly or slowly. But if we have the urge to stop, it's from our *own* volition. So, the very nature of a circle doesn't imply either going forward or stopping. In the world, it's known as taking responsibility for our actions, which is a scary concept for many people. That's why I love this museum. It's a circle and only the art, what we see and are moved by, is meant to stop us."

Junie's eyes welled up and she laid her head against Pickle's chest. "Oh God, Pickle. How could you know that I needed those words right now? For someone to say something that wasn't soothing? Just hard and true." She paused, not looking at him, but stayed close. "All the trouble I've caused everyone. You must think I'm such an idiot."

He pressed his face into her orange hair and breathed deeply. Grapefruit. "You're no trouble. You're certainly no idiot. And that was an obnoxious lecture. It's just that I've thought about these things and I don't get to say what's on my mind a hell of a lot. I'm preaching to myself more than to you. C'mon. Let's go."

They walked the few blocks to the Eighty-Sixth Street crosstown bus and rode together to the West Side. Pickle resisted the impulse to chat and Junie, also quiet, seemed content to just be with him. When they neared the brownstone, Pickle stopped at the corner.

"You won't come in?" she asked, but he knew she was being polite. And he'd had enough too, which was a surprising realization for Pickle.

"I have to get uptown."

She walked down the block, waving to him without turning her head. Pickle stood watching her, making note of her small hips, swinging arms, and narrow shoulders. Then he noticed that her left foot was badly pigeon-toed, and he suddenly felt gutted out. Her parents, apparently, had not made sure she was acceptable to the public at large. That was the very least a parent could do—*should* do. To make certain the child began life on level ground and equal to others, with feet that were straight and aligned and proper. He watched her foot and its strangled slant until she let herself into the brownstone. Fix the damn foot, people, he muttered to himself.

He pulled out his cell phone and called Lance, who picked up on the first ring. "What?"

"It's me. Did you work it out?"

"You're off for six weeks."

"Good."

"Are you okay?"

"Never been fucking better."

"Somehow, I doubt that, but whatever."

Pickle pulled a Mets cap out of his back pocket and headed over to Riverside Drive, then north to the Bridge Apartments.

15

SHE ENTERED THE BUILDING AND WIGGLED HER fingers at the doorman. Karen didn't bother stopping—she had a set of keys. Riding up in the elevator, she dug around in her purse for lipstick and a mirror to check her makeup. Then she realized she could use the reflective brass wall of the elevator. Her face appeared tarnished by the cold metal, her lips the same color as her complexion. She threw the lipstick back in her purse.

Karen walked toward the apartment at the end of the hallway, noting that the building was making much-needed improvements to the décor. Dreary teal-green wallpaper that had been peeling for ages was recently replaced with a French grey grass-cloth. And she saw that the outdated fluorescent lighting had been swapped out for modern ceiling fixtures. Never too late, even for a building like this.

When she reached the apartment door, Karen slid her key into the cylinder, turned, and pushed. As usual, the door was warped, so she gave it the necessary shove with her hip. She stopped up short, yelping a weak cry. "What are you doing here? I thought you'd be at work."

"*Obviously.*" Pickle, in bed, leafed through a *World of Interiors* magazine. He was naked, or seemed to be; the sheets exposed only his torso. He threw the magazine on the floor, scissored his legs back and forth, and yawned with his arms stretched above him. Then he lay on his side, propping himself up by one arm, and grinned at Karen. "And what, pray tell, are you doing here?"

"Why aren't you at work?" Karen threw the keys in her purse and slammed the door shut.

"Ouch! The neighbors don't like the doors slamming. And by the way, fuck you."

"I was going to leave you a note with the answer. About the brownstone."

"Coward."

"Yes," she concurred.

"Well, it's good you're here. 'Cause now we can discuss all the little details that will, no doubt, crop up due to your answer. Which is what?"

Karen pursed her lips. "Well . . . yes."

"Yes, what?"

"Yes, we'll start your renovation."

"Good. When?"

"Monday."

"*Very* good. How long?"

"Ten to twelve weeks."

Pickle pulled himself up to a sitting position and jammed a pillow between the wall and his back. "No good, Karen. It's gotta be faster."

Karen threw her arms up in exasperation. "How, for Christ's sake? I've told Patrick it's a rush job. Anyway, it's a miracle we even had the manpower to start on Monday."

Pickle shook his head like gooey molasses. "I can tell already you haven't pressed this hard enough."

She plopped into the chair at the table. "That's not true—I practically manhandled Patrick to get him to agree. It was very difficult and humiliating."

"Bullshit. He works for you, right? So, it's a matter of giving orders. And I know that's not a problem for you. Bossing people around is the second-best thing you do."

"*Idiot*," she spat.

Karen decided to shut up. A brawl was about to erupt and she wasn't up to it. Instead, she looked out the window from the quiet of thirty-two floors up. She saw head-to-tail snaking lines of cars—but traffic still managed to move incrementally. She imagined a toxic odor from catalytic converters filtering up—yet this was undetectable in the apartment. The roar of noise below never stopped—though she heard none of it. Then she remembered the jumper and Junie, and tried to find the exact location. There it was, halfway across the bridge—the enormous sign on the New Jersey-bound side. That's where the cables dipped down to their lowest point and where Jacob ended his life.

In spite of that tragedy, and this current difficulty with Pickle, she was glad for it all because of Junie. The brownstone gently rumbled with Junie's movements late at night. The morning roar of water through the pipes was the sign that she was up and about. Music she selected seemed to indicate her mood for the day. When Karen returned from work, dishes had been washed and carefully stacked onto the shelves, something Junie understood was important to Stan. All of this trace evidence was within reach, and felt intimate. She could see, smell, touch, and hear all of it if she wanted. The notion buoyed Karen. Not like up here in the clouds, a million miles away from anything alive.

Pickle broke into her trance. "Does Stan know yet?"

Karen sighed. "Yes."

"How'd he take it?"

"Like a lamb."

"Ahhh. I can just imagine." His eyebrows twitched up and down—Groucho Marx style.

"You pig."

"Defending him now?"

"I've *always* defended Stan." Karen sniffed and pulled a Kleenex from her pocket. She shoved the chair back, flipped off her shoes and propped her bare heels on the edge of the desk.

"God, stop that whimpering right now," he demanded. "I don't buy it."

Karen blew her nose. "It's really jammed up down there. Going west. Wonder what happened."

"A truck broke down on the Cross Bronx about twenty minutes ago. Right underneath the building. I've been listening to the scanner all day."

Karen cocked her head at him, curious. "So, why *aren't* you at work?"

"I told you, that's my business. How's Junie doing?"

"Better, I think. Stan said she went out for a couple of hours yesterday, in the morning. That's the first time."

Pickle snickered. "Oh yeah? Where'd she go?"

"She didn't say. I'm trying not to interrogate her. And Stan doesn't care."

"No surprise there."

"Leave Stan alone."

"Okay. I'll leave Stan alone. But I'm not about to leave you alone. C'mere."

"No."

"Don't make me get out of this bed, Karen," he warned.

Karen began to relent. But as she stood, she noticed the black-and-white image from the wedding. Oddly, it was taped to the refrigerator. She laughed and pointed to it. "What the hell is that doing there?"

"I tripped over it the night of your last big drunk. It was under the bed, where it probably should be right now."

Karen started toward the refrigerator.

"Don't mess with my shit, Karen. I've got it just the way I like."

She felt his sudden quick warmth. Pickle pressed his body into hers, against the refrigerator, forcing her cheek to rub the gloss on the paper, the cool of the metal just behind it. He held her there, reached around and cupped her breasts in his hands.

With her cheek sticking to the paper, and unable to focus, Karen saw a blurred version of the McArdle trio. But a faint smudge appeared in the background she'd never noticed before. Now she recognized the silhouette—their mother.

Karen had received a call from their mother and traveled out to Queens, expecting to have a future mother/daughter-in-law discussion. But she had been wary because Mrs. McArdle had advised, "Come alone, dear. And don't tell anyone."

The entrance hallway of the apartment was impossibly dark and cluttered. Karen sidled past ceiling-high stacks of old newspapers and her shoes felt sticky on the worn carpet. She'd actually wondered if she'd stepped on chewing gum and checked the soles of her shoes, with her hand on the wall to keep her balance. No gum, but her fingers came away from the wallpaper oily from years of built-up cooking grease. She followed their mother into the living room and waited while she re-strapped the oxygen mask to her face. Four lamps were on, but the room remained dim; drawn shades kept the daylight away. Karen sat on the sofa opposite their mother, who had slumped into a frayed recliner.

Shortly, after some generic niceties, their mother began to speak with a conspiratorial tone, as if between the best of friends. "I'll get to the point. You're a smart girl. You've been with Pickle for about a year now, and I see you like him."

"Yes, Mrs. McArdle, I do. Though, I'd like you to know that I love him."

"Well, I can see he loves *you*. But I'm not so sure about you." She stopped to put the mask to her face and sucked in more air.

Karen's armpits went damp. She knew to say nothing. It was another rule she'd learned from her own mother: don't play until the opposition exposes their hand.

Their mother nodded at Karen and smiled with a smirk. "Okay. No response from you. Which I expected."

Karen stilled herself and clasped her hands together, trying to direct all her nerves into her fingernails—an outgrowth which felt nothing. That was the best way to invite her mother for help: focus on the dead parts of her body.

Their mother continued in a voice strangely devoid of inflection. "I have a proposition for you. My son Stan, he likes you. I could see that at our little get-together a few weeks ago. He and Pickle look the same. So, that part will be easy. But Stan is special. I worry about him.

Pickle? He can take care of himself. Always could. Stan, not so much. See where I'm going?" Their mother took another gulp.

Karen looked down at her skirt—vintage Carolina Herrera. The day of that gathering, when she and Pickle had finally introduced themselves as a couple to his family, Stan had complimented her on this same outfit. His attention to her clothing had surprised Karen. Later that night, as she and Pickle lay in bed, she'd found herself wondering if Pickle would ever notice what she wore, or more importantly, would he ever understand why she considered couture clothing an art form. Karen found herself feeling pleased that Stan had appreciated something she loved.

As Karen waited for their mother to continue to reveal her plan, she noticed that her palms had made indelible sweat marks on the silk fabric. The skirt was now destroyed and she'd have to throw it away.

"I have money for you." Their mother stated it like the letter of the law—an inalienable truth.

Karen took in a quick gasp and their mother laughed.

"Don't be so surprised. The boys don't know about it. I won it in the lottery a year ago." She pulled a savings passbook from her pocket and tossed it over to the sofa. The wafer-like pamphlet slipped down the back cushion and Karen picked it out with two fingers. She didn't want to look at the amount, though two million was a lot more than she'd expected.

Karen felt a slight movement on the sofa and a small depression appeared next to her. She placed her hand on the cushion. It was hot to the touch. Karen's insides began to shimmer with what felt like the thin gold flakes of a thousand prospectors. Her own mother's presence pushed against her skin and then engulfed her body. When she felt the complete fullness, Karen then heard a lower-pitched voice emerge from her own throat.

"Just how do you think this might work?" Karen's mother asked skeptically.

"It's easy. You go to Stan and make him fall for you. You're a smart cookie—you know how all that works. And Stan will go along. I know my son." Their mother nodded with assurance.

Karen's mother, a cold strategist, asked the obvious questions, however perfunctory. "But what about Pickle? I love him. He loves me. What about that?"

"Don't worry about Pickle. He'll get in line. I know my other son."

Karen's mother understood all about uncomfortable arrangements, and knew to bring the negotiation to a swift conclusion. "Okay, I'll do it. But I want the money first. Once I have it, I'll go to work."

Their mother shrugged, as if unbothered by trifling details. "Why not? You're a good little actress—you'll do it just right."

And then it was all over. Karen resumed possession of her own body, her shoulders settled down, and she realized she'd been holding her breath, even as her mother spoke from within her throat. The essence of the agreement disturbed Karen. But not enough. She was grateful that her mother showed up to give her the courage to tack strictly to rules that had been laid down when she was a child. This mother of hers, dead or alive—and she wasn't sure which—was the only person in her life who'd ever shot straight.

Pickle's hands made their way from Karen's breasts to her waist and down her thighs. He dragged the hem of her skirt up and slipped his hand into her thong. The photo came loose and the black-and-white memory fluttered to the floor—a confused paper airplane.

"That day? It belongs on the floor. C'mon. Come to bed." Pickle said, as he kissed the back of her head. He pulled away from Karen, grabbed the paper, crumpled it in his fist and tossed it over his shoulder.

"Not today. I'm not in the mood."

"Your *mood*? This is a happy day. We should be celebrating, be-cause I'll be in the brownstone soon. We'll be closer—right on top of each other, in fact."

Karen stripped off her clothes and fell into bed with Pickle. The sun's low-setting trajectory, pierced by the cables of the bridge, splayed prison bars across the walls.

16

PICKLE STOOD ACROSS THE STREET AS A CREW of demolition guys finished jiggering an enormous garbage receptacle into place directly in front of the brownstone. The bin occupied three car lengths of precious real estate and Pickle knew things were about to get ugly.

Alternate-side-of-the-street parking is a cruel ballet, danced twice a week according to NYC Sanitation schedules. Residents lucky enough to work at home can conceivably double-park on the opposite side, wait for the sanitation truck to sweep the empty side, and then quickly re-park in the spot they just vacated. Pickle glanced at his watch; that time had now arrived, and car owners flowed from their buildings like hungry cockroaches scurrying toward something delicious. The late stragglers soon realized they were without a parking space due to the offending receptacle.

Pickle looked away, trying to distance himself as the cause of the inconvenience.

He'd been standing there since eight a.m., waiting for the lights to flicker in the brownstone. Karen had called the night before; they'd have a start meeting in the morning after Patrick's men and their gear were loaded inside. Pickle wanted his presence felt from the beginning of the renovation. After all, a building was being altered for him, and his life was also undergoing a seismic shift.

He downed the remainder of his cold coffee, crushed the cardboard cup, and threw it a few feet away into the gutter. Then, seeing the street sweeper approaching just down the block, he thought better of this, picked up the cup, and tossed it into a trash can on the corner. At the same time, he noticed a light pop on in the basement front room of the brownstone. Junie. Pickle gave her two minutes and then knocked on the door to the lower entrance.

Karen had installed planters at the outdoor vestibule, with all manner of spring flowers sprouting up and flowing down, surrounded by budding boxwoods and small blue spruces for year-round greenery. When Junie's door swung open, the scene resembled a Fragonard painting straight out of the Frick Museum. Orangutan hair (and that, Pickle had finally decided, was the only word that did her mop justice) billowed around her shoulders. Her white cotton nightgown was deeply crinkled from the night in bed. Junie might as well have been pumping her legs on a rope-and-board swing in the middle of a Giverny meadow. The Doodles skulked behind her and then raced out to tinkle against one of the planter boxes.

"Doodles! Not here, buddy!" she reprimanded. "You know better."

"He does, but doesn't care—never has. And by the way, he prefers his formal title—*The* Doodles. You'll get more out of him that way." Pickle winked.

"I'm trying to teach him his Ps and Qs about pee-pee and poo-poo."

"Good luck with that."

They stepped inside. Darren, the Design Within Reach guy, had indeed delivered. Pickle stepped into a mid-century modern jewel. The old bones of the brownstone provided a timeless envelope for the furniture's clean, crisp lines, in dusky taupe with a touch of navy blue here and there. Even the artwork on the walls, some of it culled from the upper floor, no doubt (and probably released only after huge resistance from Stan), held the space together with a seamless fusion of styles.

As they stood in the front room, Pickle nodded with admiration. "My God, this place has changed. Karen really knows her stuff. Is it comfortable for you?"

"Yeah, it's wonderful. She went out over the weekend and bought everything I'd need. I've never lived in a place so perfectly suited to, well, me. Speaking of high-end appliances, do you want an espresso?"

Pickle was massively caffeinated at this point, but stifled a burp and accepted. Junie grabbed a robe and dug her arms into the sleeves. As she tugged her hair out from the back of the robe, she beckoned to him to come into the middle room. She machine-pressed espresso into two demitasse cups. Pickle helped himself to a teaspoon of sugar and opened the half fridge to see if she had milk—only cream. Stan considered milk to be degraded cream and would never tolerate anything remotely watery in his house. He topped his espresso off with a dollop and they settled onto Plexiglas counter-height stools.

Pickle immediately felt intrusive, out of place, and rushed ahead with an explanation as to why he was even there. "They're starting the renovation today."

"Yup, Karen told me. Are you excited?"

"I am. But nervous, too. I've lived in my apartment for so many years."

"Where do you live?"

"The Bridge Apartments."

"That's a weird name," she commented.

"They're the apartments that stand right at the New York side of the George Washington Bridge."

"Oh—" Junie looked down at the mention of the bridge.

"I'm sorry. That's why I was able to respond so fast that night."

Junie shook her head rapidly. "I don't want to think about that stuff. The mornings are the only time I'm free from those sorts of thoughts."

"Okay. Sure."

She took a deep breath, and then sheepishly smiled. "I didn't tell Karen and Stan about our museum trip."

"Oh?" Pickle said with a blank expression.

"Yeah. It's not that I intentionally kept it from them. More like they didn't ask. Plus, it sounds like they're dealing with a lot right now. They argue all the time. What's going on there? I mean, do they even like each other?"

Pickle squirmed. "They're married. All couples argue, right?"

"It's worse than that. She yells at him . . . I feel sorry for him."

"Oh, please. Stan can take care of himself. Try not to take it too seriously. It's the way they let off steam."

"I don't know. I just stay out of the way." She rubbed her eyes of sleep and gulped down her espresso. "But there's something else: I feel odd around Stan."

Pickle slumped further into his chair. He didn't relish discussing the world according to Stan, Part One. But he decided to accommodate her. "How so?"

"Well, it's weird. You guys are twins."

Pickle chuckled. "Right?"

She smiled at her own obvious statement. "When I look at Stan, I expect him to act like you and kind of *be* you. And then he doesn't, or isn't. Hard to explain. But it's unnerving."

"Yeah, you're not the only one who's said that. But here's the thing: You'll get used to him. Just don't expect too much, is all I'm saying."

"Of course. Good advice."

Junie leaned in closer to Pickle. "But it comes down to feeling more comfortable around you, Pickle. See, you took my statement that night."

She stopped and began to fiddle with the collar of her robe. Pickle was aching for her to continue because he felt a compliment collecting in her head. "Go on?"

"That night at the police station, you seemed to say all the right words. I've been thinking about that since our museum trip and I guess I wanted to thank you."

"It's my job."

"Well, you're very good at it."

Pickle wanted to shut this down. He didn't want her to feel indebted to him. No. When Junie ultimately did come to him, it would flow from an impulse she couldn't control. He imagined that first she would be curious about him, and he knew she already was. Then she would consider him a friend—they were close to that, as well. As a lover, casual at first would suffice. Then the most pristine love imaginable would blossom. This love would feel shocking, even catastrophic, like a tsunami pointed directly toward his heart. It would knock him down and wash him clean. It would feel pure. It would look gorgeous. It would sound fizzy. It would taste . . . well, something like that.

Pickle broke into his own fantasies. "Are you up for another Pickle McArdle New York City sightseeing extravaganza this week?"

"Sure. But don't you have to work?"

Pickle pounded his chest in a mock ape gesture. "I'm a big shot—king of the asphalt jungle. I do whatever I want."

"Okay, then. What do you suggest?"

He looked carefully at her hair, for what seemed like the thousandth time. "How 'bout the Frick? Wednesday morning?"

Junie clapped her hands. "Oh, I haven't been there in such a long time. That sounds great."

"Then plan on lunch afterwards. Maybe we'll hit the Viennese café at the Neue Galerie."

Footsteps clomped down the stairway. "Junie! Look what I brought you."

Karen rounded the corner carrying several garment bags draped over her arms. She stopped and stiffened. "Pickle."

"Karen?" Pickle responded tersely.

She tossed the bags onto Junie's bed and then joined them to pour herself an espresso and have a bite of biscotti. The Doodles jumped off the sofa and scrambled around the corner, expecting something, anything.

"You're early," Karen scolded.

Pickle ignored the comment, looked Karen up and down, and gave a cat-whistle.

"Look at you. I feel honored that you dressed up for our meeting today. You look amazing. Doesn't she, Junie?"

"She really does," Junie agreed with admiration.

Karen bristled, and turned to Junie. "I brought down a couple of outfits I think you'll love. When we go up for the meeting, why don't you try them on and see if anything suits. Oh, and I've cancelled our dog walker—could you see to The Doodles today?"

"Of course. Stan's going to work?" Junie asked.

"Yeah, and he's getting his bandage off later this afternoon. Seems he wants to rejoin the land of the living, which is good, because the office needs him."

This was typical Karen: railroading everything and everyone while pissing all over anything within ten miles. Reminding Junie of how indispensable Stan was? Completely unnecessary. And trying to lure her with fancy overpriced clothes? Utterly ridiculous. Not to mention reprehensible. Pickle looked at his watch and began to muscle Karen toward the stairway.

"It's almost time," he warned.

"Whatever," Karen said.

They climbed the stairs in silence, his hand pushing at her lower back. Work, he saw, was already well under way. Plastic zippered shields hung from ceiling to floor. Construction guys milled about, chatting about the start of baseball season. All Mets fans, apparently.

Patrick arrived just as Stan emerged from the back bedroom and they all ascended to what would be Pickle's lower level. As Karen reviewed the details of the electrical and plumbing specifications with Patrick, Stan and Pickle walked to the front windows.

Pickle sized up his brother's navy blue Zac Posen suit and plaid bow tie. "So. You're going in today."

"Yeah. I'm sick of myself at this point. If I stay in this house any longer, I'll start drinking again," Stan said.

"You've been sober?"

"So far."

"Karen too?"

"So far."

"Huh. Will it last?"

"Who the fuck knows? Day at a time . . ."

"That's what they say. But what's the difference this time?"

Stan shrugged. "Does it matter?"

"I guess not."

"I hesitate to say this, but . . ."

"What?"

"That girl down there."

"Junie? What about her?" Pickle felt a tension build in his throat, like he was on the verge of a sneeze.

Stan perched on the dusty windowsill, then quickly stood up again and brushed off his backside. "It's hard to pinpoint. She's getting to me. I wouldn't say in a good way, though Karen spins it like that. She's been down there nonstop with some outfit or another. Dressing the girl up. You'd think it was Halloween, but for Project Runway. But here's the thing: the girl's down there. And I'm aware she can hear me when I walk around."

"So?"

"Well, it's an odd sensation—to know that someone you don't know at all is in your house day and night. And she's listening."

"What do you mean, *listening*? How would you know that?"

"It's a feeling I have. What is this girl doing in my house?" Stan said, shaking his head with disbelief. "Karen. She can really be so pushy."

"Have you even talked to her?"

"Junie? Not really. Well, maybe a little . . ." Stan shuddered and opened the window a crack. "I don't want to talk about it anymore. I feel clammy. Plus, I'm getting this blasted bandage off today and I'm a wreck about it."

"Stan, that's called *progress*—a good thing."

As Stan walked away to join Patrick and Karen, Pickle stared out the window and tried to imagine having this view in just a few weeks. Looking across the street onto the second floor of another brownstone, pretty much the same as his, he noticed a woman in a pink T-shirt working at her computer at the dining table. The woman concentrated on the screen, picked up a cell phone, spoke about two sentences and then slammed it down on the table. She stretched her arms over her head and yawned. Took a swig of something red from a wine glass. Drinking in the morning? The woman shut the laptop and shoved it to the side. She lay her head down on the table. Eventually her shoulders trembled, and it became clear that she was sobbing.

He heard his name being repeated—Pickle—over and over as they discussed his future at the other end of the room. He looked in the direction of his name and saw Karen, Stan, and Patrick flocked together like agreeable geese, pointing to construction plans and walls not yet built. "Pickle wants this. This would be good for Pickle. Pickle needs . . ."

Pickle, Pickle, Pickle. The peppered "Ps" drove into his ears, beating inside his skull. His breathing became rapid and then bottomed out to where he could barely catch any air. White dots clouded his vision. He rubbed his eyes. The woman across the street was gone now and he wondered where she was. To the kitchen for more wine? To the bathroom to blow her nose and rinse her face? To the bedroom to shut out the world? Then, he saw her front door open. She emerged with four standard poodles. They were apricot—close to Junie's hair color. Leaning with his head against the pane of glass, Pickle followed the woman, dragging the dogs toward Riverside Park. And he listened to the sound of his name from across the room.

For the twins' seventh birthday party, ten children sat around a dining table covered with a grimy plastic tablecloth. Their mother could afford only one cake, so she'd split it in half and dragged each section to either end of the table.

For some reason, a few of the kids began reciting the nursery rhyme, "Peter Piper Picked a Peck of Pickled Peppers." Their mother picked up on the frenzy and roused the children into screaming the ditty at the top of their lungs. Pickle wanted them to stop, as did Stan. Both twins cupped their hands over their ears, tears streaming down their cheeks. Stan had his own reasons for breaking down—but for Pickle, he heard his birth name—Peter—being destroyed.

Pickle knew that Peter was a biblical person—a saint (whatever that was)—and had been crucified upside down. Apparently, Saint Peter didn't want to be killed in the same manner as Jesus, who'd died, upright, on the cross. Pickle had toggled this story together from random Sunday-school classes his mother made the twins attend until she'd grown tired of getting up early every Sunday. Initially, Pickle had no idea who Jesus was either, though entire classes had been devoted to this Jesus person, who, it ended up, was the Son of God. But Peter! He was *special*—because not only was he Jesus's friend, he was also an upside-down saint. But Pickle's name, Peter, went to the devil on his seventh birthday, when he became known as a joke in a nursery rhyme.

"Pickle? Pickle? *Pickle!*" Karen was yelling at him. He looked up, confused.

"Do you want an elongated toilet?" Patrick asked. "We're marking out the location of the door swing."

Pickle strode over and stood directly in front of Patrick, almost nose to nose, and yelled, "How the fuck should I know? Do what's right. And get this shit done in four weeks."

Patrick jerked back, vaguely bobbing his head with lowered eyes.

Pickle heard a noise at the stairway. Junie appeared at the top of the stairs, dressed in an outfit Karen had worn to his apartment a few days before the accident on the bridge. He remembered because he'd removed it from her body himself and had thrown it across the room. Karen had screamed at him for not respecting her things. He told her it was just a dress, for God's sake. They'd fought hard and then fucked immediately after.

He ran down the stairs, passing Junie. He could smell Karen's perfume—musk—embedded into the cloth, now presumably all over Junie's skin. Once he got out onto the sidewalk, Pickle sat on one of Karen's planters. The woman from across the street was returning. The dogs seemed happy enough, no longer straining at their leads. Pickle looked up to find the sun, and then walked in the opposite direction.

17

THE LIPSTICK BUILDING, NAMED FOR ITS TUBE shape, glistened as spears of sunlight glinted off the imperial red granite façade. Karen and Stan stepped out of a cab and she shot a glance to the top of the building. What she wouldn't give to be up there—in the blue yonder—flying with a sharp-eyed hawk, or just a flock of dumb pigeons. Birds found freedom when a warm wind lifted them away from the dangers on the ground. The notion appealed to Karen; she wanted to escape.

The meeting had dispersed quickly after Pickle's tantrum. Patrick expressed dismay, doubting he could work for such a brute. Karen stepped in to placate him with assurances that she would act as a buffer. Stan wandered over to the front window to focus on anything but the discomfort of the drama that had just unfolded. These men. They behaved like a couple of temperamental musth elephants she was forced to herd with a ringmaster's whip—trunk-to-tail and tail-to-trunk.

Karen had grown up with men, lots of them; they filed into her home every weekend. The high-stakes poker games began on Friday evenings after she and her sister, Betsy, finished dinner. They ended late Sunday mornings, just in time for the weekend lineup of football games, when the men would then ease back into sobriety.

While the men bet their money around the dining room table, Karen and Betsy lounged in the adjoining small den watching TV, which was always kept at a low volume so Karen could hear when her father called on her to provide something for the men. It was important that she remain obedient—vigilant, really—a girl who, as the oldest, was ready to do her father's bidding, all so the poker games could flow without interruption. With the curtains drawn shut, night eased into day and back again to a longer night. No one seemed to notice and that was the point.

Karen learned from the men's banter that for some reason aces were the best, kings the next, and so on down the line. But there was something called a royal flush that she understood had great power. A flush was a feeling of blood rushing to her head or water down a toilet and in a secret way, she enjoyed the contrary associations. Still, she kept her eye on the progress of the game, and noted her father's knee under the table. When it jiggled a bit faster, this usually meant he was "up." If there was no movement, he was "down." Her father's quiet legs, like stiff, uncooked spaghetti that could snap with little effort, kept Karen particularly on guard.

It was all so beautiful and perfectly choreographed, a timeless Ashton ballet. The cards, held in the men's chubby fingers, spread out like wings of a preening peacock. Their gold rings weren't on the usual ring finger (and so she assumed they were all bachelors), but on the pinky, with heavy chunks of metal swallowing small stones in the center that occasionally caught the light of the dining room drop chandelier. The men, even as they sat for many hours, remained in constant motion by gathering their cards into a stack and then re-fanning them through-out the game. This was how they dissipated their tension—by manipu-lating the cards, flicking the edges, placing them down on the table and stretching their muscled arms over their heads, cracking their knuck-les, rubbing their hands back and forth. And always the laughter that sounded to Karen like boulders crashing down from a mountaintop, heavy and dangerous. These men were serious people, and the weekend was the most important time of the week for her father.

He called to her with a quiet whistle, like the whoop of an exotic crane. Karen jumped up in the middle of her B movie to provide fresh liquor for the men, whose glasses now held only thin slivers of watery ice, chinking at the bottom of the glass. Karen knew the alcohol by the tint: scotch looked like urine, bourbon looked like honey, and vodka like water. This was Karen's expertise, and it was easy. All she needed to do was scoop up the glass, assess the diluted color, drop in a few cubes of ice, and then refill. Returning to the dining room, she placed the freshened drinks to the side of each man, having memorized who got what. Once Karen knew she had the ability to stay ahead of what the men needed, it really wasn't all that bad. Because the men, she came to understand, were fairly predictable.

Karen and Stan headed for the back door to their office suite. This discreet entrance allowed them to settle in before the dramas of the day pressed. They marched single file down the long hallway, lined on both sides with hundreds of tubes of red lipstick sitting on the chair-rail lip. Stan believed in continuity of concept—both macro to micro—inside and out. Indeed, every woman in the firm was asked to wear red lipstick as an homage to the building. To help facilitate this odd unwritten rule, the lipsticks were there for use, should anyone forget to bring their own.

Stan stood at his office door threshold, with one foot in the hallway, the other in his office. "What should I do first?"

"Sift through the emails. Suzie's saved the ones you need to answer personally in a separate folder. Start there. Then we'll have a staff meeting at two to get everyone up to speed."

"Do I have to be there?" Stan pouted.

"Jesus, Stan, of *course*. You don't have to say anything—just listen. And think about the Kinsey project. We have another meeting with them in a week. It's a biggie and we want to lock it up. I put our bid proposals, drawings, and concept sketches on the credenza behind your desk. Come up with one more concept—over and above what we've already given them. And remember, you're going to get that bandage ripped off this afternoon."

Stan paused before he went into his office, and scrutinized the lipsticks that ran down the hallway. "Karen, have someone fix those—they look sloppy," he said with irritation.

"Oh God. The cleaning crew must have done that."

"Well, fire that crew!"

"Stan, these people are part of building maintenance. We have no control over them."

"The *hell* we don't. I'll hire my own cleaning staff. I can't walk into this chaos. Totally unacceptable—"

She slapped her hand over his mouth. "Done? Go into your office. I don't wanna see you 'til two."

Karen poked her head into the large communal room where all the work pods were arranged in an open plan, which supposedly encouraged better communication. The staff seemed to be working with heads down. Still unseen, she retreated and snuck into her office.

Karen had designed her office to reflect her personal taste—constructed femininity, she liked to call it. Nothing like the firm's tightly boxed concept of what a *McArdle* design represented. Yet, while Stan's palm print remained the masthead of the firm, Karen's input was the small engine that added a distinct third dimension. Perhaps the bravery of crossing centuries, a contrary color combination, or an unexpected curve. Her office, while offensive to Stan, helped draw a psychic line in the sand in their partnership.

After pulling the blinds down at the glass partition, thereby blocking the view, she locked the door, slid off her heels, and tugged a cashmere blanket down from the top shelf of the closet. She lay down on the loveseat, shivered, and drew the wool up to her chin. Stan was in the office not ten minutes and Karen felt completely wrung out. She reached over to her desk and punched a button on her phone. Suzie answered immediately. "Karen?"

"Stan's back. Don't bother me unless there's a fire. Get the staff prepped for a two p.m. meeting. Buzz me precisely ten minutes before." She hung up before Suzie could respond, and though Karen closed her eyes, her mind continued to paint pictures from the past.

Karen's sister usually stayed in the den when their father whistled for Karen to make the rounds for the men. That helped because when she returned, Betsy would get her up to speed on what had happened on TV while she was gone. But one late night, Betsy followed Karen through the dining room, on her way to the bathroom off the kitchen. The men never looked up when they passed by, and Karen understood this was the way the men remained clever and kept their wits. Betsy tried the bathroom door at the far end of the kitchen, which she found locked. Karen began preparing the liquor and ice for the men, while Betsy waited for her turn. Then a man emerged from the bathroom and smiled at the girls.

"Oh, dear God. What have we here?" The man, staring at Betsy, sang the words with a soft voice only the girls could hear. He took a quick step forward. Betsy tried to sidestep the man, but he grabbed her by the arm and pulled her into the bathroom. Karen was initially rendered immobile with surprise. But when the man began to close the door, she ran over and jammed her foot at the saddle to prevent the door from shutting. The man had Betsy perched on the front of the small pedestal sink. He'd pushed her skirt up to her underpants. Karen noticed Betsy's thighs, covered with golden hair, bleached by the summer sun. The man stroked the fuzz.

"Dear God, little girl." The man implored Karen with his easy eyes. "I'm just asking for a few minutes, is all."

Karen took Betsy under the armpits with both hands and pulled her away. The man dropped back and leaned against the bathroom wall. She noticed the man swallow and something on his throat slid up and down. That's when Karen noticed the man's lips—rigid and thin with no trace of red at all. Betsy gripped Karen's middle with her legs and the girls tangoed back into the kitchen. Karen heard her father's voice.

"Drinks, Karen. What's the holdup?"

She released Betsy and pushed her forward, watching until she crossed through the dining room, reached the den, and fixed her eyes on the TV. The man stayed in the bathroom, but kept the door ajar by about an inch. As Karen lined up the glasses, poured the liquor, and added ice cubes, she heard the man urinate. The flow staggered, and it made her stop for a few seconds, until the toilet flushed. Then she entered the dining room, followed by the man with the sharp bump at his neck and no lips. Karen placed the glasses on the table, and the man slid into his seat.

"Dear God, you've got a couple of sweet girls, Dan."

Karen's father didn't look up, but grunted at the man in agreement. "Yeah, they're just fine."

Voices, coming from the other side of the glass wall, now roused Karen, as Suzie directed some staffer away.

"No, don't disturb her."

"But I need her approval on this before the meeting."

"We can't bother her. Karen used the 'fire' warning. That means emergency."

The day she had failed Betsy; *that* was the real emergency. When she'd heard the noises, and walked up the stairs, and saw the man's back. He'd turned to her. She knew him. His easy eyes and his bobbing throat and his rimless mouth and the familiar twist of words she could never forget.

The phone buzzed. Karen reached up to stab at the intercom.

"What!?"

"Karen, it's three minutes till two."

"I told you ten minutes!"

"I've been buzzing you for five solid minutes."

"Oh. I'll be right there."

Karen glanced at the clock and saw that she'd slept deeply for another hour. As she roused herself and smoothed the wrinkles in her clothing, Karen felt the heaviness in her belly. She was confused; her mother entered only when conditions were dire. Karen then remembered the dream she'd just had.

She was about to enter a stage from the right wing. It was a performance of a play, though she'd never acted before. The stage manager gave her the cue and as she walked out, she became blinded by the footlights. An actor sat in a chair at the front edge of the stage with his back to Karen. This man, she surmised, was Stan. As she approached him, she became unnerved by the possibility that the man might actually be Pickle. Adrenalin rushed into her neck and head. She was no actress and even worse, wasn't sure which twin was sitting in the chair. How was she to understand her "motivation" if she didn't know who her leading man was? Then her mother entered her body. Her belly pushed against her tightening skirt waist and the extra flesh on her arms rubbed against her shirt. Her mother took control of her hand and moved it to brush the top of Stan or Pickle's head. The hair was oily with an old-fashioned pomade and she grabbed onto it. She pulled the head back and looked at the upside-down face. Her leading man was Betsy's abuser—his lips now full and smiling, outlined with red lipstick.

Karen walked down the hall and entered the large conference room. She was thirty minutes late. Stan, well into the meeting, held the staff rapt with his ad-hoc presentation. They barely looked her way. Her stomach was now empty, her body weightless in a way she imagined birds might feel. She took her seat next to Stan and stared out the window, trying to locate those birds in flight. *These men.*

18

PICKLE'S DOORMAN GAVE HIM THE SIGNAL: A two-fingered cap salute meant Karen. And it made Pickle giddy-happy. He even skipped the mailbox room; catalogues could wait. He whistled as he walked down the hallway to his apartment. The tune? "The Greatest Love of All."

He saw Karen sitting at the window with her back to the front door. She straddled the chair backwards, her legs spread wide, reckless. Pickle spied her Jimmy Choo pumps, living in separate corners of the room. As he stood behind Karen, they observed the end of rush hour; cars and trucks poured like liquid into New Jersey and all points west.

He sniffed the air. Karen took a drag of a joint, held it in, then blew it to the ceiling. Pickle sighed as he batted the fumes away from his face. "Pot is the same as booze, Karen. Your sobriety is officially broken."

She spat out a fleck of pot leaf. It hit the window and she rubbed her thumb over it, wiping the remnant on her knee. "Stan's been checking my breath. I needed a drink. So? Pot."

Pickle kissed the top of Karen's head, then threw his coat on a wall hook and waited. Something was gathering, and he wasn't sure how the weather system was going to break. He patiently watched her as she continued to stare through the fat cables of the bridge, into the distance. Then she turned to Pickle and her voice took on a wistful lilt. "Stan and I used to laugh at all those people in New Jersey—with their spoiled children and stultified lives. We used to feel so goddamned good about ourselves. Even drunk."

"Dear God. Is this gonna end where I think it will? You on all fours, sobbing? Me handing you hankies?" Pickle ripped a square of paper towel from the roll on the kitchen counter and threw it at Karen. It floated to the floor, lazy, four feet from his target.

"You are so *horrid*." Karen's back stiffened as she spit the words at the window.

"Sure," he said.

Karen stood, turned around, plopped back down and crossed her legs. She swung her leg, at first slowly, and then it picked up speed, like a dangerous tool: a pickaxe. Just as quickly, she halted the momentum and took another deep toke.

"Well, *I* need a drink. I'm parched." Pickle leaned down into the sink and cupped a gulp of water without a glass. Still bent to the faucet, he turned his head toward her. "I may be horrid, but you're so fucking beautiful. Especially when you're drunk. Or stoned."

Karen snorted. "I hate it when people say that to me. The beautiful part."

"People? How about me?"

"You, most of all."

Pickle straightened up from the sink, dragged his hand across his mouth, and rubbed the excess moisture into his hair. "Okay, Karen. Go ahead and get nice and fucked up. Give me everything you've got. I can take it. Because today? I'm in a good mood."

She stuck her tongue out. "Blah-di-da-di-dah."

"Don't you wanna know why?"

"I couldn't care less."

"Maybe. Maybe not."

Pickle walked to the bed, which was made up hospital-style, the corners tucked with a tense precision. He'd been fastidious of late and had cleaned the daylights out of the place just the day before. Books had been stacked by size, narrowing as they ascended on the shelves—a technique Stan had taught him. The room smelled slightly of Pledge, now disrupted by a patina of weed. He sat and leaned back on his elbows.

Karen looked around, as if noticing his housekeeping skills for the first time. "You did a good job on this place. I didn't think you had it in you."

"You underestimate me, Karen. That's one of your few flaws. And mistakes."

She eyed him, unsure. "Okay, I give up. Why are you in such a jolly mood?"

"I'm seeing Junie tomorrow."

Karen scrambled off the chair, flipping it to the floor, and threw the lit joint at his face. Pickle batted it away. The roach bounced off the wall and landed in the middle of the room. She jumped on top of him, causing them to fall backward onto the bed. Pickle fended her off—her arms, her hands, her nails, her legs, her knees, her feet—all of which she aimed in the general direction of his crotch. Finally, she straddled him and pounded halfheartedly on his chest, like a disinterested ape.

"You bastard." She whispered the words like a secret.

Pickle wrested Karen up and over onto her back. He located the roach, stamped it out, and scuffed it to the side of the room. Then he slid back onto the bed and gently laid his leg over her belly. He imagined Karen saw this as hostile—and meant to hold her down. But he was entitled to a little self-defense. After all, she was behaving like a Saturday-night punk.

"Now tell me, dearest. Why on God's green earth do you care if I see Junie?"

She stared at the ceiling, panting. "I don't know. It's not Junie. Not really. I'm trying to make sense of all this. I mean we're together—practically a couple, for Christ's sake. But now you're forcing the brownstone and I don't see how that's going to work out. I'm very sad."

"Don't be sad. Nothing's gonna change."

"Yes, it will. You know it will."

"Jesus, Karen. Stan doesn't know and unless you fuck things up, he never will—not from me, anyway. And forget about Junie. She's a non-issue."

"But you're moving *in* with us. How does that even work? It's insane. I want to break it off with you. That's why I needed a drink. Or something." Karen grabbed a corner of the top sheet and wiped her eyes.

"You're getting worked up over nothing. We'll be discreet. It's not that hard. But I'm curious. If you really *do* want to break up, then why do you care if I see Junie?"

"You fucker."

"I'd like an answer to my question."

Karen closed her eyes.

Pickle prodded. "Nothing's *happened*."

"But something will—"

148

"You don't know that, and even if it did, so what? I'm the cuckold-ed one; you've got Stan *and* me. Now you want to have Junie, too—as some sort of surrogate sister? You're a possessive, greedy bitch."

"I have to protect her."

"From me?"

"Maybe. I don't know. I'm confused."

"Clearly."

"I'm serious, Pickle. I can't go on with you. It's wrong."

"Oh, dear God. Boo. Fucking. Hoo."

"I detest your sarcasm."

"Well, I'm at a loss for any other tactic, because none of this makes any sense. You're creating drama where there is none. Except in your head."

Karen sat up and faced Pickle. "My life has been falling apart for ages. You haven't been paying attention. I just need to get things straight."

Pickle laughed. "Get things *straight*? Thus, the pot—"

"*You're disgusting!*"

Pickle crossed his arms, thinking. Then he poked Karen with his big toe. She looked at him, and he knew she expected a solution. It was good to be in control, for a change.

"Okay, Karen. Here's what. Do you think I'm just some rag that you can wring out and decide it's too dirty to use, after all, and toss in the garbage? Do you really believe that I'll let you end this? Do I have to remind you that you have so much more to lose?"

She leaned forward, fell onto him and sobbed into his chest. Pick-le wrapped his arms around her and breathed in her hair—musk—not grapefruit.

He nudged her forehead with his chin. "Look at me."

"I can't." She snuffed.

"I have to know that you see me."

She tilted her head up and swallowed some snot.

"Don't you know me?"

She nodded.

"That's right. I'm your husband's twin brother. We're identical. Except for the red mole, as you well know. I will continue to fuck you until the time comes when I see fit to stop. And nothing, not Stan, not the brownstone, not Junie, not even you, can change that."

Karen squeezed him tight. She kissed him and her viscous snot smeared across his face. They fell back onto the bed. Unzipping his fly, Pickle pulled himself out. She hiked up her dress and he tugged her underwear down. He looked at her collarbone and kissed the hollow. He noticed a mascara smear on her damp cheek and licked it off. He watched her chest rise and fall, gradually slowing. Hovering over her, Pickle waited for Karen to open her eyes. And when she finally did, Pickle entered her.

19

PICKLE PULLED OUT FOUR SHIRTS FROM HIS closet. After tossing aside three as weak options, he selected a light blue number and ironed the daylights out of it. He dressed slowly and with precision: a sport coat and tie, his shoes spit-shined and trousers edged. He made a final overall check in the mirror and tugged down on his shirtsleeve cuffs.

His face would require more drastic measures. Karen's handiwork stared back at him in the bathroom mirror. During their scuffle the previous night, she'd managed to give him a crescent-shaped scrape on his cheek. He debated whether he should shave, which would, no doubt, sting. Instead, he pulled down some of Karen's foundation makeup, sitting on the top shelf of the medicine cabinet. A dab here, a dab there didn't quite do the masking job needed; it looked obvious, with a much darker tone than his Irish complexion. So, he pumped a palm full, smeared his entire face, and hoped that between the makeup and his day-old beard growth, Junie wouldn't notice the scratch. Or at least not say anything.

He wolfed half a bagel while riding down in the elevator, and then fretted over the poppy seeds he was sure were stuck in his teeth. Ten blasts of Binaca, swirling the liquid around his mouth and then a spit to the sidewalk, would have to suffice.

The Frick was Pickle's favorite art collection in New York City. He'd arranged to meet Junie at the center of the former mansion, called the Garden Court, and was particularly eager to share the art in the Fragonard Room. Those paintings, known as *The Progress of Love*, depicted courtship in an era when women were revered for their refinement, for their subtlety, and for their demurring objections. That's the way he saw, or idealized, Junie—as one of those pale lovelies, pumping their legs on swings knotted to a cantilevered tree limb, reading a book of poetry in one hand and holding a suitor's advances back with the other. These eighteenth-century women were the original multitaskers, Pickle laughed to himself.

She was already waiting for him, sitting on a marble bench, dressed in black leggings and a blousy purple caftan top that draped below her knees. Thin calves poked out of the vivid color and disappeared into her ankle boots. She'd not bothered to fashion her hair in a braid this time. Instead, her curls had been set loose, going wild like rattlers all around her head. Yet, the overall effect was, strangely, sophisticated and very New York. He gathered himself up, walked over, and stood in front of her for several seconds, waiting to be noticed. She was engrossed in a slim volume of Raymond Carver short stories. Pickle nudged her boot with his wingtip. Startled, she quickly placed the book in her satchel and rose to greet him.

They stood opposite each other, about two feet apart, not sure which way their bodies would, or should, move. The kinetic confusion pushed laughter first out of Pickle and then Junie joined him. They giggled hard, gasping. They laughed about absolutely nothing. Nothing and everything.

Pickle cupped Junie's elbow to guide her into the first grouping of enfilade rooms opposite the Fragonard section. Their movement from one work of art to the next felt loosely timed, almost like choreography in early stages, the exact steps not yet finalized for performance. With this blossoming symbiosis, the visual effect felt serene, as if strolling along the Seine in a Seurat painting.

He'd held the Fragonard Room back for last. By now, the space had filled up with Europeans taking a tour. The guide's voice, obnoxious with an Oxford-like smear of knowledge, annoyed Pickle. He didn't want this blowhard distracting them from what he felt was the pure intent of Fragonard's art.

Junie stopped a few feet into the room and grabbed Pickle's hand. He looked down, and noticed the direction of her gaze. *The Pursuit.* Pulling her toward it, they stood before the enormous oil painting and all sound seemed to recede. He felt like Tony with Maria at the gym in *West Side Story*—the room all echo and blur—dancing a tentative rumba between naive lovers. Minutes must have passed. Then Junie allowed him to pull her away. They left the building, his arm draped lightly across her shoulders.

They began their walk north to Eighty-Sixth Street. The warm noon hour made them both perspire and Junie swept her hair up with a clip at the top of her head. Pickle, at least a foot taller, had a bird's-eye view. He wanted to touch her hair, rub the strands back and forth between his thumb and forefinger to gauge its tensile strength. But he resisted. Instead he wiped sweat from his brow with his palm and rubbed "Bobbi Brown Nude" onto the back of his pants leg.

They entered an empty Café Sabarsky, where a waiter ushered them to a corner table, and Pickle immediately ordered strong Viennese coffees and two Sachertorten. Junie took in a shuddering breath, her eyes wet and vulnerable.

She began, hesitantly, to explain. "I'd only seen graphite drawings in the Brooklyn Museum. Fragonard. Jacob and I went there a lot to see them. And when you said we'd go to the Frick, I'd forgotten about the Fragonard Room."

They'd spoken almost no words to each other since meeting at the Frick—and that felt just fine. Now, the quality of her voice brought Pickle back to the night at the precinct, when her emotions had splattered all over the small room, one second a howling anguish, the next as banal as spaghetti and meatballs.

"Those drawings were important to us. There was something tender about each stroke of red chalk and the intention of each line. But it wasn't just about the lines, because there were thousands. It was more that you could follow each one and see exactly where it ended. It's hard to explain but I see now, with just a bit of distance, that sometimes depression allows you to see only one small thing at a time. Minute by minute. And with the Fragonard, line by line. You focus in and sweep everything else aside. Because you simply can't take in any more. Those Fragonard drawings helped us."

He wasn't expecting this and was at a loss, out of his league. Pickle looked down and stared at the grey marble tabletop, tracing a black vein until it reached the edge of the table and died. Junie reached up, and let her hair fall; some tendrils dropped in front of her eyes.

"Tell me about the Fragonard at the Frick. How do you reconcile all of that in your mind now?" Pickle asked.

"No. I want to hear what you think."

The waiter came with their order and they set about fixing the coffees to their liking. Junie dug into her torte and he took a few deep gulps of his coffee. The café began to fill up with the sounds of chair legs scraping the stone floor, and waiters crashing through the swinging doors to the kitchen.

"Another lecture? You sure?" Pickle asked, skeptical.

She nodded after a few seconds. "I think so . . . yeah."

Pickle leaned in so she could hear him over the din. "Well, this is off the top of my head, and based on what you've told me just now. But I'm also thinking of your statement at the precinct. So, putting the two bits together—"

Junie interrupted, exasperated. "Just *tell* me, already. Stop with the caveats. Plus, you're sounding like Stan." She immediately saw the wound in his eyes. "Sorry."

"Okay. It's actually pretty simple. I see your experience with the two Fragonards—the graphite and the oil—as a metaphor for change. Or maybe transformation. Now you're able to *see* a fully fleshed-out work of art. Not a monotone line drawing, however detailed and intricate it might be. But a textured oil painting with color, whose edges are blurred and ill-defined. That's the way of life—it's messy."

Pickle splayed his hands out in a "voilà" gesture. She clapped.

"And I'd like to thank the Academy and my agent . . . blah blah blah," Pickle joked.

His stomach was empty, the bagel now long gone, so he took a bite of his torte and immediately felt a rush of sugar stack on top of caffeine. Junie reached forward and rubbed some chocolate from his chin. He was happy for the touch.

She looked at her finger and frowned. "Pickle. Are you wearing *makeup?*"

"What's that?" Pickle pulled back from her, their easy intimacy broken.

"There's some beige stuff on your face!"

"Oh. I can explain. I had a bit of a scrape last night . . . on the job."

"What!?"

Pickle waved it off. "No, no. Nothing like that. I got a scratch, and shaving stung this morning. So, I ran out to the drugstore and got some of this makeup. Obviously, the wrong shade."

"I forget what you do. How awful."

"Well I'm usually not in danger, at least not anymore." He cocked his head to one side. "No big deal. Okay?"

She put her fork down and licked her lips of chocolate. "Pickle, I have to ask you something."

"Shoot."

"What happened to Jacob? Did you find him?"

"Oh, Junie . . . *Now?*"

Her chin quivered. "I've got to know. See, I've got to get the thought of him in the Hudson out of my mind. I need a new picture."

Ouch. She missed him. Of course, she wasn't over him. It seemed that every single woman in his life was glued to a man, but he was never that man. His mother and Stan—that unholy alliance. Karen and Stan and the fact of fucking his twin brother's wife—with plea-sure. And now Junie with this loser Jacob. How could he get rid of this annoying gnat with one swat?

"Well, only if you're really sure."

"I'm sure."

Pickle scooted his chair back, creating the distance that would bring authority to his voice. He became a cop: calculating, cynical. The finest badass in New York City, as Karen liked to call him.

"We decided to keep it from you—Lance and me. And you have to understand, you weren't his next of kin, so we weren't legally obligated to inform you of anything. I probably would have told you sooner if it wasn't for the fact that my brother and Karen took you in. You were in good hands, so I figured there was no rush. But if you say you're ready, then okay."

"Tell me."

Pickle hid his hands underneath the table. They were trembling, so he stuck them between his knees and squeezed. "The good news is that he was found the next day—which was a blessing for all the obvious reasons. He was intact. And his wallet was still in his pocket, so we didn't need any other identification. Understand?"

"Go on."

"Lance contacted Jacob's family in New Jersey. They said he'd been out of touch—estranged—for some time. So, they came in and took him—his body. Lance asked them about you, wondering if they wanted to get in touch about services and stuff. But they told him they didn't know anything about you."

Junie's head snapped to the side; she frowned and eyed him suspiciously. Pickle noticed, but rushed to continue. "Lance handled all of that part. I never met them or talked to them."

"No. Wait—that's not right. Jacob told me they knew about me. Even though things were bad between him and his family, they'd been in touch."

Pickle cleared his throat. He stared at her and counted three seconds.

"Well, according to Lance, I don't think that was the case. He said the family had not known of his whereabouts for years. Junie, people are strange—you know—especially when there's a mental illness involved."

"What do you mean? What are you *talking* about?"

Pickle put his hand on Junie's forearm. She jerked it from him, as if withdrawing from a scorching burn. Slowly, he dragged his hand back. "Well, his family said that Jacob had been diagnosed with bipolar disorder. And that he'd dropped out of sight many times."

Junie put her hands over her eyes, rocked back and forth and began to whimper. Pickle pulled his chair next to hers and pried her hands off her face, enveloping them in his palms. He threaded his fingers into hers.

"You didn't know that, did you? That he was bipolar?"

She shook her head, once each way.

"We see this kind of thing a lot with suicides. Secrets can't be hidden anymore. And it's toughest on the living, those they leave behind."

"Poor, poor Jacob. I'm trying to see it now . . . maybe . . . in a way . . . yes . . ."

Pickle let her work it out. She'd get there—believe him—in no time at all. It was the type of information that made an awful situation, a suicide, go down easier. The guy was off his fucking rocker. Simple. But Pickle wanted to make sure. "Junie. There's one more thing you should know. And I hesitate, but I think it'll be best in the long run for you to know everything now."

"What? Yes. Yes. Just tell me." Her voice went from alto to soprano.

He had her—all soft in his fists—and he squeezed. "Jacob didn't work, right? Lance found no source of income for him."

She stared at him with her mouth open—confused.

"Why not? What did he tell you?" Pickle asked.

"Just that his grandparents had given him a lump sum when they passed away. Around the time he'd met me. I had a few different jobs at first, but he convinced me to quit. He said that he could support us on the money from his grandparents."

"Well, part of that is true. He did have money from his grandparents. But they aren't dead. They're still alive. Jacob stole that money. He'd embezzled about a hundred thousand dollars from them. That's what you were living on."

She shook her head, her eyes wild with disbelief, or perhaps the reality of a painful truth.

Pickle reached up and tucked a few strands of hair behind her ear. "I'm very, very sorry. This can't be easy."

They stayed in that position, like figures frozen in a midstream gesture at Pompeii. Suddenly Junie shoved her chair back and stood up. "Pickle, let's go . . . No, wait. I have to go home—I mean to the brownstone."

"Sure. I'll take you in a cab."

"No. I want to go by myself. I can't be with anyone. Please understand."

"Okay, of course. Let me pay the check and I'll get you into a cab."

Pickle looked around for the waiter, spotted him, and then gestured for the check. When he turned back she was gone. He spied Junie outside on the sidewalk, frantically flapping her arms, attempting to hail a cab. Pickle stayed back and watched until a taxi pulled up. She lowered her orange head and dipped into the backseat, just like a perp. The cab made a U-turn and headed toward Fifth Avenue.

Pickle sat back down and finished his torte. Reaching over to Ju-

159

nie's plate, he scraped off the remnants of her half-eaten slice, dumped it onto his plate, and licked his fork. The noise from the restaurant surged to a cymbal crash. Pickle tried to single out one conversation that he might grab and follow, but it remained a saturation of sound— all the voices mashed together by a noise compactor. He yelled for the waiter and ordered another torte and a triple espresso.

20

WITH DAY THREE OF THE RENOVATION COM-
pleted, most of the large debris from demolition had been dragged
down and dumped into the bin in front of the brownstone. But silt
was insidious and even though the workers swept at the end of each
day, they'd return the next morning only to refill the space with air-
borne detritus.

Karen stood on the top step of the brownstone and shoved three
Fresh Direct boxes to the side. Stan, she saw, was preoccupied on
the other side of a zippered plastic shield, trying to arrange the bottom edge to his liking with his toes. He deftly grabbed the plastic by
scrunching his digits and pulling. Karen observed with admiration; his
dexterity was impressive.

"Don't get too crazy with that," she called to him. "I need to get in,
and there're some boxes out here."

Stan, startled, noticed her through the film of the shield. "Thank
God. It's you. This filth is just too awful. Boxes?"

"Groceries. They must have left them out here because of the plastic thing."

"Okay, I'm going to count to three. Or maybe five. And then I'm going to unzip. Get yourself and all that shit in here in under ten . . . no, eight seconds."

"Eight seconds, ten seconds. Five minutes. It doesn't matter. Just go to the back of the house. Don't watch. I'll get in. I'll mop. You'll never know the difference."

"Well that's just not true. I *will* know. But you're right, I can't watch."

As Karen waited for Stan to sequester himself in the bedroom, she heard music coming from Junie's floor below—that damned Mahler 5th again. This morning she'd been playing Beethoven's 6th—*The Spring Symphony*—a musical depiction of rebirth. Something must have happened to Junie.

When she heard Stan slam the bedroom door, Karen unzipped and stepped inside, kicking the boxes in with her. She saw that all was, in fact, immaculate. They'd hired their cleaning woman, Gloria, to come at the end of each day to make sure their living area was habitable—in the way that suited Stan—pristine.

Disgusted, she yelled toward the back, "There's nothing amiss, Stan. Perfectly clean. Come out!"

He poked his head out of the bedroom, looking doubtful, then scuffed through the hall in his slippers with The Doodles bringing up the rear. Karen dragged her finger across the entrance console table and displayed the pad of her index finger for emphasis. "Nothing."

Stan's eyes narrowed, still not convinced. "Well, not really," he said, pointing to the boxes. "Now those beastly things have to be dealt with."

Karen gawked at his arm. "Ohhhhh no. No. No. *No*. Get that sling off right now. The doctor told you to keep your arm moving. You're not to coddle yourself. Otherwise, recovery will be slower, and we can't have that."

"But I'm afraid. I feel vulnerable. Someone's going to hit my arm. I just know it."

"I get that, but you have to try. And get out of that robe, for Christ's sake. It's beginning to creep me out. Let's go, I want to have Junie up for dinner."

She jogged around the boxes, turned Stan about-face with her hands on his shoulders, and walked him into the bedroom. Stan sat on the bed and let Karen take over. She gently removed the sling and pulled him out of the robe, one arm at a time. Selecting an orange cotton sweater from his chest of drawers, she began to consider how best to get his arms into the pullover and commit the least amount of pain.

"Wait, Karen. The color's not right."

"Why not? Orange was at the top of the stack. I thought that's how you and Gloria had color coded for use."

"We're in the middle of changing my concept."

"Why? I love the way this drawer looks." Karen stifled a yawn.

"It's too Sister Parish. You know, the Howard Johnson colors?"

"You lost me."

"You should know this, Karen. The Howard Johnson restaurant was her first job. Blue and orange. Then she went to the Kennedy White House, but that was years later. Didn't they teach you this shit in design school?"

"Shut up."

"Anyway, when I see this particular orange, I think of pancakes or some other foul food."

Karen covered her mouth in mock disgust. "Oh, my *God*."

"Get the dusty lavender sweater out—I think it's third down—right after the cerulean blue and the lemony citrine. And make sure you fix them so they're perfectly lined up. And put this orange one back . . . um . . . seventh down. I think. No, wait a minute. If I take the lavender out that means—"

She swatted the sweater to the floor and sunk onto the bed next to Stan. "Dear God. Deliver me."

"Oh please, Karen. It's *colors*, not the atom bomb. Jesus. Get a grip."

"I'm trying. But between you, the office, the clients, the vendors, the trades . . ." Karen's tirade diminished to a whisper. Stan draped his bad arm around her shoulders and began to massage her neck.

She looked at him suspiciously. "See? Your arm's fine, you little faker."

"What the hell's *wrong* with you? Just quiet down and help me with the sweater."

Karen repositioned herself in front of Stan and got him into his clothes. She picked up the orange sweater and began to fold it carefully, then balled it up and stuffed it at the bottom of the stack when Stan wasn't looking—*whatever*. As Stan struggled to get his shoes on, she went into the kitchen to put away the groceries.

Once dinner was under way, Karen went downstairs to rouse Junie for the meal. The music had gone silent, and Karen assumed she was reading or napping. Oddly, as she turned the corner at the bottom of the stairs, a cold draft blew at her feet. Junie's entrance door to the street was ajar, and a few birds had stationed themselves at the threshold to take a dust bath. Karen shooed them away, closed the door, and locked it. Then she peeked through the open crack of the bedroom door, almost afraid of what she might find. Junie was in bed, but awake and staring at the ceiling. Her hair, saturating the pillow, resembled a medusa.

Karen gingerly sat at the bottom of the bed. She laid her hand on Junie's leg, which felt unusually bulky. Junie turned toward Karen. "What's happening?"

"Dinner. Are you hungry?"

"I think so."

"Okay, wanna come up?"

Karen suddenly felt wary, not only because Junie didn't move a muscle and her facial expression didn't add up, but also the open front door. It might have been an oversight but now she was in doubt. On an impulse, she pulled the covers halfway back to discover that Junie was still dressed in her outdoor coat. After tugging again, Karen saw that her boots were on, as well. The bedsheets were soiled from street grime. Clearly Junie had returned to the brownstone, not bothered to even close the door, and simply crawled into bed. All after her date with Pickle.

Karen tugged off the boots, pulled Junie to a sitting position, stood her up, and removed her coat. She wrapped a wool scarf around Junie's shoulders and directed her to the stairs.

"Go up. Ask Stan to set the table. Or you do it, if you want. Okay?"

"Sure." Junie walked up the stairs slowly with her hand on the banister, for balance it seemed.

Karen went to work stripping off the sheets. She took fresh linens out of the closet, remade the bed, and covered the whole thing with a new Frette comforter she'd recently purchased. She plumped the pillows and karate chopped them, after arranging them at the headboard. Then she tackled Junie's bathroom, wiping all the surfaces: the floor, the sink, and tub. She brushed and flushed the toilet and doused Clorox into it for good measure. The mirror needed Windex, so she sprayed that too, rubbing hard. She gathered all the soiled paper towels and dumped them and the contents of the wastebasket into one big plastic bag and placed it outside at the front vestibule. Finally, Karen grabbed a feather duster and whipped through the entire floor, making sure all surfaces were dust-free.

She lay back on the bed and punched in a call on her phone.

"What the fuck've you done to her!?" Karen shouted.

"Dearest. How are you?" Pickle's voice cloyed.

"Don't play games with me. I'm serious."

"So am I. What's up?"

"You know very well."

"*No* idea what you're talking about. What's the problem?"

"Junie, that's what. I just came down to get her for dinner, and she's listless. She barely spoke—like she was in a coma."

"Too generic. More details, please."

"She was in bed under the covers with her coat and boots on."

"Maybe she was cold. I sleep with a heavy sweater on sometimes."

"She had her *boots* on, Pickle."

"Wearing your boots to bed does not a coma make. Did she speak?
"Yes."

"Then she's not in a coma."

"But she only said one word. Or maybe a few, I can't remember."

"Okay, what was the last word she said?"

"Um . . . 'Sure.'"

"She said 'Sure'? That's not so bad. Sounds like an affirmative to me. A positive word. So, she was agreeing to whatever you said before?"

"Well, yes."

"Okay, so let's review: Junie was in bed, which in and of itself is not so unusual, because according to *you*, she's been sleeping a lot since she moved in. Right?"

"That's true, I guess."

"Then we see that she's in bed with her coat on, which indicates that she was cold, but the weather did drop about ten degrees today. Plus, the front door is open a lot from the renovation. So, one might surmise that the brownstone is, in fact, chilly. Am I right again?"

"Possibly."

"Great. Then we have the issue of wearing boots in bed. Let's just toss that out for now."

"Fuck you."

"So what the hell's your problem?"

"I'll tell you what my problem is. She was with *you* this morning."

"So? We went to a museum."

"You? A museum?"

"Yeah. The Frick, if you must know. Then we went to the café at the Neue."

"Humph," Karen grunted.

"Then she went home in a cab. All very innocent—and worldly. When's the last time *you* went to the Frick, Karen?"

They were silent for several seconds, and Karen couldn't recall the last time she'd been to *any* museum.

"Now you listen to me." Pickle's tone changed—like gravel. Karen rolled over to her side and pulled her knees into her chest.

"Do I have your attention?"

"Go on." Karen wheezed out the words.

"What I do in my private life is none of your fucking business. I don't pry into your marriage. In fact, if you think about it, I almost *never* inquire into that area of your life. Do I?"

"I guess not."

"Correct. In *double* fact, I would characterize my restraint as so super-fucking-human, it verges on insane. Because no man in his right mind would have, or even *could* have, exerted the willpower I have."

Karen closed her eyes, and tears plopped onto the new comforter. She heard Junie and Stan clomping around above. The Doodles's claws flew across the ceiling. She felt left out. Abandoned.

Pickle's voice lowered to a whisper and she strained to hear. "That's right, Karen. No answer is necessary. Don't even bother. But get this straight . . ."

Her eyes were at the level of the Frette logo. She inspected the ornate stitching that for some reason made this comforter worth about four thousand dollars. She wondered what the hell was so great about the stitching, and was it really so damned beautiful? And what the fuck was she thinking, spending money like that? What normal person spends four thousand dollars on a *blanket*?

"You're on notice. Stay out of my private life vis-a-vis any woman, including, and most especially, Junie. Okay?"

"Right."

"Now that we've dusted up that little mess, I'll expect you at my place on Sunday at, let's say, about four?"

"You're really mad at me."

"Yeah. But what the hell do you expect after that display the other night—trying to break it off."

She tried to imagine him smiling into the phone. "Okay, Pickle. Sunday."

"Good. And wear red."

Karen had never cared about Pickle's casual girlfriends. In fact, she was rarely even aware of them. Once in a while, clues were left behind: a piece of clothing—maybe a sock, or a hairbrush with long brown strands. Even a smell—unmistakably female. But he'd never, she was fairly certain, made an emotional commitment to any woman other than her. He was taken with Junie, yes, but did that really matter? She could not think of an answer.

Karen's hands rattled a bit as she lay on the bed. Her red lipstick was now smeared all over the frighteningly expensive bedcover. She stretched out, taut, and then re-tucked herself into a ball, willing her body to settle down. Birds squawked in the back garden. She'd filled the birdbath just that morning and could imagine the critters performing their daily ablutions, flapping the day's dust off their feathers.

She stepped out the back door and walked to the end of the yard. Lights in the kitchen shone bright, and Stan and Junie's heads bobbed around as they worked to get dinner on the table. They lingered a few minutes at the window by the sink and had a conversation that lasted too long. Then Stan smiled at Junie. Or so Karen thought; with the distance, she couldn't be sure.

She wanted to fill herself up with something, anything to distract her from her pain, but not her mother. She picked up a trowel and stabbed into a plastic bag of fresh soil she intended to use over the weekend to plant annuals. With a clump of dirt at the tip of the tool, she brought the earth close to her nose and smelled its musty odor. The garden loam held a perfect proportion of silt, clay, and earth—

potentially delicious. The trowel found its way into her mouth, as if pushed by an invisible gardener. And maybe her mother *was* here—but no—she remembered that her childhood yard had been perpetually overgrown with crabgrass. Nothing of beauty survived where she grew up.

Karen bit down. She chewed hard and heard the deafening crunch against her molars, driving deep into her ear canal. She swallowed and felt each lump individually as the back of her tongue forced the earth down her throat. The soil, somehow moistened, reached her stomach.

Her eyes scaled up the back of the building and she noticed that Pickle's two floors were faintly lit by construction bulbs left on by the workers—just a hint of yellowed tungsten. The whole house would soon glow a brilliant white and the brightest bulb, living right above her, would be Pickle. It was a catastrophic future—possibly much worse than drinking every day. Then her mother's rules popped into her head and Karen took the inventory: be pretty—no—be beautiful. She had that down pat. And she was lovable. She'd made damned sure of that, too. She'd even gotten the money. But sneaky? That's where she'd fallen short.

21

A CONSTRUCTION SITE TYPICALLY EXUDES A distinctly male smell—not exactly body odor, more an amalgam of sweat, dirt, and pheromones, or the flex of muscle against the pressure of a deadline. Karen was reminded of this the next morning when she bumped into Patrick in the foyer of the brownstone. His men filed past them, after having gathered in groups outside on the sidewalk to wolf down their last bits of egg sandwiches. Karen and Patrick followed them, and their gamey essence, up the stairs to the second floor.

"It's going well, right?" Patrick looked around, impressed with the amount of work his men had accomplished in just a few days.

Karen pulled him to a corner, handed him a cup of espresso, and stared out the window. She could feel Patrick studying her, obviously puzzled by her quiet demeanor.

"Ya got me. What's up?" he asked.

Karen gave a rueful smile. "How many men do we have on-site now?"

"Not including the electrician and the plumber who're set to start Monday? Eight. A big crew, just like you asked. And they're all here today to finish up final demo stuff and load in Sheetrock and studs.

We can close up the walls as soon as the trades finish."

Karen put her hand on his shoulder and looked him squarely in the eyes. "Okay, Patrick. I want you to hold everything off . . . including the plumber."

Patrick stepped back. "*Why?* I pulled in every marker to even get the plumber here next week! You want the whole crew gone, too?"

"Not everyone—keep a skeleton crew. Maybe just the electrician and one other guy. But no plumber."

"What in God's name is going on here? I don't like working this way."

"It's very complicated. I just want to slow things down. Please, Patrick. I know I threatened you, and I feel awful about that."

"I have to be honest—I didn't like it either. We've worked together a long time, Karen. You must know by now that I'd do just about anything for you."

"Yes, and I was under terrible pressure that day. But things have changed. Just work with me on this."

"Jesus, Karen. You seem weird. I'm a little worried about you."

Karen's feet itched inside her Louboutin shoes. "I'm just not sure this is the right time for Pickle to move in. I need to back him off. But we have to do it in a way that he'll swallow. Construction delays are acts of God. Force majeure, so to speak. He'll understand that. It's important for him to believe that we can't control it."

"I don't know, Karen. Pickle's pretty sharp. Do you think he'll buy that?"

"He has to. And you'll be great. Tell him it's a problem you've just discovered with the building, and that you can't proceed until it's resolved."

"*Me?* No fucking way. The guy's a brute. The way he practically roughed me up on Monday? No. If he asks, I'll refer him to *you*."

"Okay. That's fair, I guess. I can't expect you to lie for me."

"I hope not. And to be honest, I'd prefer that he just stay off-site—away from me and my guys. I really think there's something off there."

"Well, he *is* his brother's twin." She laughed, trying to make light of the exchange.

"Nah. Stan's a puppy. There's nothing wrong with Stan . . . other than his obvious stuff. Once you get used to it, he's actually pretty reasonable. Almost predictable. Pickle, though? I can honestly say I have *no* idea who the hell he is."

Karen stared down at her fancy shoes, her Stella McCartney dress, and her manicured fingernails. She felt a new level of embarrassment—as if her family Ponzi scheme had just been exposed. "I'll try to control Pickle," she mumbled. When she looked up, Patrick was already out the door.

22

SATURDAY MORNING, PICKLE STOOD AT HIS WIN-
dow to the western world, scanning traffic crossing the bridge as usual,
and felt the burden of his unstructured days. The hours stacked up
one after the other, and, being off the job, Pickle found it increasingly
difficult to keep track. Monday? Saturday? What was the difference,
really? He felt adrift, without the ballast of his crew.

He'd woken up early, thinking about victims who'd need a support
call, only to remember that someone else had taken over his caseload.
Then he'd spent the next few minutes lying in bed, regretting taking the time off at all. Pickle loved the force of the city and the sway
of people—some days turbulent, others unbearably tedious. The un-
predictability required him to wear different skins based on someone
else's troubles. He was good at it. But he wasn't there. And as a result,
he felt a deflation of his power; perhaps emasculation was a more ac-
curate term.

On an impulse, Pickle got in his car and drove onto the Queensboro Bridge, toward the land of affordable houses for cops: Doug-
laston. And Lance. Halfway across the bridge, Pickle considered the
confusing options of roads that converged within a quarter mile of

each other—the BQE, the GCP, the LIE. He cast aside those high-ways and, instead, took the country road for locals: Queens Boulevard.

Queens had always seemed a confounding borough to Pickle; vague borders of the small towns bled into one another. Sunnyside suddenly birthed Woodside, then Maspeth evaporated into Elm-hurst. But landmarks, rather than town lines, helped to orient Pickle as he drove east. The White Castle at Fortieth Street, where he'd once picked up food poisoning, was still in business. He slowed to a crawl as he drove past Calvary Cemetery. Markers of death, lined up like stone dominos, were a sobering reminder that a few of his friends, killed in the line of duty, had been buried here. Just at the end of the graveyard, Pickle made a right turn onto Fifty-Eighth Street and headed south toward the granite factory. He looked at his watch: nine fifteen. It would be sadistic to wake Lance this early on his day off, anyway. Pickle worked his way through the streets, sniffing out the correct turns.

Life for Pickle's family had quickly bottomed out, very near to poverty. They'd moved from working-class Nassau County to low-er-class Elmhurst, Queens when the twins were about to enter high school. His mother was not an educated woman and held a string of low-wage jobs, finally landing something stable as an office helper for a granite fabrication company.

She was lucky for the steady employment with decent people, and occasionally gained some measure of pride from directing customers into the huge factory. And when she was given the responsibility to actually show the slabs—that was a very good day. Enormous rig-gers gripped the two-ton slices by means of rubber clamps and pulled them out for closer inspection. She'd then discuss the slabs with customers who thought she knew what she was talking about. But most days she fielded phone calls from architects and designers who purchased the product on behalf of their clients. And every evening she'd return home covered in fine silt, a by-product of the immense granite cutters. That malevolent dust was, no doubt, the cause of her emphysema and subsequent death.

In spite of their downward slide in economic status, high school in Elmhurst cemented hopeful life trajectories for both twins. Stan, not surprisingly, received full scholarships, first to college and then to architecture school. Pickle completed a year of community college before joining the police force. Yet, despite their divergent paths, the twins understood that they were forever bound together in life. By Pickle's measure their struggles had evened out: Stan battled with his obsession demons and Pickle endured his devil of a mother.

He drove up onto the sidewalk in front of the stone yard. Hundreds of remnants stood stacked against the side of the building. He got out of the car, walked among the hunks of Mother Earth, brushed his fingers over the edges and felt the dust that had killed his mother. Pickle noticed his hands becoming moist and the silver silt clouded into a thin slurry. Rubbing them together, Pickle ground the grit further into the creases on his palms. This was the exact texture on his mother's hands when she'd return home every evening.

Entering the office, Pickle was greeted by a woman sitting in what had been his mother's chair. It looked like the same one, anyway—very worn and ripped at the top edge of the back. He glared impatiently at her.

"Hi, Stan. We didn't know you were coming. Marcel's in the yard with another client. Can I offer you an espresso?"

"No thanks. I'll wait."

"Have a seat and I'll tell him you're here."

The woman got on the intercom that blasted into the cavernous factory. It was noisy in there, with machines working continuously, even on a Saturday. He felt his chair vibrate through the floor from the rattle of the cutters.

"Marcel, Stan McArdle's in the office."

Pickle looked into the factory through a large window. Endless rows of stacked stone created tunneling paths that ran the length of the enormous space. In order to get around, one had to walk from front to back and make the U-turn at the very end to enter the next section. Almost like a train terminal with high stone barriers.

Once the woman saw Marcel's fingers wave over the top of the stone as a signal that he'd heard, she turned to Pickle and smiled. "He should be in soon."

He didn't know what he was doing here. Just that his mother still saturated every corner of the place. And that he knew Stan and Karen used this yard exclusively for their projects. While he waited, Pickle absently fiddled with a stack of business cards on the counter and saw that this Marcel was the owner. He didn't remember him—his name wasn't familiar—and he wondered if Marcel had known his mother. Then, the door popped opened from the factory and a small, wiry man walked in with a couple.

"Okay, folks, I think you got some good options here. You got forty-eight hours and then the hold is released. Just let Jenny know which one you want in the next two days and she'll take your credit card for the fifty percent deposit. That'll secure the slab until your contractor's ready for it. Jenny, put these three slabs on hold for the Millers."

He handed Jenny a piece of paper. The couple thanked him and walked out.

The man poured himself a coffee. "Sorry for the delay, Stan. Is Karen here?"

Pickle shook his head.

"Okay, well I got those new slabs of Blue Bahia she called about last week. Wanna see 'em?"

Pickle nodded.

They walked into the factory toward the far side of the building where the loading docks were located. As they continued single file along the stone tunnels, Marcel spoke easily about the ongoing projects for the firm.

"I didn't wanna bury 'em just yet, 'cause I knew she'd wanna see 'em straight off. But Stan, it's nice to see *you* here for a change. It's been a while."

They'd finally reached the slabs he wanted to show Stan—gorgeous swirling blue slices.

"You wanna see the ones behind? They're bookends, or identical, for the most part. I can call Rocco over and he can pull 'em easy enough."

"Not yet. Give me a few minutes."

"Sure, Stan, sure. Rocco's just over there. Give him a whistle when you're ready. Okay then." Marcel backed away.

Pickle faced the stones and tried to imagine what it would be like to know which one was the best. They all looked the same to him. Who was to say that this one was prettier than that one? And who decided that, say, plain black granite was less valuable than these swirly blue ones, which he assumed were pricey. Who the hell got to decide all this, especially when things were, as Marcel described, identical? Because if he looked very closely, they weren't. Not really. Pickle decided right there, that this stone business was a huge scam, based on false advertising. If he were on duty, if he hadn't taken time off, he'd arrest every person in the building.

Pickle meandered through the tunnels, dragging his fingers over the surface of each stone as he passed by. They felt much colder than the air temperature and he wondered why stone didn't adapt on its own. Stone was cold-blooded, even lifeless, he concluded.

Eventually he came to the opposite corner of the building. Carrera marble loomed above him by a foot or two. He leaned into the slab with his entire body, thinking that he might have some power over this impenetrable chilled solid. He turned his head and pressed his cheek against the cool of the dusty, veined surface and waited for it to take on his heat. When the stone finally succumbed to the warmth of his skin, he then remembered that this was the exact spot where he'd met Karen.

That day he'd come to give his mother her lottery ticket. He knew she played weekly as part of a pool with people who worked with her. It was a high point of her week, as is the case with many who have no money to speak of. What—were a few bucks going to break the bank? Probably not. When Pickle saw what a thrill she got when the numbers were revealed, regardless of whether she won or not, he began playing single tickets for her. Being connected to her around the potential of an exciting possibility was his purpose; she might even anticipate his company each week. So, once a week he'd travel out to the stone yard, after first stopping at the bodega to purchase the ticket. If she ever did hit, she wouldn't have to split it with the group—it would be hers alone. Pickle imagined this as their late-in-life bond.

On that particular day, his mother wasn't in the office. She was out showing a designer some slabs—an exciting thing for her, he knew. Pickle wandered through, trying to find her. He eventually heard her voice over the top of some stones, as she described a slab and discussed cost.

"Well, this one is less money. About twenty percent less."

"And this one?" The woman pointed to another lot.

"I'm not sure. That just came in. I'll have to find out from Billy."

She turned to see Pickle observing her and stammered a bit. "Oh! Pickle. Ah, Karen, this is my son. He's a cop. Well, I'll go check on this one for you with Billy."

"That'd be great, Mrs. McArdle. Thanks."

His mother walked away, and Karen extended her hand. They shook.

"She's sweet, your mother."

"Yeah, but I don't think she knows a hell of a lot about granite."

"Oh, she does okay. I'm just browsing for a client today. Your mom's doing fine."

Karen smiled and he felt bashful. Pickle was rarely shy. That was Stan.

"So, you're a police officer?"

"Yup."

"That must be interesting."

"It has its moments, as they say. What about you? I assume you're an architect?"

"No, I'm an interior designer. A step *below* an architect. As they say."

She was beautiful. A stunner.

"Well, I'm just here delivering her lottery ticket. I'd better give it to her before I forget. It was nice to meet you . . ."

"Karen Wells."

"Miss Wells, then."

He began to walk away but stopped, surprised by her next words. "There's a great Italian coffee shop across the street. I could use a cup. Care to join me?"

Pickle, momentarily confused, hesitated. His mother was returning so he rushed ahead; he didn't want her in on the exchange. "Sure. Why not? But, why don't I meet you out front? You go ahead and finish up with my mom."

Pickle walked toward his mother, shoved the lottery ticket into her hand, and headed for the exit.

"Thanks, Pickle. See you next week?" his mother called to his back.

"Sure, Mom. Next week."

They fell in love. Karen, very hard and fast. Pickle, a bit slower, more tentative, but eventually just as deeply. It was the best thing that had ever happened to him, but he knew, not in a million years, would it last. He didn't dare tell his mother. Or Stan.

Pickle jumped as Marcel approached him with a clipboard and pen. "Anything, Stan?"

Pickle didn't hesitate. "Yeah. I'll take all ten slabs over there. The blue ones."

"Okay. The Blue Bahia. A fifty percent deposit on those alright?"

"No, go ahead and charge it all. You've got the credit card number, right?"

"We sure do."

"Good. Karen'll call you with the details."

"Sure, Stan, Sure. Not a problem."

Pickle walked out with the same display of authority Stan would deliver. He started up the car and eventually pulled onto Queens Boulevard, back toward the city. There was the White Castle, and, hungry, he pulled into the parking lot and sat for a while. The last time he'd been here was, also, the day he'd met Karen. They'd had coffee across the street from the granite yard and made plans for a proper first date. Then he'd stopped at the drive-in section of the White Castle to get a hamburger for the trip home. By the time he'd reached the Apartments, Pickle was feverish and ill with food poisoning. He couldn't work for the next couple of days.

Pickle pulled out his cell and called Lance.

"What," Lance snapped.

"I'm in Queens. Near you."

"Yeah?" Lance sounded dubious.

"Yeah."

"You wanna come over? Debbie's cooking something. You could stay for the meal."

"I'm not sure."

"Okay . . ."

Lance's voice was becoming drowned out by background music playing on his end. The volume suddenly surged into the phone, the tune from a memory Pickle couldn't quite locate.

"Lance, what's that music?"

"Fuck. The kids've been binging on *The Wizard of Oz* all morning. It's the poppy song. They love it for some reason." Lance muffled the phone and Pickle heard him scream, "Kids! Turn it down."

"Lance, wait. Don't turn it down, I wanna hear it. What's the poppy song? Which one is that?"

"You know. Dorothy's asleep in the poppy fields, then the snow falls to wake her up, and the little people sing that song. 'Out of the forest. Out of the thickets. Into the sunshine'... or some such shit."

"Is it on the tube? Or video?"

"Video. They're addicted. This'll go on all weekend. I'm going crazy... I don't believe in the good witch anymore. Neither does Debbie."

"Wind it back. I wanna hear that song."

"Where are you? You don't sound good. I'm comin' to get you."

"No. No, I'm okay. Just do it."

Pickle heard Lance drop the phone on the table. "Brittany! Go back to the poppy song. Uncle Pickle wants to hear it."

Lance came back on. "I'm putting the phone close, okay? Can you hear it now?"

Pickle set his phone on speaker and, closing his eyes, slumped further down into the seat as the poppy song filled the car. Voices floated, the pitch too high to be reasonable, and he almost wanted to hang up. But he listened.

Shortly after they'd fallen in love, he and Karen had channel surfed late one evening and happened upon the beginning of *The Wizard of Oz* on TCM. He was embarrassed to admit that he'd never seen it before; his childhood had not included such rites of passage. As they watched the credits roll at the end, Karen was weepy from what he saw as a stock Hollywood ending. Home was not worth crying over as far as he was concerned. Pickle told her he considered the little people his favorite part of the movie because they represented the best part of humanity. Whenever they sang, danger, or any sense of gloom, was swept away, if only temporarily. This was a humble notion, yet optimistic, he'd explained. Karen found this hilarious, and accused Pickle of being naive. She laughed longer than he'd liked.

"Pickle. The song's over. Are you there?" Lance asked.

Pickle thought about the granite slabs and how confounding the whole place had been. So many pieces of stone. They were, he had to admit now, as good as identical. But for some reason, after being scrutinized, one was chosen as special. The perfect one. And what was he doing at the White Castle, anyway? In Queens.

"Yeah. I'm here," Pickle mumbled.

"Fuck, Pickle. You know I can track you . . ."

"No, Lance. I'm okay. It's just this: who gets to decide what's good and what's bad?"

"What do you mean—good and bad?"

"You know—if things are almost the same and you have to make a decision, then how? How do you decide?"

Lance sighed audibly. "The first choice is usually the right one. You just go with your gut."

"Right."

"Does that help?"

"Yeah. It does. I'm good now."

"Glad to hear it."

"I'm goin' back home."

Pickle decided to go ahead and have a meal at the White Castle. Odds that the food would make him sick again were remote.

23

THE AFTERNOON SKY TURNED DARK WITH
threatening rain clouds, and a slight ache hovered at the back of Pickle's head. He turned over, reached for the Excedrin he kept on the
bedside table, and forced down two pills without water. His cell phone
lay buried somewhere beneath the covers. Rooting around under the
sheets, his big toe finally hit something hard and he dragged it up with
his foot. No calls. No texts.

He traced the outline of the phone with his fingertip and noticed
his blackened palms. He'd not showered since the trip to Queens the
day before. Throwing back the sheets, he surveyed his torso and saw
that stone silt had abraded much of his chest during the night. His
skin was red and almost blistered in certain areas. But then he remembered dreams where he was swimming in thick volcanic pits, his body
flailing around as he tried, unsuccessfully, to drag himself out. He'd
wake, only to vaguely sense the sores on his body, before slipping back
into the muddy sinkholes of dreams.

Rising up, he headed for a soapy, stinging shower and then gingerly blotted his body dry. He scrambled and ate some eggs, stripped
and remade the bed, and dressed in new trousers and a pressed shirt.

Clouds finally released a horizontal rain pelting his window as he waited for Karen to arrive at four.

The brownstone had a seldom-used landline on Junie's floor, installed for emergencies in case the cells didn't work. Sitting on the edge of his bed at three thirty, Pickle dialed the number. No one picked up—not a surprise. But he doggedly persisted, and on the fourth try, after letting the phone ring at least ten times, Junie answered with a tentative, "Hello?"

"Junie?"

"Yes?"

"It's Pickle. I had no other way to get in touch, so I hoped you'd pick up."

"Oh. When it kept ringing I thought it might be some emergency, and Stan is out with The Doodles."

"Karen's not there?"

"No, she left for the office a couple of hours ago. I think they have some new project starting."

"Oh. Well, that's good—I mean about the project."

"I guess . . ."

Pickle coughed and checked his cuticles. He pulled breath spray out of his pocket, considered a spritz, then threw it across the room; they were on the phone.

"How are you?" he asked.

"Good, I guess."

"That's good."

"Yeah . . ."

"Well, the reason I'm asking is that you were upset after the museum and I wanted to check in on you."

"Right. Um, I'm doing better."

"That's good."

After a few moments, he heard her sigh. "Look, Pickle. What you told me? Don't feel bad. It was really hard to listen to, but I needed to hear the truth. At least now I know."

He closed his eyes and smiled. "Well, I *am* sorry. It had to be a shock, the way Jacob was and all."

"Yeah, that's for sure. But let's drop it."

Pickle was relieved to get that preamble tucked away. "So, how's it going over there?"

"Well, they've been working upstairs, if that's what you mean. It's nice to have the activity around. Anyway, the noise keeps me from sleeping so much."

Pickle heard her yawn and he laughed. "Are you tired now?"

She giggled, "I guess so—must be!"

"Listen, Junie, I wanted to know if you'd like to take in a show and maybe dinner after? On Wednesday—a matinee? Do you like Broadway shows? Do you even want to go?"

"That's really nice of you, Pickle. I haven't been to many, but yes, I think I would like that."

Pickle looked at his watch: 3:50. Karen would arrive in ten minutes; she was always terrifyingly prompt, usually within a few seconds.

"Look, I have to go now. I'm at work and need to take care of some stuff. But how about I pick you up at the brownstone at twelve thirty on Wednesday?"

"Yeah, that's fine. I'll be ready."

"Okay, see you then."

Pickle lay back on the bed. His erection pushed up against his zipper and he stuck his hand down his pants to rub his crotch. Shivering, an erotic surge ran through his body. He had only six minutes remaining until Karen walked through the door, so he raced to the bathroom, dropped his drawers and began to masturbate into the sink. His knees buckled, and he held onto the sink edge with both hands to steady himself; it was pure and also painful, just the way he wanted. He inhaled his own sex odor and stifled a groan. Then he heard Karen's key in the door, turning over the cylinder. The door clicked shut and her heels pecked across the floor. He wiped his hands on a towel, pulled his pants up and walked out to see her sitting primly on the bed.

"Hi, baby," he said.

Pickle sat beside Karen and simultaneously pushed her back onto the bed. They lay face to face. He caressed her neck and dragged his fingers along the half-moon of her waist.

"I love you," Karen said.

Pickle took her face in both hands and smoothed her hair back with his palms. "I missed you. Tell me you missed me, too."

"I have."

"That's good. I like that. You're so beautiful, Karen. I know you don't like to hear it, but sometimes I need to tell you. Understand?"

"Of course. And today it feels fine." She hesitated. "But Pickle?"

"Hmmm?" He licked her neck, travelling up to suck on her earlobe, which always made her shiver.

Karen wiped off his saliva. "What's been happening with us?"

Pickle stuck his fingers into her waistband and tugged her closer. "What do you mean? Everything's fine now. You said you wanted to end it . . . but you really don't. Right?"

"Yes, I was crazy that night. But things *are* different now, don't you think?"

"How? Nothing's changed. As far as I'm concerned, anyway," Pickle said as he ran his hands over her body.

"How can you say that?"

He stopped his movement mid-motion and looked at her from an angle, puzzled. "Karen. What the fuck are you talking about?"

"The brownstone. Do you actually expect us to continue if you're living upstairs?"

"Not *this* again. I'm not worried. It'll work out."

"*How?* It's just too risky. Don't you think we should hold up on the renovation?"

"Nope. Trust me on this. Nothing will change."

They stared at each other until Pickle broke into a smile. "Okay. That's settled then."

"Not really. But that's not all."

"Oh, for God's sake. What?"

"Well, there's Junie . . ."

"What about her?"

"Don't be *obtuse*."

He propped his head against his hand and frowned. "That's not very nice. Why do you want to spoil things by calling me obtuse?"

She backed up on the bed, gaining about a foot in distance. "Aren't you falling in love with her?"

"I'm not sure—it's very early."

"Well, that's what I'm talking about. If you're going to get involved with Junie, it changes things."

"Why?" he asked, flat.

"Now you *are* being obtuse."

"How so?" Pickle's face remained impassive—not a twitch.

She abruptly sat up. "It would change everything."

"Karen, I can't believe what I'm hearing. Are you telling me that if I get involved with Junie—if I fall for her—then you and I can't continue? That just doesn't make a whit of sense."

Karen got off the bed, walked over to the chair at the table and sat down with a thump. "You're tricking me."

"No. *You* brought this up. You obviously want something from me—some kind of agreement. What that is, I have a pretty good idea. But you're going to have to make a very good case for it. So, spell it out, Karen. And you'd better give me reasons that, first, I can understand and, second, are fair and equitable."

"You make it sound like mergers and acquisitions."

"Isn't it?"

"Fuck you. I just told you I love you."

"And I—*you*."

"It wasn't the same."

"Oh? How?"

"You have to *say* it. I. Love. You. Karen . . . Just like that."

"Now you're trying to control my colloquial phrasing. Jesus motherfuckingchrist." Pickle shook his head in disgust and looked out the window. Water drenched the glass behind Karen's head, sluicing hard, unrelenting. He decided to forget that he loved her—for a few minutes, anyway. "Do me a favor. Go into the bathroom."

"Why?" she asked, suspicious.

"Just do it. I'll go with you, if that helps. I'm gonna make this easy for you because I can see this could go on for hours."

Pickle pulled Karen to her feet and kissed the top of her head, then led her to the bathroom by the hand. He switched on the light as they stood side by side in front of the sink.

She looked up at him, uncertain. "This is scary."

"There's nothing to worry about. You've been in here before—about a trillion times, actually. Now. Look down into the sink. What do you see?"

She peered down. "What?"

"Look closer."

The sink, original to the building, was the old Pepto-Bismol-colored porcelain of the 1960s. She leaned over to look, then quickly stepped back, hitting the wall. "*No.*"

"*Yes.* Now tell me what you *smell.*" He pulled her face into his chest; she inhaled.

"You bastard. Did you just have sex with someone? Somebody was in this apartment! I can smell it. I *know* that smell."

"No one was here—nothing nearly so gamey. I just had phone sex. With Junie. And she fuckin' loved it."

Karen shoved him away, ran out of the bathroom and sat on the opposite side of the bed with her back to him, her chin bowed to her chest. Pickle climbed onto the bed and scooted up behind her. He tapped her on the shoulder and she pushed his hand away.

"Why do you always put me in this position? Of being a bastard, as you so eloquently called me a minute ago?"

"You *are* a bastard."

"I'm not—not really. But let's recap. For old time's sake?"

Karen's head slunk further into her shoulders. She teetered over with a plop, lying with her back to him.

Pickle's voice took on a monotone quality, on a cusp of loving her and hating her. That was the devil that lived inside of the truth: he was rarely nice and almost never soothed. But every once in a while, heaven and hell looked, and felt, exactly the same.

"I was your love. And you were mine. Truly, you were. And, let's be honest, the sex has always been unreal—like no other. It still is, Karen."

She turned over and looked at him, her eyes bone dry. Pickle's voice caught on his next words. "Then you went and fucking *married* my twin brother."

He cleared the phlegm from his throat; his voice dropped, low to the floor. "So, you call me a bastard on occasion. And each and every time you do, we need to have a little history lesson to remind you of what a deceptive bitch you are. You said it didn't matter that he looked the same. But it turns out, you *were* attracted to him. You say you still love me. And somehow, God help me, I believe that."

Pickle rolled to his back, closed his eyes, and took her hand.

"About Junie? It's simple. I may want her. I'm not sure. But whatever happens, I will move into that house. As long I get that, everything's gonna be okay. I think I deserve it."

Pickle grabbed her torso and yanked her toward the musk of his damp shirt. Karen rubbed her face into his chest and lifted her chin to him. She smiled, then closed her eyes. Pickle shook her shoulders. "Karen?"

Her eyes fluttered open.

"The phone sex. It was Candice from Property. Not Junie." He wasn't completely heartless.

Her face turned hopeful and she wrapped her arms and legs

around him. They rocked each other for what felt like a long time. But each time she began to remove her clothes, Pickle stopped her, because he imagined that resisting sex now was an indication of a new understanding in their relationship. Maybe even a maturity, whatever that was. He knew the notion was a sound bite, of course. But at that moment, it was all he could think of to keep his heart from feeling too much.

24

KAREN WALKED ACROSS CENTRAL PARK TO THE East Side and then meandered downtown, letting the traffic lights pull her southward. She timed the pace of her gait according to the countdowns on each pedestrian walk signal. Some allowed her thirty seconds, some only ten. It felt good to give up control for the moment and let the relentlessly receding numbers dictate whether to hurry up or slow down. She was late for work and didn't much care.

Entering her office via the back hallway, Karen tossed her coat on the loveseat. It promptly slipped to the floor and she kicked it under the furniture. She was exhausted, feeling pulled apart by a million emotions, but had to get herself back on track. Work had always provided structure to her life; the jobs substituted for a pretense of normalcy. Building out and designing spaces was, and always had been, relatively simple. Living her life felt like a death-defying feat.

She perused her desk, spilling over with stacks of orders, invoices, paint chips, wood samples: the minutiae of the business. Lying right on top was the new Kinsey project—and next to that, the brownstone drawings for Pickle's renovation. She pulled out her cell.

"Patrick? You've pushed the plumber back?"

"Done."

"Great. And how many guys on-site today?"

"Two."

"Perfect. I'll call a site meeting for Friday. You, me, and Pickle."

"Whatever."

She hung up, satisfied with this bit of bother off her list, when Suzie stuck her head in the door. Suzie, third in line at the firm, worked exclusively in the office and handled every detail, from proposals and orders to invoicing. Able to visualize multiple construction spreadsheets simultaneously in her head, her knack for numbers rivaled Stan's, a fact he was loath to acknowledge.

"Karen? Busy?"

"C'mon in, Suzie. How was your weekend? Good?"

Suzie perched primly on the loveseat. "Good enough, I suppose. But listen—I just had a credit card purchase come through from Greco Granite for about sixty grand. I looked through all the projects and there's nothing about this much stone being specified, or even proposed. Then I looked at the date and saw it was run through on *Saturday*. I thought it was a fraud, so I called Marcel and he said Stan had been in Saturday morning and purchased ten slabs of Blue Bahia. That's a shitload of money to front for a client, Karen. And *which* client? Tell me what to do."

Karen quickly reviewed the weekend in her mind. They'd both slept late on Saturday. Gloria came in at noon to work with Stan on the sweater project in the bedroom, while Karen binged on *Dallas* episodes in the living room. Stan hadn't left the brownstone all day. Pickle.

She looked around the room for a few seconds, avoiding Suzie's stare, trying to figure out how to manage this. "I'm sure it's either a misunderstanding or something I just don't know about. I'll check with Stan. But hang tight for now."

When Suzie left, Karen locked her office door and called the stone yard. "Jenny, get me Marcel. It's Karen McArdle."

"Oh, hi, Karen. Sure, just a sec."

While she waited, Karen perused her bookshelves, housing hundreds of design tomes collected throughout her years of work. Three books butted out on the top shelf, not lined up with the others. She knew a flask of vodka was nestled behind for emergencies like this. She placed the phone on speaker and dragged a chair over from her desk. Standing on the chair, she ran her fingers across the weathered spines and over the protrusion the flask created. The bump felt important.

Marcel's voice popped into the room. "Karen? Suzie just called a half hour ago. I explained. Stan bought the slabs . . . That's what you're calling about, right? Karen?"

She jumped down and grabbed the phone. "Yes, but that's not the problem, Marcel. The stone is for my brownstone—not *McArdle*. It shouldn't have gone through the business account. I want you to refund the firm immediately. I'll give you my personal card. Sorry about the mix-up—Stan's just not aware of these purchasing details."

"Sure. Jenny'll take care of it. When'll you get the drawings to me? Is it a kitchen? Bathrooms? That's a heck of a lot of stone—"

"Hold the stones for the time being. We're not ready for fabrication yet."

"Okay. But Karen, is Stan okay?"

Karen, startled, pressed the phone closer to her ear. "What? What do you mean?"

"Well, it's not for me to say; I haven't seen Stan for some time. But he seemed kind of quiet—more than usual. Hardly said a word, in fact. I thought he might be sick. And the other thing is that his hands were dirty, really filthy. In fact, he had dirt all over his clothes—his face, too. And I thought—that's not Stan. Not the Stan *I* know, anyway. It's none of my business, of course. I just thought you'd wanna know."

Karen waited for her heart to stop pounding. "Thanks, Marcel. Everything's fine. He was under the weather, is all. Can I have Jenny now?"

After she'd finished with the details of the exchange, Karen climbed back onto the chair and watched her hand slide the vodka out from its hiding place. The flask felt brittle to her touch, neglected. She rubbed the silver around in her hands, then nudged the flask into the hollow of her cheek and inhaled the tarnished odor. She flinched from the musty smell. It reminded her of Pickle's words from the night before—a good friend who tells you the awful truth, when what you really wanted was the lie you'd rather live with. But you asked.

The twist cap was stuck shut. Could vodka do that to metal? Get all gummed up? She gripped hard and finally cracked the congealed-alcohol seal. Karen wiped the rim off with a Kleenex and drew her head back. Her lips opened, ready to accept the perfect antidote for her poisoned life. But nothing flowed from the flask. There were no balms, nor any comfort. And no booze. The flask was bone dry and she was deeply empty.

Karen lay down on the loveseat, pulled the coat from underneath, and threw it on top of herself. She cradled the flask, like a hungry infant, in the crook of her elbow.

PICKLE SIDESTEPPED SACKS OF CEMENT AND tubs of compound. Layers of Sheetrock lined the hallway on both sides, stopping just short of the plastic barrier that divided the work area from Karen and Stan's living quarters. The brownstone was quiet, eerily so. His adrenalin picked up as he climbed the stairs two at a time to find one guy sitting on the floor, reading *El Diario*. A radio, set to a Spanish station, softly pulsed an up-tempo salsa. Well, it *was* almost twelve thirty—lunch hour for most civilians.

Open windows allowed a strong breeze to waft front to back, and Pickle shivered from a chill. He looked around the space and the word "wow" came to his mind. Every room partition had been leveled. Silver BX electrical cables snaked through the gaps between vertical metal studs. This really seemed to be happening. In just a few weeks he'd be living literally on top of Karen. And Stan and Junie. The quiet, though, unnerved him. But what did he know about construction? Maybe they were all out at the local pizza joint.

A tall, balding man loped down the stairs from the upper floor. "Oh, hi, Stan. Just starting upstairs now with the wiring."

Pickle bristled. "I'm not Stan; I'm the other owner, Pickle McArdle. Stan's brother."

"*Oh.* Got it." The man, with an Irish accent, recovered admirably.

"You're the electrician?"

"Yeah, I'm Brendan. I work on Patrick's jobs."

They shook, after which Pickle clapped his hands to rid himself of dust. He'd dressed with care that morning in anticipation of his date with Junie, set to begin in a few minutes.

Brendan smiled and brushed off Pickle's coat sleeve. "Sorry about that, I was just about to wash up for lunch."

Pickle ignored the niceties. "What's going on here? Where is everybody?"

"I'm not sure what you mean. We're here—José and me—stringin' the electrical."

He pointed to the guy, now lying on his back, talking on his cell phone, repeating, "*Mi amor, mi amor, mi amor.*"

"No one else? Where's the crew? Where's the plumber?"

Brendan backed up a few steps. "Mr. McArdle, I'm not in charge of the scheduling, so I have no idea. I've not seen anyone else since I've been on the job. I don't think the plumber has started, but I could be wrong. You'd best speak with Patrick. Or Karen."

Pickle shook his head in disgust and pointed to the guy on the floor. "Shut him up, for Christ's sake. *Mi amor?* What the fuck!"

A few uncomfortable moments passed before Brendan continued. "Well, I came down to take my lunch, like I said."

"Right, you go ahead. I'll take a look around."

Brendan dragged José up by the hand and they left. Pickle fumed. No workers? No *plumber?* He punched in Karen's number and then immediately hung up because Junie was calling him from the lowest level.

"Pickle! Is that you?" she shouted.

"Yeah, it's me! Stay there. I'll be down in a minute. I have to make a phone call."

He took the stairs two at a time and by the time he reached the top floor, Pickle was furious. What kind of fool did Karen take him for? Pickle, chagrined, remembered the excitement he'd felt when Karen and Stan had presented his floor plans shortly after they'd purchased. It was a formal affair; they'd all gathered at a table in their office as Karen spread the rolled drawings out in front of him. Then, over the course of an hour, Stan and Karen had explained their vision. Suzie took notes. He'd felt like one of their special clients being given the royal treatment. And the design *was* perfect: An enormous master bedroom with a luxurious bath/spa, complete with a claw-foot soaking tub, separate shower, and his-and-hers sinks. Light flooding down from three skylights above. Walk-in closets lining the back of the building. Built-in bookcases on the bed wall. They even seemed eager to please him. What a joke, he thought.

He braced himself against a grimy brick common wall and tried to regulate his breath—in and out. Then, staggering to the back of the building, he looked out onto the backyard garden. The buildings across the way were completely suffocated with ivy, and then he noticed some movement. Junie was outside with The Doodles, who was sniffing every last bush before he deigned to pee.

He punched Karen's number again. It went immediately to voice mail. "Karen. I'm in the brownstone and I have to say, the progress is *amazing*. And the place is buzzing with workers—ten, maybe fifteen, no, twenty guys all swinging their hammers. And the *plumber*. What a lovely guy! I couldn't be happier. Junie and I are off to a show and dinner." Pickle shoved the phone into his back pocket. Let her stew.

He skipped down the stairs and found Junie sitting outside on the front steps of the brownstone. She wore the exact same outfit as the day he'd met her at the Frick: black and purple against her orange hair.

Pickle studied her. "Jesus. You don't have any clothes."

She let out a weak laugh. "I know. But Karen's going to take me shopping soon. She's got incredible taste."

"Right." Pickle stared at the ground, blinking hard. The day was overcast, dreary, and he continued to feel a vague unease, as if he was on the verge of a bad flu. His vision was compromised—nothing came into complete focus, and his back ached. He'd purchased tickets to a play at Circle in the Square, but now wondered whether he could sit in a theatre for three hours.

"What's wrong, Pickle? You look sad all of a sudden. Don't you want to go? We don't have to, you know."

"I'm sorry, but I guess I don't. I wanted to see you, but right now I don't feel up to sitting through a play."

Junie pressed her hand to his forehead. "You're clammy and slightly hot, maybe feverish. Come inside. I'll get you some aspirin."

She led him into her lower floor and sat him down on the deep sofa from Design Within Reach. When she went to the bathroom for aspirin, Pickle bent down to untie his shoes and kicked them away. He arranged the pillows, tossed a throw over himself, and lay down. The Doodles, who was snoozing in the corner of the room, perked up, wagged his tail, then jumped up on the sofa to nestle onto Pickle's feet.

Junie returned with a glass of water and two tablets.

"Take these."

"Thanks. I just want to lie here for a while."

"Don't worry. We're not on any schedule."

Pickle swallowed the aspirin, then sank back into the pillows. Junie pulled over a club chair and sat down. She took his hand—letting it rest in hers. Pickle noticed her fingernails were bitten to the quick, the cuticles bloody. She withdrew her hand and balled her fists. They exchanged an uncomfortable glance, as if each was acknowledging the other's private failings, and Pickle sensed for the first time that they might have more in common than he'd imagined.

Light from the windows glowed behind her head, causing that lunar aureole he'd seen on the South Sidewalk. He couldn't quite make out her face, though the fuzz of her hair was enough. This gauziness seemed to relax him, and as his eyelids eventually began to droop, his breathing slowed, too.

Junie shifted to get up, and he started forward. "No. Please stay. I don't wanna be alone right now."

"Okay, Pickle. I know that feeling."

"You do? How?"

She sat back in the chair and propped her feet on the edge of the sofa. The Doodles looked back and forth, apparently confused as to whose feet he should now occupy. Junie nudged his belly with her toes and he fell back onto Pickle's feet.

"How can I explain this? The last few weeks, I've stayed to myself. Down here. But I knew Stan and Karen were up there. Even when they went somewhere, I knew they'd return—that was enough. I didn't need contact, didn't want it for the most part. The *idea* of it was good enough."

"But what about Karen? You've gotten close?" He couldn't help himself.

"Oh sure. Karen's a really special person. We talk occasionally. And in a way, I do feel close to her. But, I see her and Stan as a unit. I'm the third wheel."

This immediately eased Pickle's fears; it was satisfying to know Karen's status.

"The odd thing is that I wasn't aware until just this moment, when you said you couldn't be alone, that I had been wanting some contact. I guess I was looking forward to seeing you." She hesitated, and then looked down into her lap. "My time with Jacob—we didn't see anyone. It was always just the two of us. And the isolation felt normal. But now that he's gone, I see that even as we lived together, I was very lonely."

The Doodles scrambled up the length of Pickle's legs and stuck his nose in his crotch. "And this one?" Pickled asked, pushing the dog's snout away.

She reached over and scratched The Doodles's ears. "This dog has just about saved my life."

"Junie . . . I'm glad you didn't go over that night." Pickle, embarrassed, rubbed his eyes.

She nodded once.

He started to say more, then thought better of it. He wasn't sure if she should, or even could, hear the things that were on his mind. He pulled his arm over his eyes to dissipate the moment.

"What?" Junie asked.

He aimed his voice toward the ceiling; it was easier that way. "I've seen a lot as a cop. You can't imagine. Human cruelty is just too much. And what a bullet can do to a body is indescribable. Even when you see it again and again, it's new and fresh and awful each time. But for me, the most painful deaths are the suicides. It's one thing to come upon a murder—gruesome as it is. But that's a death inflicted on another, so the victim retains a certain dignity. I see it as the soul staying intact, for lack of a better way to put it. But a suicide? Well, that person did it to himself. It's the most violent expression of self-hatred imaginable. And that soul was destroyed a long, long time before the actual act."

Pickle turned to her. "They know that about me at the precinct— that I'm good with the suicides. I always catch those cases."

Her body was now close to his. She'd leaned in to listen as he spoke, because his voice had diminished in volume. He realized he was treading on private ground, but he had nothing to be sorry for, and nothing to lose.

"Most people don't see death very often. But you have. You're an expert," she said.

He could smell her breath: mint. "No. I'm no expert—not nearly. It's just that I've understood that witnessing people at their saddest is a privilege. It's the only way I can do my job."

Junie stood up and reached behind him to pull out the cushions at the back of the sofa. She shoved him back and snuggled herself alongside him, in front. Then she wrapped the blanket over them both and grabbed a throw pillow for her head. The Doodles jumped on top and straddled them.

He'd never told Karen much about his job, which was typical for cops. But the odd thing was that Karen had rarely asked. He'd revealed more to Junie in the last half hour than in all the time he'd been with Karen. And though Junie's body was similar to Karen's in size and contour, and conformed perfectly to his, the real difference seemed to be his penis. It remained disinterested, even as her butt pressed against his groin. He pushed Junie's hair down and flopped his arm across her waist.

"I'm very tired. Can you sleep, Junie?"

"I could sleep forever," she murmured.

26

KAREN SAT ACROSS FROM HER BANKER, WILLIAM, who reviewed her accounts. She was the money honcho in the family; she monitored all transactions and also decided when and how much they'd put into investments, and any planning for the short and long haul. Stan sniffed around occasionally, but for the most part, he ceded control to Karen. His trust in her was part of her con, like three-card monte on the corner of Fifth Avenue and Fifty-Seventh Street—in front of Tiffany.

William swiveled the computer screen toward Karen. "See? I can move sixty grand from the savings account to cover the credit card expense you mentioned. That's not a problem."

"But I'm going to need more available cash . . ." Karen, talking more to herself, paused. "William. Let's look at the Zed account."

William leaned back, tapping his fingers on the desk. "Are you sure? You told me that account was never, under any circumstances, to be touched. I'm just reminding you."

Karen felt her face burn with embarrassment. She'd asked William to fight her tooth and nail if she even *mentioned* the Zed account. Play dumb, she'd begged him. Throw me out of the office, she'd pleaded. Well, he was just doing his job.

"That's true. But I just want to see how much I've got now. See, Stan and I are pulling reduced salaries from the business because we've taken on new staff. We're in an expansion phase. I just want to peek at it . . ." She let her voice trail off with her bullshit reasoning, none of which was actually true. As William nodded with banker-like concern throughout her little speech, Karen then wondered why she felt the need to make excuses to yet another man. It was *her* money. Sort of.

William closed out the current screen and opened up a new one. Karen stepped behind him and leaned down as the screen appeared. Just under five million. The aggressive investments she'd asked for and a generally inflated market had yielded more profit than she'd expected. She smiled. "Wow. Okay, William. That's it for now."

"Always a pleasure, Karen."

When Karen left the bank, it was past one o'clock and she was hungry. Rain had begun to fall, and she didn't have an umbrella, so she stepped into a nearby Le Pain Quotidien for lunch and an espresso. After ordering, she dumped her purse on the floor at her feet and pulled out her phone and a notebook to take notes on incoming emails and texts. The communal-table seating suited her, and listening to other conversations came as a welcomed distraction. She let her eyes drift all over the crowded room and became engrossed in the minutiae of strangers' lives: one having a fight with her mother; a straight-up networking meeting right across the table—the two people obviously having just met, gripping their coffee cups.

Karen remembered the fingers clearly. Her father had allowed Betsy to go to bed at midnight, but Karen stayed up into the morning to refresh the drinks and keep the men happy, loose, the way her father wanted them. In the early hours, when the TV programs no longer interested her, Karen stared at the men's hands from the distance of the den—the way they rubbed the green bills. She saw beauty in how they tossed those bills to the center of the polished table, and the way the bills eventually piled high like the gentlest of mountains with springlike green growth. One man would win, and his fingers would spread wide and extend over the mountain of green as he raked in his winnings. The talking ceased; there were losers. Then the men would start over, the jokes and slim chatter resuming into a renewed point of neutrality: no winners, no losers. There was now a fresh set of potential winners hovering over a naive hope. Luck always had a reset button.

Eventually the sun blasted in through the living-room windows, whose shades had been raised on the second night, as nature's marker for the end of the games. The men meandered to the front door. As her father shepherded them out, Karen considered what the pile of bills meant to her father. He usually won big. And as he stood outside their front door, stretching his legs, getting ready to nap through Sunday ball games, Karen tentatively touched the bills. They didn't belong to anyone. Not yet—not until they actually nestled themselves inside her father's wallet. This money was still the universe's bank account. She stood in front of the green pile and worked it all out in her head. No, it really didn't belong to her father. Karen grabbed a few bills—just enough to make her fingers tingle and her hands feel full, but not enough that her father would notice the dent in the pile. The idea emerged from her own imagination, and this pleased her. But she sensed her mother nearby, nodding with approval.

Karen's phone buzzed with an incoming text: Lance.

Where is Pickle?

No idea

Calling u now pick up

She immediately cut Lance off. "Why are you calling me? I'm not Pickle's babysitter."

"Where the hell is he? I've been calling him on and off since Saturday."

"Isn't he at work with you?"

"You don't know. Seriously?"

"Know what? Shit, Lance, I'm not a mind reader. And I'm in a meeting!" She looked around the restaurant. People were beginning to stare.

"Pickle took six weeks off."

"What?" she whispered.

"Yeah, he asked for the time off right after that jumper incident on the bridge. I shouldn't mention this, but he was also talking about retiring. Then I got a weird call from him on Saturday morning. He was near my house. In Queens. He didn't sound like himself. I've been trying to get in touch with him ever since. He won't answer my calls, my texts. Nothing. *Obviously*, you're a last resort . . ."

"Fuck you."

"Just answer me, Karen. Have you seen him?"

"Yes."

"Well?"

"He seems fine. What do you want from me?"

"But you didn't know he'd taken time off?"

She hesitated, not eager to admit being in the dark. "No . . . I didn't. But Pickle doesn't run every tiny detail of his life past me."

"Karen, cut the bullshit. Taking off six weeks and contemplating retirement is not a detail. Look, just tell him to call me. At least now I know he's alive."

"You're making too much of this. He's fine."

She hung up before Lance could shoot back a rejoinder, and saw that she had a new voice message from Pickle. Twenty guys at the brownstone? The *plumber*?

The waitress placed her food on the table. Karen shoved two crisp twenty-dollar bills into her hand and walked out.

27

PICKLE AND JUNIE LEFT THE BROWNSTONE AF-
ter their nap and strolled down Broadway toward Columbus Circle
and the Time Warner buildings. The monolithic glass façades reflect-
ed cumulus clouds lumbering across the sky. Walking the full circum-
ference of the towers, Pickle pointed out the perfect site planning: no
matter the vantage point, angles of the buildings aligned with elegant
precision. As he observed the structure with Junie, he couldn't help but
smile to himself—maybe he was his brother's twin, after all.

Arm in arm they continued south, drifting yet steady, like a deep
ocean current. During the course of an hour they bumped into much
of New York City. Carriage horses on the perimeter of Central Park
munching oats from buckets strapped to their noses. Single merchants
wedged into one-room import shops selling crystal beads by the plastic bag. They sidled through the theatre district, shoulder to shoulder with tourists. Then Penn Station appeared, still slightly seedy and
reminiscent of earlier days, but buoyed by the adjacent neon glow of
Madison Square Garden.

At Twenty-Fourth Street, they hung a right and eventually
found themselves near the West Side Highway. The stairway to the

High Line appeared and on impulse they climbed to take in a view of the Hudson River. Pickle and Junie avoided the northern aspect and the bridge. Instead, they headed south toward the New Whitney Museum.

Simultaneously, they became ravenous and gorged on falafels sold from a pop-up cart. Then, reeking of garlic, they feigned offense at each other's breath. Pickle pulled out his trusty breath spray and doused them both liberally. He pressed an extra tube into Junie's hand for future such dilemmas and she stuffed it into her pocket, giggling.

They needed few words. More like grunts of acknowledgement when they saw some indigenous plant of mutual interest or spied a speck of a sailboat far off on the water. Junie peeked at him at intervals and they both laughed for no plausible reason. To laugh guilelessly; to walk with insouciance; to simply breathe the air and see without terrible, yet necessary, blinders—this was a peace Pickle had not felt for some time. Yet within the safety of their intimacy, slivers of memories pierced Pickle's mind. He tightened his grip on Junie's arm.

Pickle and Karen had quickly grown serious and a dinner had been arranged for Karen to meet his family. She'd pressed him for this next step as a formal indication of their commitment to one another and future together. As they sat on the bed and finished up a meal of Chinese cold noodles, they had discussed how the McArdle family might impact their love.

"So? I knew you had a brother, and now I know he's a twin. What's the big deal?" Karen asked with indifference.

Pickle stared into his clasped hands and wondered how to explain the impossible. "You have to understand that Stan and I really are *identical*."

She laughed. "Do you also have a psychic connection? That kind of thing?"

"Don't make fun of this—I'm serious. Most people can't tell us apart. That's rare when identical twins reach adulthood. They usually gain weight at different rates . . . or one goes bald sooner. Stuff like that. But with me and Stan . . . I'm just saying . . . some people find it unnerving."

"I'll brace myself." She poked him in the belly.

"I know it sounds like I'm overblowing it . . ."

"Are you? Maybe you *are*."

Pickle got up and walked to the window. He'd needed the view to give his mind the space to gather the right words. She'd brushed it off, too easily. But how could she know, really?

"What the hell is this about, Pickle?"

He couldn't look at her. "What if you're attracted to him? We look the same."

"Pickle, love doesn't work that way. I love *you*. I'll meet your brother and that'll be that."

He tried to control the quiver in his voice. "I'm white-knuckling this."

"No, not my he-man of a cop, the biggest badass on the New York City police force. I'm with *you*. Now. Forever."

He felt Karen's arms surround his waist from behind and they didn't talk about it again.

Junie slipped her fingers into Pickle's hand as they approached Gansevoort Street and the end of the High Line. Pickle jumped. "Your hand is freezing!"

He grabbed both her hands and blew his hot breath onto her palms.

She scrunched her nose. "Yuk! Your breath is still garlicky!"

"Those falafels *were* lethal. But at least we both had them. Okay. New rule: if one of us eats garlic, the other has to also. Deal?"

"Sure." She pushed both her hands into his coat pockets, now facing him.

As much as he wanted to, Pickle wouldn't put his arms around her. Instead, he looked down into her face. "Don't move. I wanna stare at you for a while."

Junie waited several seconds, then crossed her eyes. "Had enough?"

"Never."

They left the High Line and started back uptown on Ninth Avenue. As they walked, Pickle's phone buzzed in his back pocket. Someone had been ringing him over and over. He gave in and took a look: ten hang-up calls from Karen.

That first family gathering had been benign enough, though Pickle saw that Karen was, initially at least, unhinged by their identical looks. But he was used to that reaction and was then relieved that she seemed to recover quickly and relax. The meal went well, mostly because Karen was a great conversationalist and had a knack for making every single person in a room feel that they were *the one*. Even his mother took to her and was obviously proud that she'd met Karen first at the granite yard, insisting that she was the matchmaker.

When Karen and Stan discovered that they worked in the same field, Pickle couldn't help but notice that they'd put their heads together over coffee and dessert. The old feelings of exclusion surfaced and he feared the worst. But afterwards, when they were alone again in Karen's apartment, Pickle was relieved that he still felt loved, and he was not aware of any shift at all from her. Except that in the coming weeks, their sex life ramped up: more frequent, more experimental.

Karen became an aggressive instigator with a new desperation in her physical attraction to him. But he loved it; he was the luckiest man he knew—for a change.

A few months later, when their mother was finally dying from the gifts of the granite yard, Pickle and Stan went out to Queens for what would end up being their last time together as a family. She was drifting in and out of consciousness as they sat bedside. Realizing that she probably had less than a week left, the twins went to a diner on Queens Boulevard to discuss the logistics of their mother's impending funeral.

Slipping into a booth, they'd ordered burgers and fries. Before the food came, though, Stan had several straight shots of whiskey. The diner, oddly, had a liquor license—probably a grandfathered holdover from a mob occupation years ago. They'd eaten slowly, and quietly agreed on some basic plans. It was simple really, because she had nothing and the brothers were the only survivors. Simple enough.

Pickle had noticed the booze that night. "Easy does it, Stan. That's your sixth shot. Remember, I'm the law. I shouldn't let you drive like this."

"It helps, that's all."

"You mean with Mom?"

"Yeah, there's that. But other things, too . . ."

Pickle let that comment sit on the table. Stan usually came out with personal disclosures in his own time; he couldn't be pushed. But he became suspicious when Stan began arranging dozens of napkins he'd pulled out of the holder, making a complicated pinwheel design. Stan was usually able to control his tics in public, but there he was, organizing the angles, then redoing it when he detected an unacceptable flaw. Something was off.

"Okay, Stan. I give up. What other things?"

"Pickle . . ."

"Stan?"

"I'm not sure how to tell you this—"

"Stop. Fucking stop right there." Pickle swept the napkins off the table with a violent slash of his forearm. They took forever to flutter through the air and onto the floor. And in those endless seconds, Pickle understood everything—including his own mangled name and that he was born an identical twin—a life sentence that just wouldn't release its chokehold. He took his gun out of the holster, his badge out of his breast pocket, and carefully laid them down on the Formica table. Sitting back, with his hands folded in the prayer position on the lip of the table, he waited.

Stan looked at the ceiling. "I'm sorry. It just happened."

"I'm sure. The mighty hand of God reached down and took control of your dick and her pussy. As innocent as the baby Jesus himself. But as the Lord is my witness, I want my gun on the table so that when I fuckin' kill you, they'll know it was me. I swear *to God*!"

Stan dropped his head to the table, hands covering his face, and sobbed. A few patrons had already moved from the surrounding tables. The waitstaff stacked up at the door like a firing squad. The line cooks warily looked through the serving counter. Only a booth jukebox could be heard—"Be My Baby," by the Ronettes.

Pickle slapped Stan's arms away from his face. "Shut your yap and that slobbering. You're *drunk*. I'm taking you home."

He grabbed his gun and license, pulled Stan to his feet by the back of his collar and dragged him toward the front door.

"What the fuck're you all looking at!?" Pickle screamed as he walked forward, holding his badge in front of him, not moving his head in any particular direction. "Can't you recognize a punk when you see one? He's a thief! He just confessed and I'm taking him in."

The night was almost complete, with a thin glow hovering just above the western Hudson. Junie and Pickle rounded the corner and the first floor of the brownstone was ablaze with light. They stood on the steps for a minute, watching a horizon of burnt orange become evening blue. Junie pulled him up the steps, but he held back.

"No, Junie, I've gotta go. You must be tired, anyway. I know I am—I don't think I've walked that much in years."

"It *was* a long day. But really lovely, Pickle."

"Yeah. I'll call you in a few days. It'll take me that long to recover from all this garlic!" Pickle heard his own voice apply a jocular pretense. Then with a short wave of his hand, he turned and walked away. Junie stayed put, watching him, he knew, until he got to the end of the block and turned out of sight.

Pickle called Karen, who picked up on the first ring.

Her voice rang cold, crisp. "It's about time."

"I'm returning your eighty-seven calls. What?"

"Well, first, you have to call Lance."

"Don't tell me what to do."

"He called *me*. He's worried."

"He'll survive."

"Whatever. I'm just relaying the message."

"What else?"

"We have a site meeting with Patrick tomorrow morning. Nine thirty."

"Okay. Make sure Stan's there, too."

"No. Stan has something at the office. It'll be just the three of us."

"Wrong. I want all four of us there."

"Pickle, it's not *necessary*."

"It is *fucking* necessary. And you know why."

Karen didn't respond.

"You picked up the message from me, right?"

Silence.

"That's what I thought. Good!" Pickle continued, his voice a breezy lilt. "I'll see you in the morning. Oh, and come to the Apartments tomorrow night. About eight. I miss you."

28

STAN WANDERED AROUND THE LIVING ROOM, gathering all the art books they owned on Antonio Gaudi. He'd announced that he'd indeed come up with a spectacular concept for the Kinsey project and was pulling images to present at the client meeting the next morning. Karen leaned over his shoulder and peeked into Stan's imagination: the gesture of a shallow arc, the rough outline of a cityscape, the color of a chill-grey sky as the backdrop tableau for the Basilica in Barcelona. She settled herself on the sofa and, now from a distance, watched Stan think for several minutes.

"What's all this have to do with Kinsey?" Karen finally asked, as Stan flipped through a book of birds indigenous to Spain. "Explain, please."

"No idea. I'll know tomorrow morning when I present."

How she envied Stan's comfort in not knowing. Certainty was something Karen strove for, but had failed spectacularly from a very early age.

The next time Karen had heard the noises upstairs, she was certain she knew what they meant. The sounds, though curious, were very normal, and surely nothing at all to do with Betsy. Or the man.

The occasional scraping sound at the ceiling from the floor above, was simply the house creaking. And the low hooting sound may have been from an owl outside. She'd taken a bird dictionary out of the library to further support her conclusion. Leafing through the book, Karen imagined the hoot was from an owl that was native to the area. Yes, that was probably the sound she'd heard: the Great Horned Owl. And because she'd never heard anything remotely resembling Betsy's voice, Karen then wondered if Betsy was, in fact, ever in that room at all. Karen convinced herself that she knew all of this for certain, and that she'd more than likely dreamed the whole thing.

Shortly, she found herself once again upstairs and the door was ajar. Yes—she heard the owl hooting, and the house sounds. All very normal. But then, as she peered through the crack, Karen immediately understood something awful: she'd been wrong.

He turned his head and smiled, and Karen froze. Suddenly the thin view from the crack of the door zoomed away and she felt, in her mind, that the man was small and in the distance, across a canyon. He seemed to take one hundred steps to reach her, it went so slowly. Then there he was, with his hand on hers, and she was in the room, placed in the corner.

"You can look or not look. I don't care. But, dear God, you gotta stop spying on me. Understand, little girl?"

The man turned his back to Karen and the floor scraping and the owl sounds continued. She was careful to not look directly at Betsy. Instead, she turned and faced the corner to scrutinize the cracked paint and a tiny ant, which crawled back and forth, uncertain which way was best.

Karen wasn't sure how long she'd spent at the corner, it could have been under a minute, or an hour. She'd taken a journey: out the window, to her backyard, to her best friend's house, to the dolls her father threw away, to the alcohol she'd sipped and didn't hate, to the joker on the card she'd kissed, to the dresses her mother had abandoned in the closet, to the boy down the street who wanted her to kiss him, to the teacher at school who'd touched her breast, to the other teacher who'd seen it and turned away. And then she'd ended up back in the room, not in the corner, but at the ceiling. As she hovered, she saw her own body crouching low to the ground, following the ant, with her hands over her ears.

Then the man became still, and Karen came back into her body. It was over: a rustle, a smoothing of bedcovers. She felt the man's hand on her head, his fingers like talons.

"Little girl? Now you know. So, you're part of it. Okay? You're part of it."

The Doodles jumped off the sofa and positioned himself on top of Karen's feet, his signal to go out. Karen took a deep breath. "Stan, listen. I think we have to reschedule the Kinsey meeting."

"What? Why? I'm ready for this one. For a change."

"I spoke with Pickle. Patrick and I are meeting him here at nine thirty tomorrow. Pickle wants you here, too."

"Huh. It's not necessary. Everything's on schedule, right? What's his problem?"

"I don't know. You know he gets a bug up his ass when he feels neglected."

"How on Earth could he feel neglected? We're doing the damned renovation . . . Nope. Kinsey is too important. Plus, I'm excited about it. Which I almost never am anymore. I'll call Pickle—"

"No. No, let me take care of it. And, yes, you're right. Kinsey's too important."

Stan went back to browsing Gaudi. Suddenly, he stopped and looked up at her. "Karen, the weirdest thing happened today."

"What?"

"Well, I was in the office feeling stressed-out as usual. Then Suzie came in. And you know how I don't like to see the staff until after one, if at all. And it was eleven thirty. I glanced at the clock and she began to apologize. But the weird thing was, after she apologized, I just told her it was okay. Then, I told her to go ahead and tell me what the problem was. Which she did. And it actually *was* something that needed to be addressed before one. So, I answered her, and she left."

"So?"

"Well, right then, I was thinking about booze. But not that I wanted it because someone had screwed up my schedule. Which would usually be the case. This time I just noticed that I wasn't drunk. And I wasn't hungover. And Suzie didn't really bother me. I mean, she did a little bit. But not too terribly."

"Right?"

"Right. But here's the main thing . . ." Stan paused for effect.

"What?"

"It all started with that girl downstairs. Ever since she's been here, I've felt . . . calmer. She's irritating—don't get me wrong. Like that music right now. It's killing me."

Stan paused to listen more closely. "What *is* that, anyway?"

It was deliriously happy noise and Karen knew that Junie had been with Pickle earlier that day. "Bruno Mars, 'Uptown Funk,'" she said without enthusiasm.

222

"That's so weird. I hate it. But somehow, I can cope with it. And listen to *this*. I don't want to drink."

"Wow."

"Crazy, huh?"

"Crazy."

"So, Karen. Don't let that girl go anywhere. I know I resisted her in the beginning. I admit I've been difficult. And maybe even a little mean to her. But now, she's got to stay."

"Of course."

"Whatever you do, she *stays*."

"Yes, Stan."

Stan shoved the books toward Karen. "Call a messenger for early morning. I want these ready for the staff. First thing. I'll take The Doodles out."

As long as she'd known him, Stan had never planned anything for the next day. That was her job. Karen found herself resenting his sobriety.

29

THE TONY UPPER EAST SIDE WAS NOT PICKLE'S style—not even his planet—but he'd made himself swallow it when he and Karen had first been a couple. She'd lived in a one-bedroom in the East Sixties, complete with semicircular driveway, posh doormen, and marbled everything. They'd dine at restaurants in the area and a thick scrim would descend to keep the cop separated from the man he imagined Karen might actually marry one day. This new man he impersonated made an effort to dress a bit better, curse a lot less, and fold his hands whenever he spoke. Now, after walking for hours with Junie, Pickle found himself in front of Karen's old building and remembered the truth about exactly what kind of person he'd become.

The traffic had been light the day he and Stan had returned from the diner in Queens. He'd thrown Stan in the backseat, knowing he'd cry the entire ride. Pickle hadn't wanted to see that; he could barely stomach hearing it. But once they were on the Queensboro Bridge heading toward the city, the hum of the suspended roadway seemed to chasten Stan. He fell into a heavy sleep, leaving Pickle to his wide-awake reality of being a newly single man.

He'd double-parked in front of Karen's building and thrown his police tag on the dashboard. Stan was out cold, in a mad-drunk coma, and poking him in the head elicited only a moan. Stan batted the air, with a slurred "Wanna sleep." Maybe he'd had more than six shots, maybe seven or eight; Pickle couldn't recall. But Stan's current state was immensely satisfying. Let the fucker sleep through his misery and then wake up to a bomb inside his head.

He sat for a while, not sure of what he intended to do. He looked at his watch, then up at her window. Karen's lights burned; she was home. Pickle finally pried himself out of the car and opened the trunk. Along with handcuffs, a crowbar, and other tools of his trade, a blanket had been shoved all the way to the back. He dragged it out, rattling the metal implements around, and shook it free of God knew what. The wool smelled of oil and gas, and, oddly, smoke. But he threw it over Stan anyway, knowing the filthy fabric would offend him deeply when he woke up. After slamming the car door as hard as he could, Pickle walked into the foyer of Karen's building.

The doorman looked nervous. Of course, Pickle thought. The poor slob wasn't sure how to address him: Pickle or Stan. Then he realized how preposterous this was because they were identical. And his predicament cloyed deeper; specifically, the man he now knew himself to be. How he wasn't worth a damn and how his brother always outperformed him in every possible way he knew of, or might imagine.

"Karen Wells, please. Tell her Mr. McArdle is here to see her."

Pickle headed for the elevator before the doorman had a chance to nod to him for admittance. He felt reckless, fearless in the way a criminal does who thinks he'll never be caught, so he proceeds to commit the crime with blithe confidence. He'd seen it a million times—a mindset just shy of madness. Yet he'd rarely heard of a reason for why people committed crimes, other than some distorted version of deep unhappiness. Sadness was certainly making him brave. And now he knew the very best reason to hurt: insanity. He'd lost everything and the thought made him stark, raving mental.

The interior of the elevator was mirrored on three sides. Pickle stared at himself and made a pleasant smile for the sake of the camera that was surely aimed on him. Stan smiled a lot and Pickle had never understood what was so damned funny all the time. An insipid smile was all he could muster; now they'd mistake him for his brother once the carnage was over.

Instead of pressing Karen's floor, he went to the floor above hers. He silently opened the stairwell door and walked, one tentative step at a time, down to the lower floor. Opening the door to the hallway a crack, he saw Karen leaning out of her doorway facing the other way, toward the elevator, waiting for Mr. McArdle.

He grabbed her from behind with his hand over her mouth, pressing the nub of his gun into her back. She didn't resist, rather, sank into it, and they twisted together into her apartment. After flinging her with both hands into the back of the sofa, Pickle pulled up a dining chair, turned it around and straddled it. He placed his gun on the coffee table. "Don't say a fucking word," he warned.

Karen obeyed, her face pinched into itself, obviously with fear, maybe tinged with regret. They stared at each other until Pickle swallowed and looked away. He realized this would be the last time he'd see the inside of this apartment, and suddenly thought better of his straddled seating position because he was becoming aroused. How base, how banal, how truly disgusting he was at that moment. He didn't want Karen to see how he was mixing love with desperation, and lust with violence, and hope with sadness, and finally, how his need to possess her had turned into a desire to hurt her. All of this distilled, much too easily, into the blood flow to his penis.

Pickle turned the chair back around, sat properly, and folded his hands to brush the moment away. This was to be a formal interrogation, for the record, and he didn't want to make any mistakes.

"Tell me he's a goddamned stallion in bed. Though for some reason I doubt that. Tell me he's just plain-old better looking. Oddly, I could deal with that. Tell me he stimulates your mind. That actually sounds reasonable. Tell me you're a crazy, sadistic bitch. We both know *that's* the truth. Just tell me *something* that'll make me understand this. Because if I don't get a good answer, I swear to God, Karen, one of us is going out of this apartment in a body bag. And right now, this very minute, I honestly don't care which one."

She took in a shuddering breath. "Where's Stan?"

"Fuck Stan."

"Is he okay?"

"If you cared anything at all about him, why'd you get him to do this filthy job for you? *Why?*"

"He wanted to do it. Tell you. He said you'd take it better from him."

"You're a liar, Karen. You don't know my brother very well. He's never stepped up to a confrontation in his life. That's what *I* do. You're confusing us. Not a good start to a blissful relationship."

She shifted on the sofa, pulling her legs underneath her.

"That's right. Get nice and comfortable. I can see this is gonna take some time," he sneered.

"Pickle, it's simple. We just clicked."

"Clicked? Like my gun?" Pickle scoffed at the irony of her words.

"Do you need to keep up with your terrorist threat? Or do you want to hear?"

Pickle closed his eyes and nodded.

"Remember when I went out to see your mother?" She paused, and Pickle couldn't imagine what might come next. "Well, Stan was there too. We had lunch after and talked for a long time . . . about design and all of that . . . we have a lot in common."

"So, this is a business transaction? Stan's *business*?"

"It's not business."

"Then what?"

"Where's Stan? I have to know."

"You're in no position to demand anything. But as a courtesy, he's in the backseat of my car in front of this building, sleeping off a monster drunk."

She looked toward the window and sniffed. "Okay."

"See, Karen, here's the part you just don't get. Maybe one day in the near or distant future you will, but right now you are in very iffy territory. So, listen up. My brother had to drink himself into a stupor to tell me he was fucking you. My brother is not capable of this kind of bald-faced, shank-in-the-back-of-the-neck treachery. I know him very well. You'll never know my brother like I do. Ever. As long as you live. This *had* to come from you. And here you sit with your flat brown eyes, and your perfect blonde hair, and your knockout figure, staring me down. Trying to shovel your cock-and-bull story up my ass that it 'just happened.' Well, I'm here to tell you that in life, nothing *ever* just happens. I'm a cop, remember?"

"Don't remind me."

"Oh. *Now* it comes out. You fucking snob."

"I'm not a snob, but you're threatening me. That's what cops do."

"I haven't threatened you. The gun sits on the table. I haven't beaten you up—though God knows I could still be provoked. I've only asked for an answer. A reason. And you've given me nothing. Wait. Correction. You've shown me that you're a conniving, cold-blooded bitch. I suppose *that's* your answer."

"I suppose it is."

"Are you?"

"What?"

"A cold-blooded bitch?"

She looked down at the floor, then lifted only her eyes and he expected them to land on his face. Instead she looked at the ceiling, toward a corner of the room, without moving her head. A trick he'd never seen before.

"Yes, Pickle. I'm a cold-blooded bitch." Her voice was lower than normal.

He leaned over and took the gun off the table, tossing it up and down in his right hand, like a baseball he might casually throw to a son.

"Get undressed."

"Don't be ridiculous."

"Don't worry—it'll be a quickie. I'm good at those, remember?"

She got up and started toward the front door. Pickle grabbed her arm and jerked her close to his body. She didn't wince. In fact, her face was devoid of any expression and it unnerved him. He squeezed her arm, hard, just to get some kind of juice out of her. Karen bit her lip but gave no other indication of pain. He hated her for a self-control she'd never exhibited before. Who *was* this woman?

"Think, Karen. This can be over in eight minutes or eighty. Your call. But it's gonna happen."

He reached toward her neck to unbutton her blouse and she pushed his hand away. "I'll do it." The voice, from the bottom of a canyon.

"That's better." Pickle holstered his gun, sat on the sofa and watched her.

She stepped out of her shoes, dropped her skirt to the floor, slipped off her blouse, unsnapped her bra and wiggled out of her underpants. Naked, she quickly straddled him. She closed her eyes and her fingers stroked his face in a perfunctory way. He noticed her eyeballs do something strange behind the lids—rising up into her brain. He shook her shoulders but it had no effect on her. Still, his erection pushed forward with an urgency he wasn't expecting.

"I hate that you can do this to me." Pickle pushed Karen off his lap and walked to the door. She stood naked in front of the window, hands on her hips, as if she were posing—a willing participant for a voyeur across the street. Her eyes, trained on him, almost frightened Pickle.

"Who do you see, Karen? Am I Pickle or Stan? I know you can tell the difference. Not many people can."

He closed the door quietly behind him.

Entering the elevator, he punched the lobby button, and, riding down, instinctively kept his head out of the aim of the camera. It easily could have been awful, after all.

As he approached his car he saw Stan sitting in the front passenger seat with sunglasses on. Pickle let himself in, turned to his brother, removed the sunglasses and tossed them on the dashboard. "Stan. Look at me."

Stan covered his eyes. "I can't."

Pickle pulled his brother's hands away from his face. "I'm in hell right now, but I'll get over it. Let's get you home."

Stan sank back into the corner of the seat. Pickle pulled out onto the street.

Their mother died the next day. The wedding was two weeks later. Seven days post-nuptials, Karen was back in Pickle's bed.

As he stood in front of Karen's old building, staring at her window, he texted her.

Can't meet u tonight c u at brownstone in a m

Pickle powered down his phone and walked the city. He had all the time the darkness would give him.

30

KAREN STARED AT THE CORNER OF THE CEILING in her office. She lay on the loveseat with her legs over the back and her head dangling down, hair brushing the floor. She tried to recall the last time she was happy. Nothing came to mind, at least not in recent memory. Pickle's text, cancelling their date for that evening, had just come through on her cell. The phone now lay at the bottom of her trash basket, thrown there in a fit of despair.

And she'd prepared so carefully. First, by telling Stan she'd do an overnighter at the office to get on top of a backlog of work. That was easy. Then, she'd frittered away the afternoon ruminating on talking points for how she and Pickle might get all their confounding relationship details ironed out. A challenge, but not impossible. Finally, she'd donned a fire-engine red D&G blouse. As requested. All the while, she'd tried to avoid her bookcase and the top shelf at the ceiling. The flask, and the deadening effect the liquid would surely provide. Of course, she knew it was empty, but the fantasy felt like the most realistic thing she knew at this moment. Because now she wouldn't be going to Pickle's and she didn't want to go home. Work was out of the question. She might as well drink. Or dream.

Karen righted her body to a supine position and blood stopped pulsing to her brain. She tucked the wool throw under her chin, hoping the warmth would make her drowsy. When her eyes wouldn't cooperate by closing, or even look away from the flask stuck on the shelf, Karen reached down, picked up one of her kitten heels off the floor, and gave herself a few well-placed whacks on her skull. The pain of the welts screamed louder than the urge to guzzle, just like the backyard dirt she'd been shoveling down her throat most evenings.

She heaved her shoe across the room into the wall common to Suzie's office, leaving one more divot among the dozens that had accumulated over the last few days. In just a few seconds, she heard footsteps race up, and then a banging on her door.

"Jesus, Karen. Will you open up already? It's after seven and I'm worried . . . you've been locked in there for hours," Suzie implored.

Karen got up, grabbed her purse, and dug her phone out of the trash. She opened the door and strode past Suzie. "Fix everything," she ordered.

"What do you *mean*? Karen!" Suzie yelled into her back.

Karen left the Lipstick Building and hailed a cab on First Avenue. Around the corner from the Apartments, she hit a liquor store on Broadway and 177th Street to purchase a small bottle of vodka. An impulse, yes, but necessary. Maybe she'd drink, maybe she wouldn't— but she wanted to be prepared in case the bruises on her body didn't hurt sufficiently. Karen stuffed the bottle deep into the bottom of her purse, covering it with her makeup pouch.

The night doorman greeted her.

"Jim, is Mr. McArdle in? Did you see him go up in the last couple hours?"

"No, Mrs. McArdle, I haven't seen him. But go on up—you have the keys, right?"

"That's okay. I think I'll wait for him in the lobby."

Karen sank into one of the mid-seventies pleather chairs smattering the dated lobby and pulled out a copy of *Elle Décor* magazine from her bag. She flipped through with disinterest. How many Hamptons mansions did she really need to look at? Beige, beige, beige. Off-white. Nude. Weak colors literally made her gag. Then she spied a beautiful purple welt on her shin. Now *that* was a color she would stake her life on.

After several minutes of dismissing the design world, she noticed a pair of Nike sneakers at her feet. Pickle smiled and gently pulled her up by her hands. His haggard look startled her, but she remained silent, allowing him to say the first words.

"What the hell are you *doing* here? Didn't you see my text?"

"I wanted to talk. I just chanced it—coming up here."

"Well, I'm not unhappy to see you. But why didn't you just go upstairs?"

"I'm not sure. Can we walk a bit?"

"Huh. Funny, but I've been walking for hours—all day, in fact. And I have to pee really badly. Come up for a few minutes?"

His apartment was still immaculate. She admired the change, but it made her feel even more alienated: who the hell *was* Pickle? She sat on the edge of the bed, careful not to disturb the covers with her weight. With her knees clamped tightly together and her arms stiff at her sides, Karen tried to maintain her balance. She thought about the bottle of vodka in her bag and leaned down to dig into her purse at the floor. Her fingers fluttered against the paper label on the bottle—

there it was.

Pickle came out of the bathroom and stretched broadly. He'd shaved and combed his hair and she felt a stab of optimism.

Pickle raised his eyebrows in a question. "The Cuban/Chinese joint?"

"Sure. I could use some food, too."

He planted a firm kiss on the crown of her head, which hurt, and placed a protective hand at the small of her back, which felt fine, then guided her out the door.

The small dive around the corner was familiar. They'd eaten there many times through the years, and it was number one in their stack of delivery menus.

A favorite waiter approached. "Martini for the lady?"

"No, Carlos, just water."

"Me too, water's great. And, Karen, should we just do the usual?"

"Perfect. Go ahead."

He ordered their food, and then placed his paper napkin in his lap. Karen followed his lead. They stared at each other. She sighed.

"What?" Pickle leaned forward.

"Everything's screwed up."

"Yup."

"And I'm very sad."

"Tell me."

Karen shook her head rapidly. "Please. Don't interrogate me." Her eyes dropped to the table.

"I'm not. At least, I don't mean to. Sorry if it sounds that way."

"Whatever."

Pickle prodded with his chin. "So?"

"Well, first, I know you took off from work."

"Okay."

"Don't you want to know how I found out?"

"I talked to Lance. And I gave him shit for contacting you."

"Well, I was glad he told me."

"He told *me* you were royally pissed that he called you at all."

"That's true—I was at the time. He caught me off guard. I was so confused . . . and scared."

"Why scared?"

"Because I'm losing you." Karen's eyes welled up.

"Why do you say that? The fact that I'm having a midlife crisis . . . well . . . I'm fucking entitled. Don't you think? Can't you slice me up a little piece of slack here?"

"I guess . . . Pickle, do a recap for me. I hate them, but right now I need it."

He laughed out loud and drummed his fingers on the table. "Recap number 4001 for Karen McArdle."

"Go."

"Okay. But can we eat a few bites first? I'm gonna die from hunger."

The waiter had just brought their food, and they dug into their meals of fried chicken, plantains, and spicy rice. After several minutes of determined chewing, Pickle blew out a breath and wiped his hands free of grease. "Whoa. That shit packs a wallop."

Karen finished her bite. She took a sip of ice water and slipped her hands between her thighs. She dug her nails deep into the skin and felt warm liquid spread onto her fingertips.

"I love you. That hasn't changed for one second. Though, we've sure had some 'rough patches.'" Pickle smirked as he made the air quotes. Karen held still.

"But I'm not in control of the love part, much as I hate admitting it. You've been the gold standard, and you know I've fucked other women. But no one has come close. Truly. Now. Let me muse a bit about why I think you feel that my love, or *our* love, is in trouble. And you'd better brace yourself because this might not go down too easy."

Karen's jaw ached from trying to keep her face immutable, and she wondered whether her teeth were loose.

"First, there's the initial betrayal bomb, which you probably feel you need to continually make up for, and rightly so. And I'll admit that I press that vulnerability—perhaps unfairly at times. All things considered, though, I'd say that event has shaped our relationship. And I'm still here. You still alive?"

She nodded and rubbed the blood into the skin on her knees.

"Well, that's the easy part, because we both know all that shit." Pickle burped into his napkin.

"Anyway, it's Junie. I'm attracted to her, Karen. No surprise. But it's not sexual, exactly. Just that I'm very relaxed around her, and that's not easy for me."

Pickle paused and seemed to consider what to say next. "But I'm here with you right now. And God knows I had every reason on Earth to never speak to you again . . . that night—"

Karen held up her hands to stop him, but he reached over, slapped them down and held them to the table. He didn't notice the crimson under her nails.

"*No.* You're gonna hear this. You asked, remember?" Pickle held her hands down and squeezed hard. "That night? I never got an answer. I think that's the reason why I took you back right after the wedding. I've been expecting you to, one day, explain why you left me for Stan. Because I still don't get it . . . and I've never asked."

Pickle released his grip, took a sip of water, looked above Karen's head, and then lowered his eyes to his empty plate. His voice began to tremble.

"I've waited all this time. And for much of it, I forgot I was waiting. Then there'd be something in your face when I'd remember and think: *Now, she's finally going to tell me.* But you never did. I know something happened. And it wasn't about Stan. I feel that so clearly."

Pickle repositioned himself and crossed his legs. She knew the familiar posture: the cop—the authority on every subject known to man, and she braced herself for a noose.

"But now with Junie showing up? I suppose there's the possibility that I'm at the end of my rope. Maybe I've stopped caring or even wondering what the reason was. It might not even matter anymore."

They sat quietly, his words like logs tied to their necks. Pickle broke the stillness by poking at the barely eaten fried chicken on her plate. He took one more bite, swallowed, and threw down his fork. It clattered to the floor.

Karen coughed out a whisper. "Can we go back to the apartment?"

"Why?"

"Because I want to tell you. And I think I can do it better if we're alone."

"I don't think so. I want this public . . . I mean, in a public place. That way I can trust myself. Understand?"

Pickle shoved his plate forward, the sound like wheels screeching to a halt. The waiter appeared to scoop up the fork and clear the table.

"It was your mother," Karen said.

Pickle cocked his ear toward her, as if he were hard of hearing. "*Huh?*"

"Your mother."

"My mother made you do it," he repeated.

"In a way."

Pickle scooted his chair back a few inches. "How so?"

"She gave me money."

"*Money?* My mother didn't have any money."

"I know. But remember the lottery tickets?"

"Yeah. I bought them for her every week."

"Right. But not those tickets. The office pool. She played that one with her own money."

"So?"

"Well, they won. It was split between four people. And her share was two million."

Pickle whistled, suspicious. "That's a lot of money. Particularly for my mother. But what does this have to do with you?"

"Remember when I told you about the day she asked me to come out to her apartment? I thought she wanted to talk about our relationship. Maybe she had concerns about my age, because I'm older. So, I went. But Stan wasn't there."

"No? Okay. But what about this so-called money?" Pickle pressed, doubtful.

She couldn't remember the details; much of that day was lost because she'd not actually said the words. Pickle was waiting, thrumming his fingers on the table. She heard the cloudy din of the restaurant around her. A cluster of people stood by the entrance door. One

239

man stood apart from the others, and she knew it was him. The slope of his shoulders, the cut of his waist, the bulging veins running down the back of his forearms. He'd never come to her before, but his words, his declaration, helped her now: "You're part of it now, little girl."

Karen remembered enough to proceed. "She was blunt. She told me that she would give me the money if I went to Stan. Over you. She showed me a savings account passbook. It was there—the money; it was real."

"Yeah?"

Now the memories were gone. Then it dawned on her. Karen finally understood the last rule, and what sneaky meant: she'd make it up. "I was stunned. I argued with her—tried to reason with her. We went back and forth. But I didn't want to insult her because she was, after all, your mother. I told her how much I loved you. Which was true. But she didn't think that was important. She was very clever and so, so sure of herself. And then I thought of a way out: I explained that even if I *tried* to go to Stan, it wouldn't work because I'd never gotten any inkling of interest from him. But she said that he *was* interested. That he'd told her so."

Pickle started forward. "She said that? That Stan was interested in you?"

"Yes." It could have happened like that and in a strange way, Karen knew it was close enough to the truth. After all, her mother had been with her, inside her, speaking through her.

"Did Stan know about it? This money scheme?"

Now Karen was back into her conscious thought and she continued with what she knew to be literal reality. "At first I wasn't sure, but then I quickly realized that he didn't know a thing. Stan's pretty guileless."

"Whatever," Pickle scoffed.

"Pickle, I had a plan. I'd agree. Take the money. Go to Stan. Marry him. I'd invest the money and just let it sit. I wasn't going to use it. Then after she died, I'd go back to you."

"Lovely. Fucking great."

"You've *got* to believe me. I figured with that money, we could have a good life. I thought I knew what I was doing."

She looked around and saw that the man was gone, and she felt oddly alone in the busy restaurant. Karen stared at the tabletop, trying to compose her next words. "But then it got complicated because Stan immediately brought me into the firm. I liked his star power. I had you back at that point, anyway. All of it happened with a strange ease, like it was meant to be. But mostly, I was lazy. I had everything: Stan, the business, the money. And you . . ."

Pickle stood up, reached into his pocket and threw a hundred-dollar bill on the table. "There, Karen. You can keep the change and stuff it in your pocket. Add *that* to your stash."

Karen grabbed him as he began to walk away. Pickle swung around. "It was a mercenary transaction. That's all it was for you. I get that part. What you left out was why my mother did this."

"I can't tell you."

"Why the fuck not?"

"It's too awful."

"Fucking *try* me."

"Pickle. I still have the money. It's almost five million now. I'll give it all to you. I don't want any of it. It's money from the devil."

"Just tell me about my mother. There's nothing you could say that'll surprise me."

Karen picked up the hundred-dollar bill, rubbed it between her fingers and watched it drop to the table. When she looked up, Pickle was already out the door. She caught up with him and, without talking, they walked back to his apartment. Then, like a miracle, they fell into their usual routine of preparing for bed. Pickle ran a bath for her and she was grateful. The roadmap of her body would surely tell him everything about her pain.

When he saw the bruises all over her body and the dried blood crusted on her legs, he didn't ask. That was how they understood each other—to leave all the inward aches and outward hurts stranded in a distant place. Pickle carried her to the bathtub, lay her deep among hot bubbles and washed her. As much as he tried to be gentle, every swipe of the sponge stung. Karen kept her eyes closed; she could not look at what the power of her own hand had done.

Then, five a.m. light, yellow and thin, crept into the room and the building's traffic rumble woke her. Karen heard Pickle in the bathroom, showering. When he returned, she patted the covers for him to rejoin her. Karen shifted onto her back, pushed down the covers and finally scanned her naked body. She wasn't beautiful, and it gave her the courage she needed to tell Pickle all about his mother.

"She didn't want the money split between you and Stan when she died. It was meant for Stan only. When I asked why, she said that you could take care of yourself, that Stan needed the help. In fact, she said you didn't need anything at all—that you'd never needed her—that you didn't love her like Stan did. Because he was the firstborn and you were the burden. I didn't understand much of what she was talking about . . . just that your mother was crazy. I don't know if she was always that way, but when I realized the extent of her mental state, I saw a way to get the money, and you, too. She trusted me—we signed no papers."

Karen needed oxygen, or something restorative that might revive her as she unloaded her secrets. She rose up off the bed, dragging the sheet with her, wrapped herself in a cotton cocoon, and stood in front of the view, where everything made just a bit of sense. Pickle joined her, standing behind her with his chin resting on the top of her head.

"I went to Stan—made it happen. It was easy, easier than felt comfortable, and it occurred to me, again, that Stan was in on it. But as I got to know him I saw the limits of his ability to deceive. The worst day was the wedding. Stan and I began to drink heavily immediately—I think he knew something was wrong . . ."

Karen's voice trailed off. Pickle wrapped his arms around her and together they witnessed the first drip of an emerging morning. She wanted to wash away all the words that had been spoken, all the awful truths that were now alive in both of their heads—every tiny fact that both hurt and released them. And every rule she'd ever followed.

31

PICKLE HAD STOPPED OFF AT A CAFÉ AROUND the corner from the brownstone to load up on muffins and coffee. Before going upstairs, where he anticipated the satisfaction of blowing his stack, Pickle took a few minutes to gulp down a sustainably-sourced organic muffin and swig a weak latte with an artful bonsai tree etched into the foam at the top. His new version of life, thanks to Karen's disclosure the previous night, showed him how phony his whole existence had been—just like the pretentious food he was now ingesting.

After the requisite breath spritzes, he climbed the stairs to find Patrick and Karen stuffed into a corner of the room discussing the progress of the renovation. Brendan was at work pulling his BX cables. With each tug, the sound against the new metal studs buzzed into Pickle's nervous system. He stopped short as he remembered Karen's battered body lying amid bath bubbles.

She looked up and smiled at him, so benign, so Karen. "Patrick says it's going well and we're making good progress—"

"Bull*shit* it's going well. There's nobody *working*. And *where* the fuck is Stan?" As he began his protest, Karen waved her hands at him to stop. Pickle noticed a large, fresh welt on the back of her hand; he was sure it hadn't been there at five a.m.

"Stan's at the office. I know what you're going to say, but just listen. Patrick and I have decided to bring in a crew that can work into the night to move things along. It'll be noisy, but Stan'll just have to deal with it."

"We still have the inspection," Patrick warned, directing his words at Karen, and ignoring Pickle altogether.

"Suzie will have a call into the DOB shortly. Don't worry, Patrick, I have everything under control."

"I'm not worried about you, Karen. I just want Mr. McArdle's expectations to be *well managed*."

As Patrick turned and walked away, Pickle called after him. "Patrick, there's coffee and muffins downstairs!"

Patrick waved Pickle off with disgust.

"He doesn't like me very much." Pickle stated the obvious.

"Can you blame him? You practically beat him up the last time you were here. Patrick's a sensitive guy."

"He's in the construction business, for God's sake. I'm surprised he doesn't have a thicker skin."

"Drop it, Pickle! Anyway, it isn't a mob business anymore. There's an understood decorum with high-end construction now. You're lucky he didn't walk off the job."

"I wasn't that bad. All this posing. Jesus."

"Oh, *please*. Can we stop all of this?" Karen pleaded.

Pickle decided to give her a bone. "Okay. Listen, about that granite . . ."

Karen feigned surprise. "Ah! The mystery purchase."

Pickle ignored her. "I want it everywhere. Bathroom, kitchen, every surface. Make a dining table out of it. Whatever. Use it all up."

"Why? I can save most of it for other projects. It won't go to waste, if that's what you're worried about."

"I'm not worried about that at all. I *want* to use it."

"But it doesn't make sense, design-wise," she insisted.

The Doodles walked up and jumped up onto his legs, clawing to be picked up. Pickle scooped him up, buried his face in the fur at his neck and inhaled. Grapefruit. Junie. He plastered a Jack Nicholson/ Here's Johnny grin on his face. "It makes perfect sense. It reminds me of Junie's eyes."

Pickle didn't wait for her reaction. Instead, he began to pace, trying to get a feel for the space. He noticed, as if for the first time, that the ceilings were quite high. And Pickle imagined color everywhere— he'd dictate to Karen exactly what colors to put on which walls. Her design advice would get no traction, because he meant to make this space entirely his.

The Doodles squirmed as Pickle waltzed around the room, now sure of a future that had been out of reach just yesterday, and he tightened his grip on the dog. They ended up at the window to the street. He hoped to see the woman with the standard poodles. But she wasn't there—the curtains closed tight. Pickle released The Doodles, turned, and walked the length of the brownstone back to Karen, who seemed to still be recovering from the sting of his Junie comment.

"Karen, can we get one floor completed immediately?"

"What are you talking about?"

"Well, what if they finished the top floor first—completely? Then I could move in sooner. The bathroom's up there, and that's all I really need. I don't cook much, but if I needed to, I could use your kitchen. Or Junie's."

"No. That's not a cost-efficient way to do the job. Construction is carefully timed; you know—when we do one thing, we do it every-where. If we did it the way you suggest, it would almost be like doing two renovations, and really expensive."

Pickle bore down. "But that's not an issue now—the money. Right? Because now I know there's money lying around. *Lots* of it."

Karen shifted her weight from foot to foot. "Well. That's true."

"Karen? Don't fuck with me. Not now. Just say yes. That's what you need to do."

Karen nodded slowly, and Pickle began to mimic the motion. They stared at each other as their heads bobbed in unison.

"Good. So, I wanna move into the top floor in two weeks. Make it happen. I don't care if they have to work all night long. I don't care if you and Stan don't sleep for two weeks straight. Got it? Because I don't care about fucking *anything* right now. I'm going down to see Junie."

Pickle loped downstairs, taking two steps at a time, then blasted through plastic wall barriers. Just as he reached the upper landing to Junie's floor he stopped up short.

He took out his breath spray, doused his mouth, combed his hair, and loosened his tie, which he'd worn for some reason, then tightened it again. As he was about to descend, he heard strains of classical mu-sic coming up though the radiators.

"Junie?" Pickle screamed in a whisper down the stairs. There was no answer, so he gingerly proceeded. Approaching the last step, he heard the shower running. Pickle tiptoed through her private area, all the way into the front room. He made himself comfortable on the sofa they'd dozed on a few days before, and picked up *Architectural Digest*—an old dog-eared copy. Pickle leafed through last year's high-end residences from the world over, listening for the shower to conclude.

The water stopped. He heard her singing along with the music and imagined her toweling off. Perhaps she'd need two towels—one for her body and one for that mop of hair. Then maybe she'd use lotion on her legs, heels, and elbows to keep her skin supple. He'd seen Karen do just that the night before.

The bathroom door creaked open. He expected the footsteps to diminish to the back section of the brownstone, when he'd call out, so as not to startle her. But he heard a rustle of movement closer to the living room. Embarrassed, he put the magazine up to his face so that Junie could jump back into the privacy of the hallway—if she was naked. Or if she'd wrapped herself in a towel, or if she was in a nightgown, or even if she was fully clothed. All possibilities lined up in his head like crows on a live wire. He cowered on the sofa with *Architectural Digest* blinding him and his knees jammed up to his chest. Now, he regretted what he'd done—that he'd invaded her space. It was certainly disturbing, but more likely, unforgivable.

Bare feet stood in front of him, her toes painted with sparkling blue nail polish. He could see her boney ankles and slowly, from the bottom edge of the magazine, he allowed his eyes to take in her calves, slathered with a trillion freckles. She gently tugged the magazine from his hands and threw it on the sofa. Pickle, simultaneously, slammed his eyes shut.

"I'm sorry, Junie. I thought for sure you'd go back to the bedroom.

I feel awful barging in like this. Just go to the back and I'll go upstairs. Please. Let's do this over. Okay?" Pickle rambled on, his hands now covering his face.

She pried his hands off his face, but he kept his eyes shut. With her fingers like tweezers, Junie pried Pickle's eyelids open. She stood before him— naked, lithe, shivering. Drop-dead angelic. Pickle grabbed the magazine and threw it on his lap for fear he'd get an erection. Junie laughed and knelt down in front of him. He accommodated her by parting his legs so she could nestle her body into his. Her damp hair draped over his chest and he couldn't resist digging his fingers into the clumps of wet tangles.

"Pickle. Your heart is racing."

"I'm sorry."

"Why?"

"All of this."

"I'm a big girl. I heard you come down when I was in the shower—and I knew it was you."

"How?"

"Karen's the only person who's been down here. The footsteps were a man's. It couldn't be Stan, so I just figured."

"Not Stan?" he whimpered.

Junie continued to talk with her head pressed to his chest. "Nope. You know Stan won't go into basements."

Pickle distracted himself from the Stan topic by looking down the length of her back, how her waist curved in and out like a gourd, terminating at her butt.

She squirmed. "Okay, now I'm cold. And a little bashful! So, close your eyes again and I'll go get dressed."

He felt her rise up, supporting her arms on his legs for leverage, and when he was sure she'd retreated to the back, he opened his eyes and stared at his crotch, where he'd usually have an erection waging battle with his pants. But he was embarrassingly limp. Well, he reasoned, Karen *was* upstairs . . . but Junie had allowed him, for just a moment, to dip into the privacy of her body, and that was a beginning.

Junie returned in no time, dressed in a simple floral dress, an outfit he recognized from Karen's wardrobe. Unacceptable. "Jesus. I can't have you wearing Karen's clothes," Pickle said with more than a hint of indignation.

"But we're the same body type exactly. If that's all I wore for the rest of my life, I'd be very happy. And stylish."

Talking about Karen's body type was making him literally sick. That yuppie muffin and millennial coffee were exploding in his stomach and trying to crawl up his throat. "Well, it's not right. I mean . . . I'm not sure what I mean. Just that I think you should have your own clothes. Not *hand-me-downs* from Karen," he stammered.

"But it's been kind of fun, kind of like *being* Karen."

Pickle began to hyperventilate. "I don't think it's a good idea. I can't explain it other than it feels very weird."

"Well, we certainly wouldn't want you to feel weird!" Junie smiled and plopped on the sofa next to him. She continued in a more subdued, conspiratorial tone. "I've got to start thinking about getting a job. I'm bored."

"Are you sure you're ready for that?"

"I think so. The days drag. I take The Doodles for walks. He cheers me up. Don't you, Doo-Doo?" Junie reached down and rubbed the area just above his tail and The Doodles attempted to scratch the unreachable itch. "I help Karen with stuff. Grocery shopping. She's gone a lot—much more than Stan. She seems to have the brunt of the work. I googled them and it's pretty impressive. I was thinking they might have a part-time job for me. I'm not qualified for much, but I thought I'd ask them."

Pickle stiffened. "But aren't you interested in art?"

"Yeah, that was my major in college. How'd you know?"

"Oh. It was part of a routine background check that Lance did. When you mentioned a job just now, I remembered. But why not do something in your field?"

Junie swung her legs up off the floor, propped her feet on the sofa arms, and rested her calves on Pickle's midsection. "That sounds so far-fetched—the art world. Like a dream."

Pickle saw the defeat on her face, as if he'd clamped down on her hopeful idea. "It's not a horse race. Something will come up. Hey, I'm starved. I barely ate breakfast. Wanna go out? I know a place in the neighborhood where they'll let The Doodles in."

Junie grinned and fetched the dog's leash. They walked outside just as the woman across the street came down her steps with the poodles. The Doodles dragged them over and nose/butt reintroductions were made between the dogs, Vixen, Comet, Cupid, and Blitzen. Junie chatted easily with the woman, a well-known writer it turned out, with whom, it became evident to Pickle, she'd taken several walks.

Pickle stood back. The women took up topics he had little interest in, while they alternately kneeled down to attend to the quadruplet dogs and The Doodles. He looked back across the street to the brownstone—to his two upper floors. Karen stood at the window on the top floor, observing them. She placed both hands on the glass pane, as if someone was holding a gun at her back. Pickle nodded once and then, with apologies to the writer, explained that he and Junie were hungry. Locking his hand into Junie's, he pulled her away. He felt Karen's eyes bore into the back of his head, or maybe they didn't. Perhaps she was already living her other life, bossing the construction guys around. In either case, Pickle leaned over to Junie and kissed the side of her head.

32

KAREN PULLED HER HANDS AWAY FROM THE WINDOW. By simultaneously removing some dust buildup and depositing a filmy residue of oil, she'd made two turkey impressions with her fingers. She lay her cheek against the glass in between the birds, and watched until Junie, Pickle, and The Doodles dropped out of her sight line. Then she called the office.

"Suzie, I won't be in till later this afternoon. When Stan comes back from the Kinsey meeting, tell him I'm at the brownstone, supervising stuff."

"But he likes to unload with you after he has a big presentation." Suzie whined.

"You'll be fine. Just stay with him. He'll talk it all out. And take notes for me. In fact, act like you're me."

"Oh, God no, Karen—"

She worked her way downstairs to Junie's level and wrapped herself inside the fleece robe, which smelled of some kind of citrus. Walking into the front room, she looked at the rumpled sofa and intuitively knew that Pickle and Junie had conducted an intimate conversation here, just a few minutes before. Maybe they'd shared personal details about their lives. Karen couldn't imagine such disclosure; she'd hidden so much of her past and wouldn't know where to begin. Her brain had managed to push memories around, so that all the bits and pieces were far away from each other, at safe distances. Certain facts had poked into her elbow; others had sifted down to her feet. One tidbit lived in her little finger. Yet her own mind didn't want the story to be complete or known or even real. So, the details had been parsed out to others: Pickle knew some of the worst. Mundane facts were safe inside Stan's brain. Her mother understood her the best, but she was gone. And Betsy could still wake Karen in the night with her passive body and her blank eyes and her owl sounds. Karen had been able to tolerate *all* of this. That is, until the man had shown himself in the Cuban/ Chinese restaurant. That was a new visitation and Karen finally understood she could no longer keep all the disparate chunks of herself apart. Somehow, it had to coalesce; she needed to funnel herself into one safe person. She'd thought that could be Junie. Now she saw that possibility slipping away.

The work crashed above her. She pounded one new bruise on her ankle bone. Perhaps the last one ever. She looked out the back door and saw fairy dust floating down—it was microscopic, silver and very beautiful, as it glinted against the rays of the sun. Karen walked out to the backyard and looked up to discover the source: Pickle's windows. She lay down in the virgin soil. Spring crocuses brushed against her hair and the ground accepted her body. Karen allowed the dust to cover her, and she dreamed of a shallow grave, while her mother's robe protected her from the moist earth.

33

PICKLE CRESTED THE SLIGHT INCLINE ON THE
walking path at the Cloisters. He spied Lance talking on the phone,
standing with one foot resting on the bench seat, gesturing with his
other hand. The scene kicked him in the gut—not so much with regret, but nostalgia. Pickle knew police work—could see it a mile away.

Lance eyed Pickle with suspicion and quickly shut his phone. "I've
been waiting here for a fucking half hour. Like I have time for this
crap with you? Hurry up. I've got a shitstorm up my ass."

"Hold on there, partner. I was on the subway and there was an
incident. Okay? Not my fault."

"Whatever. So, tell me. How's the man of leisure?"

"Good. I think."

"What does that mean? You had sex with that girl?"

Pickle shook his head in disgust. "So devoid of any class whatsoever. I mean, if you could even hear yourself—"

"Wait a minute. A few weeks away from your tribe and you're all ho-
lier-than-thou? I don't buy it. You're a hound dog and always have been."

"Well. Yeah, I suppose you're right—at least from your limited
perspective."

"Talk." Lance sat on the bench and dusted the space beside him with his handkerchief, gesturing for Pickle to join him. Pickle plopped down, rubbed his hands into his face and coughed up some phlegm.

"Waaaaiting . . ." Lance looked at his watch, tapped his foot, and checked his phone.

"Well, it does have to do with Junie. But not really."

"Okay. What?"

"I'm gonna resign from the force."

"And *I'm* gonna get you into mental services so fast your head'll pop off."

"I understand your concerns."

"Don't give me that bullshit phrase. My *concerns* are that you've completely flipped your lid ever since the night that nut took a dip in the tub from the South Sidewalk. And the girl he left behind has taken hold of your dick with a vice grip."

"Ouch."

"Yeah, fucking ouch is right. And she's obviously twisting it to the point of no blood flow to the brain."

Pickle twiddled his thumbs. "Let me see. How can I possibly explain this to you?"

"No idea."

"Let me start with a question: if money were no object, would you be a cop?"

"Fuck no."

"Right. That's my point."

"What *is* this? Not everybody in the world has a job that makes the heart go pitter-pat. Anyway, money is a moot point for us slobs. Being a cop is just what we do."

"Right. It's what we do. But I ask again, if you *did* have the money, would you do it?"

Lance sighed and waved his hand for Pickle to get on with it. "No."

"So, I've asked twice, and you've given me the same answer, which proves my point."

"Okay. You have money. Is that what you're trying to tell me? Which property room did you raid? Candice's?"

Pickle crossed his arms, with a satisfied smirk. "Karen's."

Lance let out a whistle. "That sot? What about her drunken husband—sorry—your brother? Where does he fit in?"

"Well, first, they've stopped drinking . . . as far as I can tell."

"Really."

"Yeah. But this has nothing to do with Stan. I've got Karen in a choke hold so tight her eyeballs are popping. Turns out she owes me money, and I'm talking a *lot*."

"*Really.*"

"Yeah. And as soon as I collect it, which should be in the next day or two—goodbye, police force. I'm gonna give my notice."

"Wow. Does Stan know?"

"Nope. And if I play my cards right, he never will."

"That good, huh?"

"Yeah. *That good.*"

"Well, let me give you a warning. From someone who knows a tiny smidge about sneaky bitches." Lance shifted in his seat to face Pickle. "Let's say I believe there's some money there. I'll give you that."

"It's there. One hundred percent."

"Okay, fine. And let's say that you *do* get hold of this money. From Karen."

257

"I will."

"Well, remember that old adage? 'Never take everything from somebody, because when you gut them out, they have nothing left to lose.' Ever hear that one?"

"Never. Who the hell said that?"

"I can't remember. Gotti. Gandhi. Giuliani. Does it matter? You know it's true."

Pickle remained silent.

Lance pressed forward. "'Cause, I'm thinking. You say Stan doesn't know about any of this—whatever *it* is. Right?"

"Meaning?"

"Karen could spill it to him."

"She wouldn't. She's got much more to lose than me."

"Okay. But just be very sure, because women are crazy, especially when it comes to money. And sex."

Pickle dismissed him with a sniff. "I don't care about any of that shit. I really don't. I'd risk it all in a heartbeat if I had this money and a chance with Junie. Now I'm right next to the cash. And I'm gonna get it. And Junie. I've got Karen right where I need her. And it's taken this girl, Junie, for me to find out that it was there all along. I just never asked the right questions."

Kids were kicking a ball around, forbidden at the Cloisters, but they didn't move to stop them. After a few minutes, Lance placed his hand on his partner's back. "Okay. Let's do a recap."

"That's my line."

"I know, but I think you need one about now."

"You're probably right. Hit me."

"What do you know to be absolutely the truth? Rock solid?"

Pickle stared at the ground. "Karen's a great fuck," he said. "And she's been the love of my life in the worst way imaginable," he whispered with resignation.

"Right. And what about the money? Is this just on Karen's say-so? Or do you have proof that it exists?"

"So far, only her say-so. But I believe her. She told me about it under duress, so to speak."

"And this Junie? Is this really a feasible thing? In other words, is it mutual?"

"Yeah, it's mutual. She practically offered herself to me in the nude just this morning. I held back. But I could have, I'm pretty sure."

"What about Stan?"

"What about him?"

"Where does he fit in?"

"Who the hell knows? I'm fucking tired of his puss right now. I'm sick of looking at him. I'm sick of looking *like* him. Tell the truth, I'm sick of being his brother! I'm sick to death of him, and his clothes, and his superior opinions, and his hotshot business and his colors and his sweaters and his spice bottles and his counting—"

"Whoa! Bingo. Jackpot. Ball in the corner pocket. Hole in one."

"What!?"

"This whole time we've been talking? You've been flat—no juice. The real emotion comes up around *Stan*. Which means that with all your plans surrounding Karen and Junie, you're hottest around your brother. Which leads me to believe that you're not clear."

"Fuck you."

"Right. Fuck me." Lance got up and stood in front of Pickle. "Be careful, is all I'm saying. And get *clear*."

Lance wandered off, screaming at the kids playing ball while flashing his badge. "Get out of here! You know better! Go home and do some homework!"

34

STAN HAD ACED THE KINSEY MEETING; THE CLI-
ent awarded *McArdle* the project on the spot. And Suzie, who'd survived being Karen, had filled her in earlier that morning. Now Karen
was up to her eyeballs trying to catch up on Kinsey, with several rolls
of millwork drawings cluttering her desk for review. She was jotting
notes in the margins, slashing a red pen back and forth, when a familiar shadow loomed at her frosted glass door.

"Give me fifteen more minutes, Stan. I have to get these drawings
buttoned up. Okay?"

The door opened. Annoyed, with her eyes stubbornly aimed at
her work, she shook her head in irritation. "Can't you listen to me for
once? I need some time here."

Pickle walked in and sat on the loveseat. "I can wait. I've got fifteen minutes or fifteen hours. In fact, I'd wait forever for you."

"Mother of God. What're you *doing* here?"

"Well, let's see. It's Monday morning. The sun is out. The temperature is mild—no rain predicted. I slept well last night." Pickle kissed
the air in her direction. "How're you, baby? You good?"

"C'mon, Pickle, what the hell is going on? And shut the door.

Somebody'll hear you."

Pickle stuck his leg out and kicked the door shut. "Karen, I just asked after your well-being. The least you could do is to respond in a civil manner."

"I'm fine. Everything is *fine*. Now, what?"

"Come for a walk with me."

Karen threw her red pen on the desk and it rolled off onto the carpet. Pickle grabbed it and pocketed it. "C'mon, let's go."

"I'm busy. And I'm on deadline. So, no, I cannot take a walk with you." She faked a smile, tilting her head to the side.

"I just wanna go for a walk with my best girl. Is that too much to ask?" Pickle wagged his finger at the drawings. "All that shit? It can wait, right?"

"Actually? It can't." Karen leaned back in her chair.

He got up and went to Karen's closet, reached for her jacket, and held it like a bullfighter with a red cape. She gave in, slipped on her shoes, and poked her arms into the waiting coat.

"*That's* my girl. It isn't often I come to where the brain trust of the family does its stuff. All this Lipstick Building jazz? It's intimidating. Have I ever admitted that to you?"

"No, though I've had my suspicions. But believe me, there's nothing special about this place, or the building for that matter. It's just a big smokestack filled with a bunch of working slobs. Like me."

Karen gathered the rolls of drawings in her arms and pointed to the loveseat. "Sit right there for a minute. I need to give these to Suzie—she'll get somebody else to finish. Now you've got me curious, and a little excited, too."

When she returned from dumping the workload on Suzie's desk, Karen took Pickle by the hand. "Okay. Where to?"

"It's a surprise."

"Okey dokey. Whatever. Let's go out the back entrance."

As they walked down the long corridor past all the lipstick tubes, Pickle led the way and picked up two or three random tubes.

Karen swatted him on the head. "Thief," she teased.

Once on the street, they walked a few blocks from Third Avenue to Fifty-First Street and Second, when Pickle abruptly stopped.

"What gives? This better be good, Pickle," Karen warned.

"Don't worry, it's gonna be great. Let's go inside." He held the glass door open for her.

Karen looked up and around, then back at Pickle, and balked. "Wait. No. This is my *bank*—"

Before she could complete her protest, Pickle grabbed her by the arm and muscled her into the lobby. William strode out of his office and approached them.

"Good morning, Karen. And hello, Stan! It was nice to get your call this morning. I've got everything set up for you both in the back office. Just follow me." William looked back at them as they walked. "Lovely day, isn't it?"

"Oh yes, the best day ever," Pickle said.

The three settled into his office as William banged on the computer, pulling up the accounts. He swiveled around and launched into his banker spiel.

"First, let me congratulate you both on the huge leap you're making for the firm. It gives us great pride when our clients have the courage to grow their businesses. Now Stan, you told me on the phone this morning that you and Karen have decided to release funds from the Zed account. We'll need a signature from Karen, so I've prepared the papers for her to sign. Once you sign, Karen, the transfer will go through in about an hour."

Pickle held the pen toward Karen. "Let's do this, honey. We've been waiting our whole lives to use this money in the right way at the right time."

Karen grabbed the pen and quickly signed the papers. She sat back heavily in her chair. "William, could I have a glass of water, please? I'm parched, for some reason."

"Sure, let me get that for you." He left, and the door clicked shut.

"Pickle. This is theft. Or robbery—whatever you want to call it."

"Wrong. Leave the police jargon to me. Robbery occurs when you take something from a person using force. No force here. Theft refers to taking something without the person's knowledge or consent. You're here and you just signed the papers of your own free will. And let me remind you that just the other night you said, quote, 'I'll give it all to you. It's money from the devil. It doesn't belong to me. I don't want *any* of it.' Unquote."

Karen bristled. "Well, we can't talk about this now, obviously."

Pickle moved his chair closer to hers and took both of her hands into his. "There's nothing to talk about, Karen. You told me the money was mine. I thought about it over the weekend and I agree. Or would you like me to ask Stan *his* opinion?"

Pickle kissed Karen and when she tried to disengage from him, he kissed harder.

"Whoops! Sorry for the intrusion," said William, who'd just entered the room with a pitcher of water. He poured a glass and handed it to Karen.

Karen gulped the water, which dribbled onto her chin. She wiped her lips with the back of her hand, smudging her lipstick. Pickle whipped out his handkerchief, along with a tube of lipstick. Taking her chin in his hand, he carefully dabbed at the smudge and then applied fresh lipstick. "There. I can't have my wife walking around with a mussed mouth."

"That's *very* sweet." William sat back, admiring them.

Pickle winked at William. "That's why we've been together this long. We look after each other."

Karen quickly ended the meeting, saying she needed to get back to the office. Once outside on the street, Pickle backed her into the side of the building. Pedestrians sidestepped them with New York City ease—just another couple having a public spat.

"Karen, this was just step one. Step two is we go have lunch for an hour and then come right back to the bank. You're going to make out a cashier's check to me for the entire amount. Look at this as old business—just some loose ends being tied up."

Karen turned her head and stared down the block as if looking to be rescued. He shook her.

"*Okay.* Okay, Pickle."

"You'll see. It's the best thing for everyone. You've got to get this burden off your chest. So many years . . . all this time . . . it must have been killing you."

"Yeah, something like that."

"Step three: you'll come to the apartment tonight at seven. You'll sleep over. Tell Stan . . . whatever it is you always tell him. We'll celebrate."

They walked down the street and Pickle ushered Karen into a nearby four-star restaurant. She realized he'd made a reservation.

35

THE DOODLES TOOK UP RESIDENCE ON THE PAR-
lor floor at the stair landing to Junie's level, below. That small nook had become his default nesting area shortly after she'd come to live in the brownstone. Stan had grudgingly acquiesced and finally dragged the dog's bed and blanket to the landing. This was only after many failed attempts to get The Doodles to sleep at his usual corner in Stan's bedroom. The Doodles's loyalties were now clearly divided and he'd apparently found a new soul mate.

Stan nudged the dog with his big toe. The Doodles stood up, turned around three times, and plopped back down to resume his nap.

"Junie? Did you take him out?" Stan yelled down the stairs.

He'd not ventured to the basement since he and Karen had purchased the brownstone, much less since Junie had come to live with them. Now with her lurking down there, visions had tortured Stan on a daily basis—of things in disarray, of his irrational fantasies of stacked-up coffins, of the very earth that might swallow him. But mostly it was the notion that another human on the premises didn't understand him. She'd need to learn what he could barely tolerate and what was forbidden. He anticipated that it would take months of fine-tuned adjustment, and exclusively on Junie's part. Stan had been patient, or so he saw himself.

During the first week Junie was there, Stan decided that he'd simply make believe she didn't exist. This seemed the easiest solution to the reality of her presence, and it worked well for a short time. But music floating up through the radiators quickly destroyed that plan. He couldn't quite imagine music away. Gradually his brain began to clear (mostly due to drying out from the booze), and he began to notice that what felt impossible to bear or even imagine just a few weeks before, was slowly becoming stuff he could now not only tolerate, but was also, oddly, curious about. What was it about Junie, the first person perhaps ever, that made him stop caring about spice bottles and his sweaters, at least for a day or two? He hadn't even watched *Dallas* in the past two weeks!

"Yes, Stan! About an hour ago! He's good!" Junie bellowed from below.

Stan realigned the shoes at the stair landing and tucked all the arms of each coat into the body of the garments. He glanced into the kitchen to make sure the spice bottles suited him. They were imperfect, but he managed to ignore the annoyance. Then he realized that the sweater he currently wore was the same one he wore yesterday, which, just a month before, would have been an impossibility. He allowed himself to count The Doodles's toenails, just to recreate a semblance of normalcy.

They'd established their rhythm around The Doodles. With Karen at the office more and more, Stan and Junie found a symbiosis that was soft and reliable—like a brother and sister, or a single woman and her slightly androgynous male friend. The distance of one floor, physically and mentally, proved optimum for them both. And music became their tendril of connection—an invisible silk thread that spun up from the basement to let Stan know: she's awake—she feels this way today. Maybe he knew more about Junie than he'd admit to himself. And even worse (or maybe it was better), could she possibly know something about him?

Junie appeared at the bottom of the stairs and looked up at him. "Is the music bothering you? You have to tell me, Stan."

"Well, now that you mention it, could you turn it down just a tad? I'm trying to prepare for Gloria tomorrow. You know, cleaning up a bit? And it's hard to think clearly with Mozart horn concertos going full blast."

"Of course. I forgot it was even on until now." She went into her bedroom and switched off the Bose CD player, then reappeared at the stairway. "Stan, I just had a thought. Do you want me to help you? I mean, I'm not doing anything, and I'm a little bored. We could clean together. Maybe organize a little? It might be fun. And, you know—it might help me, too."

Stan looked down the stairs at her, wary. Her figure was backlit from the light at her entrance door and all he could see was the outline of her body, which he had to admit was very similar to Karen's— a thought he pushed aside. "I'm not sure about that. No. It wouldn't work."

"Okay. But keep it in mind. I'm pretty good at that stuff. You should see it down here. Everything is clean and in its place. You wanna come down?"

"No. No. I can't. But I appreciate the offer."

Just then his cell rang. Stan went into the kitchen to fetch it. It was after six p.m. and he was expecting Karen to walk in the door any minute. But he now saw she was calling. He let it ring exactly four and a half times, which, when doubled, equaled nine.

"Stan, I have to stay at the office tonight."

"Again? So many nights, Karen. *Why?* I'm waiting for you. I'm starved."

"I know, and I'm sorry, but those millwork drawings need more work after all. I found a huge mistake that offset everything by three inches, and I'm keeping the CAD person here so we can print and review. It'll take hours. I have to approve them by early tomorrow morning . . . it's just easier to stay here through the night."

"Okay, if you say so."

"Junie can come up and cook, right? Or there's leftover takeout in the fridge. Or just order in. Or you guys can go out."

"Enough, Karen. I know the options."

"Oh, and Stan, have you been upstairs to check the work at all?"

"Yeah, I went up about an hour ago. It's all fine. They started with Sheetrock for the partitions and some guys have begun the first skim on the common walls. All on the top floor, of course."

"Good. Did the bath fixtures arrive? And what about lighting fixtures? Tile?"

"Yup, it's all here. I think Pickle might actually be able to move in on his timeline. I wish all our projects could be fast-tracked this way."

"Whatever."

"Okay, let me get some dinner plans going."

"How is she?"

"Junie? How the hell should I know? I never go down there. We rarely speak. But as of five minutes ago, she seemed great."

"Great?"

"Yeah. Great. She seems different these days."

"How would *you* know? You just said you never speak to her."

"I didn't say 'never,' I said 'rarely.' Leave it at that. Christ."

"Okay, I'll see you at the office tomorrow morning."

"Okay, boss."

"So, you'll eat, yes?"

"Yes."

"You'll check it out with Junie; include her, yes?"

"*Yes.*"

They signed off and Stan listened for the music downstairs. He'd only asked Junie to turn it down, but she had turned it off. Is that what he did to people? The house was silent, save the banging of hot water pipes, but that was noise he had no sway over. He paused, remaining very still, trying to discern some other movement. Maybe she'd gone back to bed. And now The Doodles had disappeared from his nest—probably down there with her.

Stan suddenly sensed the vacancy of the house—of sound, of any life—and it felt wrong. He'd gotten used to the pulse of Junie's days and nights—the running of the shower, even the toilet flushing, as much as he hated noticing that. Not to mention the front basement door squeaking when she took The Doodles out. And the gardening she'd taken over from Karen. He admired Junie's color sense and how she grouped the flowers, which was fairly sophisticated. He'd gradually become aware of her taste in music, and he found himself curious about what she'd play each day. Just recently she'd begun to play *Einstein on the Beach* quite a bit, and Stan discovered, against his better judgement, that he liked it. And he'd just requested that she lower the volume. That had caused her to turn it off. *He* did that. And he now felt an uncomfortable regret—a nagging feeling of pulling away from another, or of controlling another person for his own whim. He asked himself why. At that moment, Stan had no answer, but he felt a shift. He wanted the air in the house to move continuously. He needed that indication of life, something he now realized he'd been missing terribly. Sometimes you don't know what you need until it is right in front of you. Even thinking this cliché revolted Stan, but he had to admit, it was true.

Stan returned to the stairway to obey Karen's instructions—to "check it out with Junie."

"Junie! Karen's not coming home tonight. Let's go to Henry's for a steak."

"Really? Sure! Give me a few minutes. I'll be right up," she called from the bedroom.

Stan dug his feet into the slippers that were lined up with his other shoes along the wall. He tentatively stepped onto the first tread to the lower level. The stair slat creaked, and The Doodles appeared at the bottom of the stairs, curious. Stan steadied himself with his hand on the railing.

"Junie! I'm coming down, okay? Was that the Chicago Symphony?"

Junie's head poked around the corner, a hairbrush in her hand. She stared at him with her mouth open. "Yes. Chicago. Wow. You could hear that? Sure. C'mon down."

Slowly, a step at a time, Stan descended to the lower level, counting each step, his heart beating, his breath steady, his eyes adjusting to the dark, and then the light.

36

THE EVENING BEGAN LIKE SO MANY IN THE PAST:
Pickle and Karen wrapped tight in a sheet at the big window, imagin-
ing the bodies traversing below on the bridge, back and forth, maybe
toward love, perhaps away from sadness. Either way, their night would
proceed, quietly and with tenderness. Memories comforted Pickle, yet
a new certainty rattled him. He would soon lose this expansive seclu-
sion forever, because words had been spoken, secrets revealed, a building was changing, and finally, dollars had changed hands.

Pickle pulled Karen to the bed. As they stretched, naked, across
the covers, he examined her face—nude of makeup, her skin flushed.
He scanned her body, now marred with a terrible healing beauty. He
traced the edges of her eyes, her nose, and her mouth. His hand then
landed on her neck, her waist, her hip. He realized right then that as
close as Karen had always been, he'd never really had her. Not in the
way that meant anything.

The first night Karen came back after the wedding, she'd floated
in, careened out of her shoes, tossed her clothes on the floor. And
cried. He'd stroked her hair and mopped her hot tears. He'd kissed her
mouth to quiet her. That night they lay across this same bed, where

Pickle had remained for the previous week. His pillows and sheets still smelled of his sweat and hard dreams, as he'd tried to accept a sad future he could not imagine. But there she was, in his arms again. No words were spoken, because the truth and certainty of their love could not be set aside by a prim wedding ceremony. And now there were new truths living between them and he wanted to figure this out, not only for himself, but for her, as well.

"Remember, Karen? I can honestly say that you are just as beautiful tonight as you were the night you came back to me. But it's more than that. Every part of you is precious, outside and inside. It has always been there. And that is astonishing. I know this now. I see it and feel it. And there's not a thing in the world that needs to change. Nothing."

She began to weep.

"Don't," he whispered. "I want you without any sadness. Can you give that to me? Tonight?"

"I can."

Finally, Pickle understood that he owed Karen something. He owed her himself.

EPILOGUE

Dear Jacob,

It's been three years since you jumped. I can still see your face in the few seconds before you went over—when you pulled away from my hand. I see that red fury in your eyes, a look I didn't understand then. I still don't, completely, but I think I've come to accept your pain and what I saw raging in your face that night. And how I really wasn't the cause of it. But for so long I had thoughts of "what if." If we'd not argued. If I'd truly understood you. All of it. The list could wrap around the planet. On many nights, I've dreamed of you being alive now, and with me. And you can be sure it's been an aching throb to wake up every day feeling, knowing, that I should have done something. But what would that have been?

I think back to the way we lived in Brooklyn—in a cocoon of sorts—carefully woven for us to hibernate within until we were ready to push out, toward death. You flew out of that cocoon into the river, and left me half alive. Oh, they were nice to me, these people in the brownstone. But what could they do? And how could they really understand? So, I tried to make believe and rise to meet their level of caring. Just to ease their worries. I was a good little actress. The days went on, and they included me in their lives; they watched me and listened as carefully as they could. Some better than others. And I fooled them for a very long time. I was surprised how easy that was. I was not okay.

Now I have a baby and I've named him after you, Jacob. We call him Coby. That was okay with his father. I thought I'd never have a child, but that's what angels do—save you and bring you a future. Now, my little Coby, who looks nothing like you, but did come from you in a way, made his Herculean effort to be born, in spite of all you and I did to kill his future existence.

I'm spending all my time caring for Coby and am grateful that I know how to love again. Coby makes that so easy. There are no questions from him, no holding back. My boy is pure love and is adored and protected by us all.

By "all," I mean everyone living here in the brownstone. Karen took a leave from her job to help me through the pregnancy and with these early months. Coby's father is still working and so is his twin brother. I feel supported by them and anything I want is okay. Which is so different than when I was with you, Jacob.

But I want you to know it was worth it—being with you. Because I know that however deep my pain was, however much I wanted to end my life—well—the joy of this baby shows me how high a love can bring me. I've learned that love comes in all guises, and some not so pretty. But it's love all the same—even terribly disfigured like yours and mine was. Now I pick up the veils when I can and try to be brave enough to look under and see what love looks like, day after day.

I'll marry Stan soon. I saw his beautiful face underneath many thick veils. We'll raise our baby to recognize and live within this wide-open world, and our love.

END

ACKNOWLEDGEMENTS

Endless thanks to my agents, Paul Feldstein and Susan Dalzell Feldstein, for their tireless support. And to Paul, particularly, for wading through multiple drafts of Pickle. Massive gratitude to my publisher, Michelle Halket, for believing in my writing and ushering my debut novel into the world with close attention and fine business acumen. Thanks to the sales team at IPG, who distributed my novel with more bells and whistles than I ever expected. My deep admiration for Liz Van Hoose, who reviewed early and late drafts of Pickle, providing feedback which proved pivotal. And last but never least, my incredible publicist, Nicole Dewey, has shown the patience of Job and the kindness of a saint. I am honored to have her in my corner.

The Catto Shaw Foundation granted me a month-long residency, where I managed to complete the first draft of this novel. Many thanks to Aspen Summer Words, Community of Writers at Squaw Valley, Tin House and One Story for the opportunity to workshop nascent pages of *Pickle's Progress*.

I am very grateful to early readers who took the time to read Pickle and say just the right things to boost my confidence: Keren Blankfeld, Helene Brenkman, Adrienne Brodeur, Kathleen Flynn, Geeta Kothari, Louise Marburg, Ralph Olsen, Simone Grace Seol, Don Shaw and Howard Welsh.

Writing is a solitary act and at times gives rise to loneliness. But I have not been alone and many have supported me, including dear friends far and wide. I fear that if I began a list, it would necessarily go on for many pages, and even then, I'd leave someone out. Please know that I have learned so much from each of you, on the page and in life. I love you all. Madly, truly, deeply.

Photo: Matt Dine

Marcia Butler has had a number of creative careers: professional musician, interior designer, documentary filmmaker, and author. As an oboist, the *New York Times* hailed her as a "first rate artist." Acclaimed interior designs include projects in NYC, Boston, and Miami. *The Creative Imperative*, her documentary film exploring the essence of creativity, will release in summer 2019. Her memoir, *The Skin Above My Knee*, was one of the *Washington Post*'s "top ten noteworthy moments in classical music in 2017." *Pickle's Progress* is her fiction debut. She lives in New York City.